Praise for the Novels
of Ralph Cotton

"Cotton writes with the authentic ring of a silver dollar, a storyteller in the best tradition of the Old West."
—Matt Braun, Golden Spur Award–winning author of *One Last Town* and *You Know My Name*

"Evokes a sense of outlawry . . . distinctive."
—*Lexington Herald-Leader*

"Authentic Old West detail and dialogue fill his books." —*Wild West Magazine*

"The sort of story we all hope to find within us: the bloodstained, gun-smoked, grease-stained yarn that yanks a reader right out of today." —Terry Johnston

KILLING
TEXAS BOB

Ralph Cotton

A SIGNET BOOK

SIGNET
Published by New American Library, a division of
Penguin Group (USA) Inc., 375 Hudson Street,
New York, New York 10014, USA
Penguin Group (Canada), 90 Eglinton Avenue East, Suite 700, Toronto,
Ontario M4P 2Y3, Canada (a division of Pearson Penguin Canada Inc.)
Penguin Books Ltd., 80 Strand, London WC2R 0RL, England
Penguin Ireland, 25 St. Stephen's Green, Dublin 2,
Ireland (a division of Penguin Books Ltd.)
Penguin Group (Australia), 250 Camberwell Road, Camberwell, Victoria 3124,
Australia (a division of Pearson Australia Group Pty. Ltd.)
Penguin Books India Pvt. Ltd., 11 Community Centre, Panchsheel Park,
New Delhi - 110 017, India
Penguin Group (NZ), 67 Apollo Drive, Rosedale, North Shore 0745,
Auckland, New Zealand (a division of Pearson New Zealand Ltd.)
Penguin Books (South Africa) (Pty.) Ltd., 24 Sturdee Avenue,
Rosebank, Johannesburg 2196, South Africa

Penguin Books Ltd., Registered Offices:
80 Strand, London WC2R 0RL, England

First published by Signet, an imprint of New American Library,
a division of Penguin Group (USA) Inc.

First Printing, November 2007
10 9 8 7 6 5 4 3 2 1

For Mary Lynn . . . of course

Prologue

Sibley, Arizona Territory

In the rear corner of the Sky High Saloon, Lady Lucky looked at the three players as she held the deck of cards in her delicate hands. "To the tall Texan," she said, offering a thin coy smile to Texas Bob Krey. Outside, a raw March wind wailed mournfully. Somewhere a loose piece of tin roofing flapped and drummed in the blue dawn light.

Texas Bob raised his eyes to her above the edge of the cards in his hand. He wore a faded blue bib-front shirt, its top button open, the bib turned down on one corner. A drooping bandanna tied around his neck covered much of his broad chest. "I'll keep these," he said quietly. The drawstring on a bag of chopped tobacco dangled from his shirt pocket.

"I was afraid you would," said a surveyor named Reid Yeager. He sighed and dropped his worthless cards on the table and pushed them away. Then, gazing off toward a rear window overlooking a littered backyard kitchen where smoke billowed madly from a blackened *chimenea,* he asked no one in particular, "Is that bacon I smell cooking out there?"

"I do believe it is," said Texas Bob, still examining his cards.

"None too soon to suit me," said Yeager. "I could eat a boiled polecat." He gathered a thin stack of American bills and Mexican pesos lying in front of him. "This game didn't have my name on it from the onset." He picked up his last two gold coins, pitched one over in front of Lady Lucky and pocketed the other in his vest.

"Obliged," said Lady Lucky, sliding the coin away to her right on the battered pine tabletop. "Better luck next time, Reid."

"Next time?" said Davin Bass, a burly livestock and land speculator. "This game's not over! I'm down close to three thousand dollars. You've got to let me get right." As he spoke he tossed two cards onto the tabletop and gestured for Lady Lucky to deal him two new ones.

"It's over for me," said Yeager, taking his bowler hat down from a row of pegs along the wall. He nodded at the pile of cash and gold coins stacked in front of Texas Bob Krey. "You want to know where your money went? Here's the culprit." He gave a mock frown. Cocking his bowler fashionably and running a thumb along under the rim, he said to Texas Bob, "I will deal with you another time, sir. Right now I'm in need of food and rest."

"At your pleasure," said Texas Bob, appearing more interested in the cards in his hand than in making conversation. "Tell Rubin to cook me up some eggs and peppers too. I'll join you after this hand."

"What, you're quitting me too?" Bass asked, giving Bob a sharp stare as he stuck the two new cards Lady Lucky dealt him down into his hand. "You can't quit while you're ahead!"

"I don't know of a better time," Bob said. "I'll be around the next day or two, if you want a chance to even yourself up."

"No, I want to even up now," Bass insisted.

"Not with me," Bob said more firmly, seeing the cattle dealer getting more cross and edgy. He gave Lady Lucky a look. "What about you, Lady? Can I escort you to breakfast?"

"I'm starting to feel set upon by snakes," Bass said before Lady could answer. Glancing at his cards in disgust, he dropped them onto the table and shoved them away.

Texas Bob reached out and raked in the pot. As he did so, Reid Yeager said pointedly to Bass, "What exactly do you mean, *set upon by snakes*?" Along with the smell of bacon, an aroma of strong coffee wafted on the air.

Bass' hands stayed atop the table, but he pulled them back closer to the edge. Along his thigh lay a bone-handled Dance Brothers revolver in a tied-down slim-jim holster. "I mean exactly what you think I meant," he said. Across the table Texas Bob stopped sorting his money and watched the two men closely.

Lady Lucky's chair scooted back an inch. "Whoa, gentlemen," she said, keeping her voice friendly but cautioning. "Everybody's getting tired and starting to

show their horns and rattles. Let's not go saying things
that are going to—"

"Shut up, Lady!" Bass growled without taking his
eyes off of Yeager, who stood only a few feet away.
"I know when I've been taken!" He glared between
Yeager and Texas Bob. "All night long these two have
worked me over good." His dark scowl centered on
Yeager. "This one builds the pot up, then folds, leav-
ing it all for his partner!" His eyes turned to Bob.
"Isn't that the way you've been working it?"

Texas Bob stared in silence for a tense moment,
then replied in a calm but cautioning tone of voice,
"You're heading down the wrong trail, my friend. I
think this is the time to gather up and go."

"Yeah," said the surveyor. "We don't want to go
calling one another names. There's been no cheating
going on here."

Lady Lucky hurriedly scooted her chair farther back
from the table. "Mr. Bass, listen to them. It's been a
long night. Let's end it wisely, huh? What do you
say?" She stood and tried to reach a gentle hand over
and pat his forearm.

But Bass would have none of it. "Keep your cheating hands off me, woman!" He jerked his forearm
away and stood up from his chair. "I'm starting to
think you're in on it too."

Behind the bar, Carlos Montoya had been observing
the situation from the moment he'd heard Bass's
raised voice coming from the gaming table. Upon
seeing Lady Lucky toss him a worried look from thirty
feet away, he'd eased his hand under the bar, cocked

both hammers on a ten-gauge shotgun and lifted it quietly.

Always when it is me working back here, Carlos remarked silently to himself. Taking a deep breath, he walked toward the disturbance. At another table a drunken Croatian miner raised his head, looked around bleary-eyed, then dropped it again as Carlos slipped past him. Outside, along the wind-whipped dirt street, lanterns began to glow in dusty windows and from within ragged tents.

At the table, Davin Bass stood and pushed his chair away from himself with the back of his leg. His big hand closed around the bone-handled revolver. Across the table to his right, Yeager's hand closed around the butt of a Colt Thunderer behind the lapel of his wool suit coat. Straight across the table from Bass, Texas Bob stood staring coolly, his hand poised an inch from the dark walnut butt of a Colt resting in a holster under his left arm.

"*Nobody* make another move," Lady Lucky said with authority, seeing Carlos arrive and stop a few feet behind Bass. Beside Carlos a fire raged inside a potbellied stove. Logs he'd tossed into the stove moments earlier now crackled and hissed and settled into place. Carlos felt the heat on his arms, his face.

"Carlos is right behind you, cocked and ready, Mr. Bass," Lady continued. "Is this how you want to die?"

"You'll die too, Lady," Bass growled, his jaw clenched, his hand white-knuckle-tight around the gun butt.

"Yes, I know," said Lady Lucky, "and it will be all your fault. You know deep down that I didn't cheat you. You're spilling innocent blood."

Something in Lady's words got through to Bass. He stood tense for a moment longer, then let out a breath and let his hand uncoil, then slip down off his gun butt. "Whew." He batted his eyes as if to clear his head. "I—I reckon I am more tired and drunk than I thought." His red-rimmed eyes went from Texas Bob to Yeager, then to Lady Lucky. He looked repentant and ashamed. "Ma'am, call him off, please," he said, giving a cut of his eyes toward Carlos, standing behind him.

"Carlos," Lady said quietly.

Beside the woodstove, feeling the scorching heat, Carlos reached his thumb over the shotgun hammers. Yet before he could let the hammers down, a log inside the firebox thumped loudly into place, like a low clap of distant thunder.

"Wait!" shouted Yeager as they all instinctively went for their guns. Each of them recognized the sound of the settling firewood immediately, but their reflexes had been set into motion and nothing could stop them. Even as the surveyor shouted, his hand closed back around his Colt Thunderer and jerked it out.

Seeing Yeager's move, Bass jumped sidelong, hoping to get out from under the shotgun at his back. He fired on Yeager just as the shotgun roared. The surveyor staggered backward, his Thunderer firing repeatedly as Bass's bullet hit him in his chest. Yeager flew backward against the wall, still firing wildly.

Behind Bass, Carlos fell sidelong into the woodstove, one of Yeager's wild bullets hitting him in his forehead. The woodstove toppled over onto its side, its door flying open and its fiery contents spilling out onto the plank floor. Lady screamed and jerked a pocket derringer from beneath her dress, seeing Bass and Texas Bob both on their feet even though they'd each been hit with buckshot from the shotgun blast.

Bass and Texas Bob fired at one another, but Bass' shot went wild, the blast of buckshot having done terrible damage to his upper back and shoulders. Texas Bob fired two shots, both well aimed, both into Bass' chest. Then he fanned his big Colt back and forth instinctively, seeing Lady Lucky's pocket gun pointed at him.

Her face pale white, a trickle of blood running slowly down the corner of her mouth, Lady managed to say in a failing voice, "Don't shoot, Texas. I'm dead already." She took her left hand from under her breast and showed him her bloody palm.

"Hold on, Lady," said Texas Bob. The fire ignited by the overturned stove had already licked long and hungrily up the side of the building and begun reaching out across the ceiling. Shoving his Colt into his holster, Texas Bob stepped over, took her in his arms and headed for the door. At the table where the Croatian sat looking back and forth drunkenly, he said, "Get up, mister. Let's go! The place is on fire."

But the miner only muttered something in his native tongue and let his head drop back onto the table. "I said come on," shouted Bob, shifting Lady in his arms so he could reach down with his free hand and drag the Croatian by his collar.

From the street the rising townsfolk had heard the gunshots and come running. At the sight of the licking flames and black smoke hissing out from under the rafters, they had already begun to form a bucket brigade. As Bob reached the front door, a townsman named Fred Kearney stepped inside and looked around frantically. "Oh my, Tex!" he exclaimed, seeing the three bodies lying sprawled around the rear gaming table. "Are they dead?"

Looking back over his shoulder at the heavy boiling wall of flames, Bob said, "I hope so, Freddy. Else they're burning alive."

On the street, townsfolk hurried to the boardwalk and helped Kearney and Texas Bob carry the miner and Lady Lucky a safe distance from the fire. "Is she all right?" a young dove from a neighboring brothel called out as Bob placed Lady's pale limp form on the boardwalk across from the dirt street.

"Get the doctor, Cheryl," Bob said, noting how his own voice had begun sounding distant to him.

"Are *you* all right, Texas?" another dove asked. Stooping beside him, she opened the blanket wrapped around her with one arm and offered to spread it over his bloody shoulder.

"I'm all right, Mary Alice," Bob said, his voice sounding weak to him. "Just get the doctor . . . for Lady." He sat down on the cold hard boardwalk. "I'm going to rest here for a little while." He stretched out as if lying down on a soft feather bed.

The doves looked at one another. "Well, you heard

him, Cheryl! Go get the doctor!" Mary Alice shouted above the sounds of excited voices, clinking buckets and the roar and crackle of the raging fire. Clutching her ragged wool blanket around herself against the cold wind, she crouched down between Texas Bob and Lady Lucky and said, "I'll stay with Tex 'til he gets here."

PART 1

Chapter 1

Arizona Ranger Sam Burrack stood in the dirt street of the abandoned mining town with his wanted list in his gloved left hand. In his right hand he held his Colt at his thigh, his right glove stuffed into the pocket of his weathered riding duster. "Dade Sealey," he called out above the whir of cold wind. "You are under arrest. Come out with your hands high." He looked from the open doorway of the vacant saloon to up along the roofline. "Tommy Rojo, you're not wanted for anything. If you'll walk out here unarmed and ride away, I'll forget that you shot at me back there."

"Ranger, you must be as crazy as everybody says you are," a voice called out from the saloon. "I don't quit a pard when the going gets rough. What kind of coward would that make me?" Boards lay strewn in the dirt where the pair had hastily pried them off of the doorway.

Sam didn't answer. He'd spoken to Rojo only to make sure the outlaw wasn't waiting for him atop a roof or at some dusty window ledge. Sam knew where the young outlaw stood. Rojo had made his intentions clear the past three days as the ranger dogged the two men's trail all the way from the old fort along the Santa Cruz River.

"Is that how it is, Sealey?" he shouted. "You're going down. Are you going to let this young man die for you?"

"You're awfully sure of yourself, Ranger! My money says you're the one who's going to die. Not me! Not us!"

All right. Sam nodded slightly to himself, knowing there would be no hidden gun sights on him. The two had no rifles. They hadn't split up and taken positions. At the hitch rail in front of the saloon, two sweat-streaked horses stood with steam billowing from their nostrils, too worn-out to make a getaway. The only question now was whether Sealey and Rojo would choose to live or die.

"You both better think it over," Sam called out, making one last attempt at sending Rojo on his way and taking Dade Sealey in alive. "With luck you could be back out in a few years, Sealey. Maybe get yourself rehabilitated, not have to spend your life with a price on your head."

"Rehabilitated, ha!" Sealey called with a dark, scornful chuckle. "I've had some kind of bounty on me my whole life. I'm worth five hundred in Kansas, two hundred and fifty in Arkansas, and close to a thousand in Texas! That's what *my* life is worth. Now you tell me, Ranger, how much is your own lousy life wor—"

Sealey's words stopped short beneath the harsh explosion of a single gunshot. Sam instinctively braced himself, his Colt coming up at a drift of gun smoke in the doorway of the saloon. "Sealey?" He stepped forward, prepared for anything. But the saloon lay in silence beneath the whirring wind.

"He's dead, Ranger! I killed him!" Tommy Rojo shouted.

"You killed him? I thought he's your pard," the ranger said.

"Not anymore! I'm claiming that reward money! You're my witness! *Yeee-hiiii!*"

"All right, Rojo, if that's the case," Sam called out as realization came to him. "But nothing's changed. Step out with your hands high."

"What about the reward money?" Rojo asked firmly. "You said yourself, I'm not wanted. If I turn his body in, I will get the money, right?"

Sam had heard no shot whiz past him, had seen no bullet raise a clump of dirt in the street or thump into the face of a building. Yet he kept his senses alert in case this was a trick, and said, "If he's dead, you killed him, so yes, I suppose you will." He looked all around as he carefully walked forward. "Now come out with your hands up. No tricks."

Stepping into the middle of the dirt street, Sam held his Colt aimed at the saloon doorway and watched Rojo back out onto the boardwalk, dragging Dade Sealey by his forearms. "I'll do better than that," Rojo said. "Here he is, dead and delivered. *Yeee-hiiii!*" He dropped Sealey's limp arms to the ground and raised his own arms high, wearing a smile of satisfaction. "As far as I'm concerned, you and I have no argument between us. Right, Ranger?" He had to restrain himself from dancing a little jig.

This was a new and unexpected twist, the ranger thought, looking at the dead outlaw's body. A bloody hole gaped in Sealey's forehead where the bullet had exited. "No arguments," Sam said. He studied Rojo up and down, seeing no gun in his holster.

Noting the ranger checking out the empty holster, Rojo shrugged. "I left my Remington inside, so's you would know I wasn't trying anything. I thought it might be a good idea. Can I lower my hands now?"

"Yes, lower them," said Sam. Playing a hunch, he added, "And while they're lowered, reach down and pull that pig-sticker out of your boot."

Rojo sighed. He reached down, raised a wicked-looking Green River trade knife from his boot well and pitched it to the dirt. "I wasn't planning on trying anything with it."

Sam stared at him, poker-faced. "Now raise your hideout pistol and toss it away," he said.

"I've got no other weapons, Ranger," said Rojo. He added reflectively, "Funny how it come upon me in a flash, standing there. All of a sudden I thought, *Man! That's a lot of money ole Dade's bragging about.* I would be a fool to not claim it, I told myself." He paused, then continued, "I'd be more of a fool to make a move against you and lose my hard-earned reward."

"I suppose you would," said the ranger, making a gesture with his gun barrel for Rojo to turn around.

"But you won't mind if I search you all the same, seeing as how you shot Sealey from behind."

"I always say a man shot on a Sunday morning is no less dead than a man shot on a Wednesday afternoon," said Rojo, turning his back to the ranger, his hands going up again. "Do you get my meaning?" he asked as Sam patted him down. When the ranger made no reply, Rojo said, "Besides, you ought to be glad to see a man turn to the right side of the law the way I just did." He looked down at Sealey's body and shook his head. "Ole Dade shoulda had better sense, talking 'bout how much he's *worth*, me standing behind him with a cocked pistol."

"I agree with that," said Sam, glancing down at the hole in Sealey's forehead. Finding no more weapons on Rojo, he stepped back and lowered his Colt. With his free hand he pulled out his wrinkled list of names and consulted it for a moment. "Where's Trigger Leonard Heebs and Mitchell Smith?" he asked.

"I don't know," said Rojo. "They hadn't showed up yet. Is there money on them too?"

Sam stared at him without answering. Then he said, "We're going to rest these horses before we head back across the badlands. Keep yourself in front of me at all times if you intend to make it back and collect any money."

Texas Bob awakened in a jail cell with Mary Alice's blanket covering him. He looked all around at the bars and out through them at the deputy sheriff, Claude Price, who sat leaning back in a chair, his dirt-crusted boots resting atop a battered oak desk. His holstered pistol lay with his gun belt coiled around it on the desk. Seeing Texas Bob look his way, Price held a slice of an apple between his thumb and his pocketknife blade and said with restraint, "Well now, look who's waking up. I reckon you didn't spill all your blood after all."

Bob pieced together what had happened in his foggy memory as he looked down at the bandage that wrapped around his shoulder and covered much of his chest. "How—how long have I been asleep, Deputy?"

Price took his time, sticking the slice of apple into his mouth and chewing it before answering. "Oh . . . about a day and a half," he said. "Doc Winslow said you're lucky you made it at all, as much blood as you lost."

Bob pushed himself up onto the side of his cot and took a second of reflection, then said, "I can get around on my own now." He stood up and looked for his boots and clothes. Spotting his shirt and gun belt hanging from a wall peg outside the cell, he walked over to the barred door. "I barely even remember getting shot," he said, looking down at his bandage. "Just a few buckshot nicks as I recall."

"A few *nicks*?" said Price with a nasty grin. "Doc said two of them went deep enough he could feel your heart beating against his bullet extractor." He carved another slice of apple and stuck it in his mouth.

The gruesome remembrance of the gunfight came back to Bob. He saw the flames, and the dead lying strewn at his feet. "How are Lady Lucky and the miner?" he asked, knowing nobody else had made it out alive.

"The miner headed back over to Cleopatra Hill, to his diggings. Lady Lucky Claudene is in worse shape than you," Price said, hoping to make Texas Bob feel bad. "Doc said it's still long odds on her ever coming to." He grinned slightly, glad to see that it worked.

"That's too bad," Bob said under his breath. He pictured the smile on Lady Lucky's face when she'd last spoken to him over the deck of cards. "Doc's a good man. Maybe he'll pull her through."

"Yeah, maybe, but I doubt it," Price said with little concern in his voice. "One little slip on you, Doc Winslow could've done us all a favor and put you down like a mad dog." Chewing, he glared at Texas Bob. "As it is, I expect you'll hang at the town's expense."

Bob stopped and stood at the cell door, his hands on the bars. "What are you talking about, Deputy? I shot that Bass fellow in self-defense." He shook the bars and added, as if Price were only taunting him, "Come on, open up." Then, seeing the serious look on Price's face, he asked, "Where's Thorn, anyway?"

"Sheriff Thorn is over in Jerome. He'll be gone a week or more." Price laid the apple and knife on the desk and stood up, hooking his thumb into his belt. He stepped over close to the cell door and glared into Texas Bob's face. "Until he returns, I'm the bull of this walk."

Bob stood firm, not backing away an inch from the bars. Returning Price's menacing glare, he said, "Careful where that walk takes you. You're wearing a badge today. But you'll be Claude the blacksmith when Thorn gets back."

"You could be dead before then." Price's voice dropped low as if to keep the rest of the world from hearing. "There's bad blood between us, Bob. I've just been waiting for my chance to get a boot down on your neck."

"Don't issue threats you can't make good on, blacksmith," said Bob, standing his ground.

"No threats," said Price. "Just stating possibilities." He nodded at the bandage on Texas Bob's chest. "If you don't get the proper attention, you could swell up and rot."

"Doc Winslow would never stand for that," said Texas Bob. He gripped the bars tightly.

"Maybe not," said Price. The nasty grin returned to his face. "But hey, I'm just saying anything can happen here." He shrugged. "Including a rifle going off while I'm cleaning it. In a small space like that," he nodded at the cell, "one little slip and *bang*! Oops, sorry, Texas Bob Krey! Is that your brains running down the wall?"

"Why, you . . ." Bob gripped the bars tighter, as if he might very well rip them apart.

Price gave a dark chuckle, but he took a step back, seeing by the look on Bob's face that at any second this wounded man's good hand might reach through the bars and grab him by the throat. "Back off, Texas Bob. Let's see if Mary Alice thinks you're such a tall stack of chips when you're splattered on the wall."

"Is that what the bad blood is about?" Bob asked.

"All this, because Mary Alice won't give a flea-bitten jackass like you the time of day? You're blaming me, Claude? You never brought it up when there were no bars between us."

"It was coming," said Price. "The bars being around you just made it easier." He took down a rifle from a wall rack as he spoke and made sure Bob saw him slip a cartridge into its chamber. "And, yeah, you're right, it is about Mary Alice—and Cheryl, and Lady Lucky and all the rest of the doves. They hardly pay me any mind even when I'm paying them, but a big bold plainsman like *Texas Bob Krey* they fawn over like some kind of royalty!"

"You'll never get away with this, Claude," said Texas Bob, seeing the intent in the deputy's eyes.

"Who's going to tell?" Price grinned smugly. "Not me, and you'll be dead. It's an accident about to happen."

"No judge is going to believe it was an accident," said Texas Bob.

"I know one who will." Price grinned again and cocked the rifle hammer. "Territorial judge Henry Edgar Bass will believe it."

"Bass . . ." Texas Bob let the words sink in with a look of contemplation.

"You don't know who it was you killed, do you, Texas Bob?" the deputy said sarcastically. He raised the rifle. "None other than Judge Bass's beloved brother, Davin Bass."

"Oh . . ." Texas Bob stood stunned for a moment, his hands easing around the bars.

Claude gave a devious chuckle. "*Oh*, indeed." He

nestled the rifle stock to his shoulder and took close aim from only fifteen feet away. "See why you're so easy to kill? I could wind up becoming sheriff, maybe the judge's fishing pal." He squinted his left eye shut. "So long, Bob."

Before he could squeeze the trigger, the loosely closed front door opened suddenly and Mary Alice gasped at the sight of Price pointing a rifle at the tall Texan standing helplessly in the cell. "Claude! What on earth are you doing?" she shouted immediately, stepping inside. With a raised foot she kicked the door shut loudly behind herself. A bowl of stew sat on a service tray in her hands. Beside the steaming bowl lay a spoon and a folded checkered cloth napkin.

Caught by surprise, the deputy stammered, not knowing what to say. But finally, lowering the rifle, he said, stalling, "Oh, this?" He turned the rifle back and forth in his hands, looking at it as if it were a child's toy. "It's not loaded. I was just showing Texas Bob how a man ought to—"

"Like hell you were," said Mary Alice. "You were getting ready to kill him!" She stepped over and set the tray on the desk.

"Take it easy, Mary," Price said with a pleading voice. "Look, I'm putting it away, see?" He hurriedly stuck the rifle back into the rack. "Like I said, it's not loaded anyway!"

"It *is* loaded. Don't believe him, Mary," Texas Bob said, speaking fast. "You're right. He was going to kill me and call it an accident. You walked in and stopped him. When you leave he'll do it anyway."

"Stop it, both of you," Mary Alice said coolly.

Turning her back to them, she picked up the checkered napkin and shook it out. "Sheriff Thorn will decide who's lying when he gets back," she said, tinkering with a spoon and the cloth napkin. "I'm only here to see the prisoner is fed."

"Sounds fair enough to me, Mary Alice," said Price as he gave Texas Bob a harsh glare.

Mary Alice picked up the tray and walked to the cell, her back to Price, who stood staring at Texas Bob. The deputy didn't notice that his pistol had been lifted from its holster on the desk and now lay on the food tray, covered by the cloth napkin. "I don't know how I can ever thank you enough," Texas Bob said, reaching through the bars and snatching the gun up at about the same time Price finally glanced at the desk and saw the empty holster.

"Oh no!" said Price as Mary Alice stepped aside.

"What about this one, Claude?" said Texas Bob from behind the raised, cocked six-shooter. "I bet it's loaded."

"No, Mary Alice," Price said sorrowfully. "Why'd you do that? You broke the law!"

"I did it because Tex is no criminal," the young prostitute said. She rushed over and grabbed the cell key from the side of the desk, then hurried to the cell door to unlock it. "He wasn't your prisoner," she said, turning the key in the lock. "He was here to convalesce. You tried to kill him!"

"You can't get away with this!" Price said, wide-eyed at the sight of his own pistol pointed at him, ready to shoot him down.

"Oh?" Texas Bob stepped out of the cell with a

grim, determined look. Repeating the deputy's words from moments earlier, he said solemnly, "Who's going to tell? Not us, and you'll be dead."

"Tex!" cried Mary Alice. "You don't mean . . . ?" She let her words trail off.

"Go get my horse and a horse for yourself from the livery barn," Bob said, not taking his eyes or his aim off of Price. He didn't want Price to think he wouldn't kill him.

"Are you taking me away with you, Tex?" Mary Alice said hopefully.

"Yes. At least until Sheriff Thorn gets back and can straighten this out." He gestured the deputy into the cell. "Now hurry, Mary Alice," he said, "before somebody shows up."

Chapter 2

Leaving Sibley, Texas Bob and Mary Alice rode south
for the rest of the day, toward a stretch of hills and
grasslands near Black Canyon. Atop a wind-whipped
ridge, looking back along their trail, Mary Alice asked
from inside her upturned coat collar, "You didn't hit
him too hard, did you, Texas Bob? I mean . . . he's
not dead or nothing, is he?"

Bob smiled at her patiently beneath his wide dark
mustache. "No, Mary Alice," he said. "I didn't kill
the buzzard, and if you ask me again in another twenty
minutes, I *still* didn't kill him."

The young woman returned his smile, looking embarrassed. "I'm sorry, Tex. I don't know why I keep
asking. Just nervous, I guess."

"I understand," said Bob, sidling his horse over to
hers. Steam wafted from the breath of horses and riders alike. "You've lost your hat," Bob said quietly,
noting the cold wind sweeping her hair across her face.

"It wasn't nothing. I'm hardly cold at all." She
pushed her hair from her cheek.

Bob took off his hat, reached over and shoved it down onto her head and drew the rawhide string up snug beneath her cold chin. "There, that's better," he said.

"But what about you, Tex?" She could already feel the warmth of the hat making a difference.

"I'm good," said Bob, adjusting his tall duster collar. To the west the sun lay low, sinking behind a green and copper line of hills. "We'll be riding out of this wind in a few minutes. I'll find a camp and make a nice warm fire for the night." He nodded toward a trail leading into a long stretch of cliffs and plateaus covered with towering pines. "I have a cabin out there in a valley nobody knows about. You'll be safe there until things get straightened out."

Mary Alice didn't reply. Bob turned his horse back to the thin trail, and she nudged hers along behind him, following silently for the next hour until they stopped for the night in the shelter of a deep cliff overhang.

"I feel like I'm inside a fancy cathedral," Mary Alice commented, stepping down from her saddle with Bob assisting her. They both gazed up at the dome of rock reaching a hundred feet above them.

"By the time the smoke rolls up the underside of this overhang, it spreads out and can't be seen, especially under a wind," Bob said.

They made a fire out of nearby dried deadfall pine and mesquite brush. After attending to the horses they shared a meal of jerked beef and coffee from Bob's saddlebags and then settled in under blankets on opposite sides of the fire. For almost an hour they lay in an awkward silence, listening to the crackle of dried pine in the low licking flames. Finally Mary Alice said softly, "Tex, is there something wrong? Don't you want to sleep up against me?"

Bob waited for a moment, then said, "I thought I might be taking advantage, knowing you make your living the way you do."

"I'm not making my living tonight," Mary Alice said in the same soft warm voice. "Tonight I'm doing what a woman wants to do—if she's with the right man, that is."

"Yes, ma'am," Bob said quietly, needing no more of an invitation. He stood up and carried his blanket around the fire to where she looked up and smiled dreamily, pulling back her blanket, making room for him.

Moments later they fell asleep, warmed by one another beneath the whir of wind above the rock overhang.

When Mary Alice awakened in the gray hour of dawn, Bob had stirred the fire back to life and reheated the strong coffee left over from the night before. They sipped the hot brew and ate a breakfast of stiff warmed biscuits that he took from a canvas sack inside his saddlebags. "How did you sleep?" Bob asked quietly, the low flames flickering in his eyes.

Mary Alice took a deep breath and sighed, giving him a knowing look. "The best ever," she said.

Bob nodded. "Me too."

No sooner had they eaten than they were back on the move, going slowly until daylight burned away any traces of silvery mist looming on the steep trail.

In the early afternoon when they'd rested their horses and ridden on again, Mary Alice followed close as Bob veered away from the trail and rode deeper into the thickening forest. Finally, looking all around, realizing that she had no idea where they were, she said anxiously, "Tex, I'm glad you know your way through here. I've been lost ever since we broke camp this morning."

"Don't worry," Bob said reassuringly. He eased his horse back until they rode side by side. "If it was easy to find, I couldn't call it my hideout."

" 'Hideout' sounds like a place where an outlaw can run to, Tex," she said, giving him a look.

"I'm no outlaw, Mary Alice," Bob said. "But there are times I feel like the whole world is dogging my back trail. All I can do to regain myself is get away, lay low out here where the only hand that can touch me is the big hand of God."

"You go from talking like an outlaw to sounding like a preacher." Mary Alice smiled as their horses walked along at their own pace.

Bob smiled easily, staring straight ahead. "My father was a man of the cloth, a steadfast Texas Methodist. Both he and my mother died of the fever when I was young, but I expect some of their ways stuck to me—his especially."

"Oh, a minister's son," Mary Alice said softly, hoping to keep this conversation going, wanting to hear more about him. "That explains some things we've always wondered about you."

"Really?" Bob looked at her. "Like what?"

"Oh, just things," Mary Alice said coyly. "Your manners, the respectful way you treat people—us girls in particular."

Bob knew what she meant. He'd witnessed the rough, crude treatment the working girls received in the saloons and brothels across the western frontier. "You girls deserve no less respect than anybody else, far as I can see," Bob replied. "Circumstance plays reckless with all of us." He gazed out through the pines as if in remembrance. "Nowhere in the Good Book does it give me the right to judge another—only myself, and even then not too harshly. Our lives are small and short. We ought to be working on how to live our own lives instead of judging how somebody else lives theirs."

The Good Book? Mary Alice sensed that not many people knew the Texas Bob Krey he had just revealed to her—certainly none of the doves in Sibley and the surrounding mining towns. She didn't offer any comment and her silence prompted him to continue.

"Besides, everybody takes a different view of the other person. Look at Deputy Price. He pegged me for a killer."

"I know that what you did was self-defense," said Mary Alice. "So does everybody else in Sibley, except Claude. I wouldn't have given you that gun otherwise."

"I know you believe me, Mary Alice," said Texas

Bob, "and I'm obliged. But without seeing the fight firsthand, you're judging it the way you want it to be. So is the deputy. He's eaten up inside because you and the girls don't pay him the same attention you do me."

"It's because he treats us like field animals," Mary Alice offered. "He's just envious of you, Tex."

"I understand," said Bob, the two following the thin trail up a rise. "But instead of him trying to better himself and his ways, he'd rather see me die." He shook his head. "That's the way some folks are. That's why I live out here as much of the time as I can." He nodded toward the widening trail ahead. "I can only take being among folks for so long, and then I've got to get away from them. The longer I stay, the more apt I am to run into trouble. This time I overstayed myself."

Mary Alice started to reply, but before she could they topped the rise and her attention was drawn to the sight of a cabin in a small clearing. "Oh my," she said, seeing a doe and her fawn straighten up from the ground, look at them curiously, then lope away into the woods. "Tex, this is beautiful." She raised her fingertips to her lips in awe.

Noting a glistening tear forming in her eye, Bob nudged his horse forward. "Thanks, Mary Alice. I'm glad you like it. You're the first person I've ever brought here. It's home for me and ole Plug."

Following close behind him, Mary Alice asked, "Who's ole Plug?"

"Plug is a wild hound who showed up one morning a couple of years back. He settled in with me and has been here ever since."

Looking around, Mary Alice said, "Where is he? Why isn't he raising a ruckus?"

"If he was here those deer wouldn't have been bedded down in the yard," said Bob. "I expect he's out hunting down a meal of brush rabbit for himself."

They rode down and stopped at a hitch rail in front of the cabin. Bob stepped down and reached up to help Mary Alice from her saddle. "Well, here's home, for the time being anyway," he said.

"Oh, Tex," Mary Alice said, throwing her arms up around his neck and hugging him as soon as her feet touched the ground. "I'm so happy you brought me here. I—I feel like it was meant to be, us having to leave Sibley! This feels like coming home." He felt a warm tear against the side of his throat.

"Whoa now," said Bob, taking her arms from around his neck gently. "Better wait until you've seen the inside. I might have left it in a mess."

Mary Alice collected herself and turned, hooking her arm around his waist and pulling him toward a path of stepping-stones leading to the cabin door. "Oh, I don't care," she said, turning more jovial. "I can clean up a mess. It just feels good to get away from Sibley for a while."

"I'm glad you feel that way," said Bob, "because it might take a few days for me to find Sheriff Thorn and make him understand how things happened. Meanwhile I want you to stay here out of sight. I don't want to risk any trouble coming to you for helping me."

"Yes, I understand," said Mary Alice in a more serious tone. "But you'll wait a couple of days before looking for Thorn, won't you?" She turned her face to his with an inviting look in her eyes.

Texas Bob smiled. "Well, I expect it wouldn't hurt to let these wounds heal a day or two before I leave." They walked on to the cabin door.

In Sibley, Raul Lepov pushed up the wide brim of his black flat-crowned hat and said to Deputy Price, "You some damn figure of a fool, you are." He rested a dirty knee-high French Cavalry boot on the chair beside the battered desk where Price sat holding a wet rag to the back of his swollen head.

"Listen to me, Mr. Lepov," Price said crossly. "My head is busting and I'm not in any mood for hearing anybody's guff. So walk easy around me."

"Walk easy around you? Why?" The French gunman chuckled. Wearing black leather gloves with the fingers cut off, he reached his hand out and palmed the deputy on the side of his head, not hard, but hard enough to make Price wince. "You let a wounded *cawboy* and a stupid *putain* bust your head and walk out of your jail." He grinned tauntingly beneath his long black mustache. "You are *un imbecile!*"

Price said angrily, "I'm in no mood for joking or sharp remarks, mister!"

But Lepov only chuckled. *"Imbecile,"* he repeated, and acted as if he would palm the deputy again.

Price flinched and ducked his head, scooting his desk chair farther away. "I'm warning you, Lepov!" he growled.

"All right, you *warned* me," said Raul in his strange

accent. "Now, why did you tell me your sad story, *imbecile*?" He grinned again.

Price overlooked being called a fool and said, "I want you to hunt him down and kill him. Bring his head back to me. The whore's too if she's still with him."

"Ah!" he said, feigning surprise. "You want him dead, this *Cawboy* Bob and his *putain*."

Price stared at him coldly for a moment. "I don't have to take this." He dropped the wet rag on the desk and started to stand.

But the tall rawboned Frenchman shoved him back down and said in a more serious tone, "Ah, but where are your sense of humor, *mon ami*? Of course I will kill them for you." He tossed a hand. "They are dead already, if I am on their trail."

"All right." Price calmed down, stared at him levelly and asked, "How much?"

"Well. Let me see," said Raul, using his fingertips as if adding up the cost. "Kill the *cawboy*, cut his head off. Kill the *putain*, cut her head off. Both heads . . . bring them back to you . . ." He let his words trail off, gazing upward, making tally. "Three hundred dollars."

"Three hundred dollars?" Price almost came up from his chair. This time Raul stopped him, poking a long dirty fingernail into his chest.

"Oui," Lepov said shamelessly. "Three hundred is not so bad, if it keeps an *imbecile* from looking like an *imbecile*, eh? Also if it keeps an *imbecile* from getting himself killed, which is what you would do." He returned Price's stare. "See, I know this *Cawboy* Bob.

I have seen him many times. He is a man to be respected."

"His name is *Texas* Bob," Price said, correcting him.

"Texas . . . *Cawboy* . . . all is the same." Raul shrugged under his black wool cape. "I kill them both, cut off their heads, bring them back, the story ends. You can tell your sheriff you did all this."

"I don't know if I'd tell Thorn I cut off their heads," said Price, considering things.

Raul shrugged again. "Tell him they cut off each other's heads, for all I care. Are you man enough to carry this through? Do you have the three hundred dollars with which to pay for my services?"

"I've been . . ." Price paused, then said, "Well, I've been saving money for a long time, hoping to someday ask one of the doves to marry me." He wasn't about to mention that Mary Alice was the dove he had in mind.

"Oh, that is so sweet," said Lepov, grinning darkly. He reached out and pinched Price's cheek roughly. Price swiped at his hand but missed. He didn't know what to think of Raul Lepov. He'd never met the strange-acting French hunter. But knowing Lepov was in town, he'd gone to the Bottoms Up Saloon and found him as soon as young Jimmy Elder came by the office and found him staggering to his feet inside the locked cell. He hadn't told Jimmy what had really happened, and he'd sworn the boy to secrecy about finding him locked up in his own jail.

"Nobody is going to hear about this, are they, Mr. Lepov?" he asked. "You see, this man was not really a prisoner. He was just a man who needed a place to sleep off some work the doc did on him and I let him use an empty cell."

"Nobody hears a word of it from me," said Lepov. Rubbing his fingers and thumb together, he added, "Now, about the money?"

"Yeah," Price sighed. "I'll go by the bank and get it. Are you ready to ride?" He stood up.

"Of course I am ready to ride, *imbecile*." Raul grinned, shooing him toward the door.

Price stopped and stood firm, pointing a finger at the Frenchman. "Stop calling me names. I'm not an imbecile. You understand?"

But Raul shrugged it off with another grin. "But it is a name I give to you, as a sign of our newfound friendship. I give pet names like this to all my friends. It is how I am. You must get used to it!" He shooed him on toward the door. "Now go, you *imbecile* you, and get my money for me!"

Chapter 3

When Price returned from the bank he counted out three hundred dollars into Lepov's hand. He watched the Frenchman walk out the front door, mount his black horse and ride away. But moments later as Price stepped onto the boardwalk, confident that Lepov had gotten onto Texas Bob's trail, he saw the black horse standing back at the hitch rail out front of the saloon where he'd found him.

Damn it! Price clenched his fists at his side and headed for the saloon, realizing he should never have given Lepov the full three hundred in advance. But on his way to the Bottoms Up Saloon and Brothel, Price saw territorial judge Henry Edgar Bass's private four-horse Studebaker coach turn onto the wide dirt street and thunder toward him, the powerful horses pounding forward at a trot.

Knowing the judge would be coming straight to the sheriff's office, Price stopped and watched the driver lean back on the reins and the long brake handle until the horses came to a halt beside him. Without so much as a greeting or a touch of his hat brim, the judge glared at Price from inside the plush coach and flipped the door open. "Get in, Deputy," he said in a tightly controlled voice.

Price hurriedly stepped inside and sat down across from the judge. "Your Honor, I can't tell you how sorry I was to have to send that telegram to you over in Hazelton, but I knew you would want to hear the news right away, no matter how painful—"

"Where's my poor brother's body?" the judge asked flatly, cutting him off.

"He's—he's in the cooling house behind the Bottoms Up, Your Honor."

The judge shook his large hairless head and looked over at the charred remains of the Sky High Saloon. "I knew someday poor Davin would meet his end at just such a place as the Sky High Saloon. Not that I'm opposed to a man taking his pleasure," he added quickly, looking along the boardwalk at a string of saloons, brothels and gaming establishments. He shook his head again. He pulled up and down on a thin chain that ran up through the roof of the coach and connected to a small brass bell mounted beside the driver's seat.

"Yes, Your Honor?" said the driver, leaning down and looking inside at the judge and Deputy Price.

Pointing toward the saloon, the judge said, "Take us behind the Bottoms Up, Wilson. I want to see my poor brother's body."

The driver slapped the reins and sent the horses forward, having to go to the far end of the wide street and circle back onto a wider main alleyway behind the row of saloons. On their way, the judge tugged his vest down over his belly and said grudgingly, "I am obliged to you, Deputy, for sending that telegram as soon as it happened. Fortunately I hadn't yet left Hazelton."

"You're welcome, Your Honor," said Price, easing down in the soft seat, liking the idea of being seen riding in the judge's big elaborate road rig. "I knew this was your week to preside there. I figured it best if I could catch you there, only thirty miles away."

"Now then," said the judge, not appearing to hear what Price had to say, "as horrendous as this is, tell me exactly what happened to poor Davin."

The deputy ran through the particulars of the shooting as the coach made its way to the rear of the Bottoms Up. When he'd finished, the judge said, "I've heard of Texas Bob Krey. I've never known of him being a ruffian, or a bully." He seemed to contemplate things. "And Lady Lucky, how is she coming along?"

"She's going to live is the last thing I heard when I went by and checked. Doc Winslow said she told him it was a fair fight," said Price. "But I've got to tell you, Your Honor, Lady Lucky is a friend of Texas Bob's." He added in disgust, "All the women in this town are *friends* of his, as far as that goes."

"How can it be a fair fight," said the judge, "when my poor brother is lying dead?"

Price didn't know how to answer. He shrugged slightly.

"And you let him get away?" the judge added in a prickly tone.

"Like I said, Your Honor," Price replied, "he was

never under arrest. He was in the cell getting treated by the doctor. When it was all done and he was awake and feeling better, how could I keep him from leaving?"

"How indeed." The judge stared at him through thick wire-rimmed spectacles. "You could have held him on suspicion until you found out if it was a fair fight."

Price scratched his head. "Well, he said it was, Your Honor."

"Oh," said the judge. "*He* said it was." He turned away and stared out through the window at the back side of the saloons and brothels, where women lounged with cigars, cigarettes and pipes curling smoke from their lips. Returning the women's waves, the judge said in a lowered tone, "I want Texas Bob to answer for this."

"I understand, Your Honor," said Price. "I'll do whatever you want me to do—"

"Are you sure he wasn't under arrest, maybe for starting the fire—maybe being held for questioning about the fire, or the shooting, or for *some* damn thing?" The judge tossed a hand in frustration.

"No, Your Honor," Price said, shaking his head. "I never arrested him for anything."

The two fell silent as the coach stopped at a free-standing stone building in the shade of an ancient native oak behind the Bottoms Up Saloon and Brothel. Price stepped out quickly and opened the thick door of the cooling house for the large ambling judge.

"Allow me, Your Honor," he said, feeling the coolness from blocks of ice stacked against every wall. The judge stopped as Price reached out and lifted the edge of a stiff gray tarpaulin covering Davin Bass's charred remains.

"Oh my," the judge said, swooning weakly at the sight of his own flesh and blood roasted to a crisp, the bullet holes hard to see in the blackened sunken chest cavity.

"As cooked as he is," Price said, trying to speak gently but failing at it, "we wouldn't have had to keep him cooled this way. I did it out of respect for you."

Judge Bass jerked a neatly folded handkerchief from inside his black swallow-tailed coat and pressed it to his nose and mouth. "Poor Davin . . . poor, *poor* Davin," he murmured. He paused, but only for a moment, then breathed deep and asked, "What about the other people you mentioned—the surveyor, the miner?"

"The surveyor was burnt up too," said Price. "We went ahead and got him into the ground straightaway. The miner is gone back over to Cleopatra Hill to work the copper holdings. He was too drunk to see anything. Anyway, Texas Bob dragged him out, so he thinks Texas Bob is the next step from a perfect saint."

"I see," said the judge, his hands tightening in controlled rage. "The women all love Texas Bob, and the miner worships him. Quite a pat hand Texas Bob Krey has had dealt him here, isn't it?"

"I'm just telling you how things are, Your Honor," said Price, still holding the corner of the tarpaulin up.

"Cover him, Deputy," the judge said briskly. "I've seen enough."

They walked back to the coach and the judge said as the driver stood to the side and opened the door for them, "Don't let me put words in your mouth, Deputy, but think real hard. In the heat of ensuing events—a shooting, a raging fire—is it possible you might have told Texas Bob he was under arrest and it slipped your mind until just now?"

Price stared at the judge for a moment as they seated themselves and the coach door closed behind them. Nodding in thought, making sure he understood what the judge wanted, he said, "As a matter of fact I did, Your Honor. I—I told him he was being held until the sheriff returned from over in Jerome."

The deputy looked relieved, knowing that no matter how he had mishandled and mistreated Texas Bob, he now had the law on his side. He could go to court if need be and tell the story as it had actually happened, adding only that he'd told Texas Bob he was under arrest. "Thank you, Your Honor. I knew Texas Bob ought to be dealt with in the sternest legal manner. I just didn't understand how it should come about, *legally* speaking."

"But now you do, so there you have it," said the judge. "Texas Bob is wanted for jailbreak, plain and simple. I'm sending out a telegram to all territorial law enforcement. This man has fled to avoid being implicated in the serious crime of arson, perhaps even murder." The judge took a deep breath of satisfaction. "Now then, I will have him caught and brought before my bench. We'll see how *fair* this alleged *fair fight* really was. I can take any fair fight and break it down so that whoever *I want* to see guilty *is* guilty, beyond a shadow of a doubt. The law knows how to deal with troublemakers like Texas Bob."

On the way back to the sheriff's office, Price saw Lepov stepping up into his saddle in front of the Bottoms Up. He wanted to jump out of the coach and go tell him to forget about killing Texas Bob—the deal was off. *Give the money back!* But he didn't. Instead, he kept his mouth shut and remained calm. Sometimes things just had a way of playing themselves out, he told himself, relaxing in the soft coach seat and watching as faces turned toward him and the judge from all along the dirt street.

Sam had first heard the sound of horses' hooves an hour earlier, moving behind him in the dry brush. Now, in the long shadows of evening, he heard it again as he gathered deadfall limbs, stacked them and built a campfire. A few feet away Tommy Rojo sat leaning back against a tree rolling himself a smoke, not offering to help with the campsite.

But that was all right with the ranger. He'd rather have Rojo sitting still where he could keep an eye on him. Looking over at Rojo, Sam could tell by the expression on his face that he too had heard the sound. Rojo gave him a wary look. "Visitors," he whispered.

"Start talking," Sam said quietly, easing his Colt from its holster.

Seeing the revolver, Rojo raised both hands chest high, and said, "Whoa, Ranger! I've got nothing to do with whoever is out there! I swear it."

"That's not what I mean," said Sam, almost in a

whisper himself. As he spoke he piled his blanket up against his saddle lying on the ground and laid his sombrero atop it. "I want you to start talking to me about something."

"About what?" Rojo looked confused.

"Anything," Sam said, stepping sideways away from the growing firelight and into the shadowy evening darkness. Seeing Rojo scratch his head, the ranger prompted him, saying, "Tell me about how you grew up." He stepped back out of the small clearing into the darkness of trees and brush.

"Well now, let me see," said Rojo, not comfortable with revealing anything about himself, especially to a lawman. "Uh—I grew up in Missouri, outside of Springfield, I believe it was . . ."

Sam shook his head, realizing that Rojo was making up every word of it. But that didn't matter, he thought, only partially listening as the young man began to rattle on. "We was all good children, my brothers and me," Rojo continued, "although we got blamed for everything bad that happened . . ."

Sam listened to the sound of slow-moving hooves in the dried brush. When the sound stopped, he peeped around the tree hiding him and watched a rider step down, hitch his horse to a sapling and draw a rifle from a saddle boot. Sam slowly cocked the Colt against the leg of his trousers, muffling the metal-against-metal click. Then he waited silently, his back against the large native oak, until he saw the dark figure move past him and stop less than three feet away. From their hidden positions both the ranger and the intruder stood listening to Tommy Rojo's conversation.

"I remember we got blamed for throwing a hornets' nest into a church house and jerking the supports out from under a walk bridge across a creek," Tommy continued. "Once they even tried to blame me for stealing the bell off the schoolhouse and trying to sell it to a band of horse gypsies—"

"Nobody make a move, or you are dead!" the dark figure called out in the midst of Rojo's ramblings, stepping out quickly and pointing his rifle back and forth between Rojo and the ranger's sombrero lying atop the saddle on the ground. Seeing Rojo raise his hands in surprise, the dark figure shouted to the sombrero, "You! On your feet! One false move and you die!"

From against the tree Rojo saw the man stiffen and freeze as the tip of the ranger's Colt jammed against the back of his head. "Drop the rifle, or drop with it," the ranger said in a calm but firm tone.

The rifle plopped to the dirt. "You are making a big mistake, you *vermine*," said Lepov. His neck poker straight, his eyes straining sidelong for a look at who stood behind him, he added, "I am not a man you want to ambush from behind."

"I'll keep it in mind," Sam said quietly. He pulled a sleek Colt from Lepov's tied-down holster and pitched it forward beside the discarded rifle. He reached around Lepov's waist from behind, pulled a big British army revolver from the gunman's belt and pitched it to the ground with the other two firearms.

Lepov's fiery tone cooled a bit when he saw his big guns hit the ground. "Listen to me, *monsieur*. If you let me go this instant, I promise I will not seek retribution against you."

"I'll keep that in mind too," said Sam. He reached his hand up under Lepov's black cape and pulled a navy Colt from a shoulder holster.

The dark French Canadian let out a sigh of resignation as he saw his last weapon hit the ground. Across the fire by the tree, Tommy Rojo puffed his cigarette and said to Lepov, "It's hard to hide things from him."

Lepov's eyes went to Sealey's body lying over by the horses. *"Mon ami,"* he said over his shoulder, his attitude having changed quickly. "I wish you gentlemen no harm. I am searching for a vicious killer. Perhaps you will be kind enough to help me?"

"Huh." Rojo blew a stream of smoke. "How do you know one of *us* ain't that vicious killer?"

Lepov fell silent.

"We're not, though," Sam said behind him. "I'm Arizona Ranger Sam Burrack." He gave Lepov a nudge forward with his gun barrel. "Take a seat. Tell us about this vicious killer you're searching for and why you're out here slipping up on folks in the dark."

"Burrack?" said Lepov. "I have heard much about you, Ranger." He stepped forward and turned around facing the ranger, his hands coming down only slightly. "You have made yourself known and respected, keeping the law and order here in this blasted furnace of a place." He sank down beside Rojo.

Sam ignored the praise and asked, "Who is this vicious killer and why are you hunting him?"

"I am Raul Lepov. I am commissioned by the deputy of Sibley to find *Cawboy* Bob Krey—a cold-blooded killer—and bring him to justice."

"I've heard of you too, Lepov," Sam replied. "I take it you mean *Texas* Bob Krey, not *Cowboy* Bob. Texas Bob Krey is no cold-blooded killer." He looked Lepov up and down appraisingly. "And since no *deputy* sheriff has the power to commission *anybody* to do *anything* that I know of, I take it that by *justice* you mean you're out to kill Texas Bob." He stared pointedly at him. "Am I understanding it right so far, Lepov?"

Lepov hedged a bit. "I think I did not make myself clear. I am being *paid* by an officer of the law to find *Caw*— I mean *Texas* Bob, and see to it that justice is served."

"I'm tired of fooling with you, Lepov. Talk straight, if you can." Sam said forcefully. "The deputy in Sibley is paying you to *kill* Texas Bob. Why?"

"I will tell you everything," Lepov said. He took a breath and told the ranger the whole story—about how Texas Bob had killed Judge Bass's brother, about Lady Lucky being wounded, and about how Texas Bob and Mary Alice had unlocked the cell and Bob had walked out of the Sibley town jail.

"My, my." Sam shook his head when Lepov had finished the tale. "I can see why Texas Bob lit out," he said, speaking more to himself than to Lepov. But then he caught himself, looked at Lepov and said, "I can't tell you not to go after Bob Krey. But I'll tell you this: If you kill him, you'll have to answer to the law for it."

Lepov shrugged and grinned smugly. "You Americans and your laws are so funny. It is the *law* who is paying me to kill *Cowboy* Bob, Ranger."

"Texas Bob," Sam said, correcting him again. "You're free to go, Lepov. The sooner the better," he added, seeing the gunman eyeing the coffeepot sitting beside the fire. "Don't come sneaking around here again. That's your only warning."

Lepov stood up with a sigh and pointed at his guns lying in the dirt. "My weapons?"

"Leave them be," said Sam. "Pick them up in the morning after we're gone."

"No, no, I must have them right now, this instant," Lepov insisted, shaking his head. "I cannot *pick them up* tomorrow. That is out of the question."

"Pick them up *tomorrow,*" Sam said strongly. "The only *question* is do you want to pick them up off the ground or up out of a deep creek?"

"But what about tonight?" said Lepov. "I will be alone in this dark wilderness, with no way to protect myself!"

"Are you afraid of the dark, Lepov?" Tommy Rojo cut in.

"Shut up, Rojo," Sam said.

"I caution you not to insult me, *monsieur,*" Lepov said, pointing a finger at Rojo.

"Get out of here, Lepov," Sam said, to keep down any trouble between the two. "You'll get your firearms back in the morning. I'll sleep better knowing you're unarmed for the night."

"Yeah," said Rojo. "If anything bothers you out there tonight, start squealing real loud. We'll come protect you."

"That's enough out of you," Sam said, giving Rojo a harsh stare, but keeping an eye on Lepov as he walked back into the brush, cursing Rojo and the ranger under his breath.

"Sorry, Ranger," Rojo said, puffing on his short cigarette. "But now that I'm a bounty man myself, I don't want the competition coming around crowding me—'specially some high-handed Frenchy at that."

Paying no attention to Rojo, Sam stared off in the direction the French gunman had taken and commented to himself, "We'll be riding into Sibley come morning. I'll see what this is about with Texas Bob. He's no killer, I know that much already."

"Maybe he wasn't to begin with," said Rojo. "But a man gets the wrong kind of lawmen down on him, they can turn him into a killer quicker than you can slap a cat."

Still staring off after Lepov, the ranger considered everything the Frenchman had told them and said, "I wouldn't agree with you on many things, Tommy Rojo, but in this case, you might be right."

Chapter 4

Deputy Claude Price stood slumped at the bar of the Rambling Dutchman Saloon, a large ragged tent that was the last in a long line of drinking establishments reaching to the outskirts of Sibley. *Damn it all.* He shook his head and tossed back a burning mouthful of rye whiskey. A dirty canvas bag hung on its strap from his shoulder. *How did I let things go so far?* he mused silently, shaking his bowed head.

Frisco Phil Page, the day bartender at the Rambling Dutchman, stepped forward, refilled Price's shot glass and asked, "Just how serious is the judge about wanting revenge for ole Davin getting cooked like a pig?"

"Why, Frisco?" Price stared at him, raised the filled glass and drank half of it. "Are you in some position of remedy? Is there some service you have to offer?" He gave a sarcastic look, the shots of rye starting to go to his head.

"I might be, when the money gets right," said Frisco, a big Colt sticking up from behind a red sash around his waist, a bar towel hanging around its butt. "I wouldn't kill a man on the cheap." As he spoke he pulled the towel up and wiped it back and forth along the pine bar top, causing flies to rise up in a swirl of protest. "But I would kill Texas Bob graveyard dead to raise myself a stake and get out of the pig dump."

"Is that so?" Price said flatly.

"Yes, it is so," said Frisco Phil, not being put off by Price's attitude. He stopped wiping the bar top. "And stop giving me your 'better than I am' belligerence. You're nothing but a blacksmith wearing a tin badge."

"Yeah, and you're a day bartender for Vinten Kriek, the Rambling Dutchman, a sick old lunger who's ready to catch a face full of dirt any day." He tapped his finger on the bar. "You best keep pouring and leave the law work to me."

"I'm pouring your drinks for free, *blacksmith*, so get civil or get out," Frisco Phil countered, thumbing himself on the chest. He picked up the bottle of rye sitting near Price's glass and appeared ready to cork it and put it away.

"All right, I apologize," said Price. "Keep pouring . . . I'm obliged to you. I'm just out of sorts right now. The judge is driving me crazy."

"Yeah?" Seeing the relenting look come to Price's face, Frisco said, "Then how about me and you teaming up and cashing in on the judge's grief?"

Price considered it, nodding, looking at the bottle of rye. "I don't see how," he said, raising the dirty canvas bag and plopping it down on the bar. Flies rose and swirled. "Here, take one. You'll see what I mean." A few leaflets slid out onto the bar top.

Frisco Phil picked one up and looked it over, his lips moving as he read under his breath.

"He's got me hammering these up all over town." Price growled with discontent.

"Two hundred dollars? Forget it." He let the leaflet fall back to the bar. "That doesn't sound very serious to me." He reached the bottle out and topped off Price's half-empty shot glass.

"Me neither," said Price, thinking about having already spent his savings on the French gunman.

"But maybe this is just to stir up a few gunmen and get them hounding Texas Bob's trail," said Frisco.

"Oh?" said Price. "You think?"

Frisco shrugged. "I think nobody is going to bring Texas Bob in for two hundred dollars." He smiled. "You've got the judge's ear. Once he sees nobody is going to find Texas Bob, let alone kill him, what do you suppose he'd *really* pay to see Texas Bob slung facedown over a saddle, both eyes bugging out of their sockets?"

Price eyed him curiously. "If nobody else can find him, what makes you think we can?"

"I know where he holes up," said Frisco, his voice dropping lower even though there were no other customers to hear him. "Once when I was out scouting a copper claim, I followed him over three miles through the long pines, him not knowing I was there."

"Why'd you do that, Frisco?" Price asked. "You're not a bushwhacker, are you?"

"Never mind what I am or ain't," Frisco Phil said crossly, his face reddening at Price's question. "The point is I know where Texas Bob and the dove most likely are laying low right now."

"Yeah? Where?" Price asked, then tossed back his shot of rye.

"I won't tell you, but I'll show you, if the money is right." He gave a wink.

"I don't believe you," said Price, setting down his empty glass and watching Frisco refill it.

"Oh, I think you do believe me, Deputy." He narrowed his gaze on Price and purred in a rasping tone, "Just picture the two of them, all alone, grunting, groaning, her panting, humping, doing for him for *free* what you could barely get her to do for—"

"Shut up, damn it!" Price pounded his fist on the bar top; his shot glass splashed rye over its rim.

"That's all I'm going to say about it." Raising his hands chest high, Frisco continued, his tone of voice growing louder, more confident, "All you've got to do is get us a deal with His Honor for some *serious* blood money, and you can skin them both and roll them in salt for all I care."

Stepping inside the tent, a hand on his hip, a hammer dangling from his fingertips, Judge Bass called out to Price in a booming voice, "What kind of *deal* is it you plan to execute with me, Deputy?"

"Your Honor!" Price shoved the empty shot glass away from himself, startled by the judge's sudden appearance. "We—we were just talking about how we might help bring in your brother's killer!"

"Oh, you want to *help*?" the judge said cynically, stepping toward the bar, holding the hammer out toward Price. "I found this lying on the boardwalk out front of the barbershop. If you want to *help*, get the rest of these reward posters nailed up all over Sibley the way I instructed you to do."

Price turned nervous. He fumbled with the canvas bag, jerking it up and trying to stuff the loose posters back inside.

"Easy, Deputy," the bartender said under his breath, catching Price's forearm and stopping him. As Price stood transfixed, gripping a handful of reward posters, the bartender said boldly, "Judge Bass, you need to hire yourself some barroom flunky to do this kind of work." As he spoke he stepped from behind the bar, the butt of his Colt standing high from his waist sash. "Better yet, you could do it yourself."

The judge looked offended, but he held back any sharp response. Instead he tilted his head back and looked down his nose at the bartender. "Oh? And who might you be?"

"I'm Phillip Page," the man replied in a calm voice. "Folks call me Frisco Phil." He stopped three feet away from the judge—too close for the judge's comfort. Yet, when the judge took a short step back, Frisco Phil took a short step forward. "I'm the one man who can bring Texas Bob Krey to you, either all at once or a few pieces at a time, till I've got him piled up in the street like cordwood."

"The one man indeed?" the judge said. "What makes you think so, pray tell?"

"Because I know where he lives," Frisco said with a thin mirthless smile. "I can ride there straightaway for the right amount of money."

"For money," the judge said, as if even saying the

word conjured up disgust. The judge looked him up and down with the same measure of distaste. Then he looked at Price and said, "Come along, Deputy. You have posters to distribute."

Frisco cut Price a harsh glance, his hand going to his gun butt and resting there. "Your Honor," said Price in an anxious voice, "this man is telling you the truth. He knows where Texas Bob lives." Price had no reason to believe Phil really knew where Texas Bob lived. But he didn't like the way Page stared at him, his fingers tapping on his gun butt. "Frisco and me can go get Bob right now and settle this whole matter for you."

"If the money is right," Frisco cut in, turning the same harsh stare to the judge. "I don't work for *flunky* pay."

The judge glanced first at the bar where Frisco Phil had been standing a moment earlier, then at Phil with a knowing look. Getting the judge's meaning, Phil said, "I've only been here biding my time 'til some man-hunting work comes along. Now, here it is. And I'm ready for it."

The judge nodded slightly, considering the offer. He was starting to realize that if this man knew where to find Texas Bob, he might be worth dealing with. He'd known of many cases where one man killed another and rode off, never to be seen or heard from again. He didn't want that. Letting out a breath, he asked, "Just what amount of money are you proposing, Frisco Phil?"

"One thousand dollars," Page said without hesitation, staring the judge in the eyes.

"A thous—" Judge Bass stood in stunned silence

for a moment. Finally, he looked back and forth between the bartender and the deputy and chuckled.
"For a minute I thought you were serious." His
chuckle turned into a short, nervous laugh, then fell
away as he saw the no-nonsense look on Frisco Phil's
stoic face. He coughed and cleared his throat. "That
is totally out of the question, of course." He pitched
the hammer to Price, who caught it and dropped it
inside the canvas bag.

"You're the judge," said Page. "You can set the
reward at whatever you want it to be. I once heard
of a judge who set rewards high, billed the territory
for a thousand dollars but only paid the bounty hunter
two or three hundred. I expect you might have heard
of that same judge."

"Are you accusing me of something untoward, bartender?" said Bass, bristling at Page's words.

"Not at all, Judge Bass," said Page. "I'm just pointing out that you have the power to appoint whatever
amount you feel is right for the man who killed not
only your brother but two other men. Not to mention
that he wounded a woman and burned down a saloon." Looking back and forth between the judge and
the deputy, he said, "For all we know he might've
forced this other woman to go with him. He might be
holding her against her will."

The judge listened closely. Page was making sense.
A thousand was not too much to ask for. Neither was
two thousand, the more he considered it.

Page stood silent for a moment, seeing that the
judge was working it out in his mind. Finally he asked,
"Well, what's it going to be, Judge?"

Bass knew that whatever amount he posted on Texas Bob's head, he could keep it a secret for only a short while before making it public information. "You're certain you can ride out straight to where Texas Bob is hiding?"

"I'm certain," said Page.

"Then here's the deal," said the judge. "I want Texas Bob brought in alive if at all possible."

"But, Judge Bass," Deputy Price cut in, "after all he's done—"

"Shut up and let His Honor finish what he's saying, Deputy," Frisco Phil said gruffly.

"Thank you, Frisco Phil," Judge Bass replied cordially, saying his name more respectfully this time. "What I'm saying is, I would perfer personally hearing Texas Bob's neck crack, dangling at the end of a hangman's knot, than to see him already dead and slung over a saddle." Looking at both men he said, "But I will take his execution either way I can get it. Am I making myself clear?"

Frisco grinned. "Clear as springwater, Your Honor." He took his hand from his gun butt and extended it toward the judge. "Then we have a deal between us?"

"I just told you the deal," Bass said coolly. He looked down at Frisco Phil's hand but didn't reach out to shake it. "Bring me Texas Bob Krey, dead or alive, *right away*, and you'll receive one thousand dollars. I can stall putting out reward posters for a few days. But if you're not back with him pretty quick, every bounty hunter in the territory will be out there looking for him."

Seeing that the judge was not going to shake on the matter, Frisco rubbed his hand on his belly as if that had been his intention. "You can consider it done, Your Honor." He lowered his hand to his side. "Once you've given us the reward money we'll get saddled up and under way."

"Reward money? For *what*?" The judge looked him up and down again.

"For what we're getting ready to do, Your Honor," said Page. "For what we just agreed to."

"I can't think of one incident in my years on the bench when this territory has paid a bounty reward before the culprit has been either killed or captured."

"The victim being your brother and all, Judge," said Page, "I figure we need at least half up front and the other half when Texas Bob is dead."

"An advance? I don't think so." The judge looked shocked at such a suggestion. "Brother or no brother, from now on this is a territorial matter. Things will now be handled in an official manner."

Bass pointed a thick finger at Page's chest. "What kind of fool do you take me for? Only an idiot would pay bounty money in advance." He looked at Price with a cruel grin, as if he knew the deputy had paid the Frenchman three hundred dollars up front to kill Texas Bob. Price felt his face sting with embarrassment. The judge adjusted his fine shiny derby hat on his head and said to the two, "Come see me when this Texas Bob business is finished—your money will be waiting."

Chapter 5

On their way into Sibley, Sam kept Tommy Rojo riding a few feet in front of him. Rojo led Sealey's horse, Sealey's body dangling over its saddle. Before all eyes along the boardwalk began turning toward them, Tommy and the ranger saw three men standing out front of a barbershop reading the poster Price had earlier attached to a tall striped barber's pole. A few yards away, two miners with their picks over their shoulders stood reading another poster out front of a closed stage depot. Farther up the dirt street, a man and two women stood reading yet another poster.

"If this is about Texas Bob Krey, somebody didn't waste any time getting his name on the wall," Rojo commented.

"Yep, so it appears," said Sam. Without further comment, the ranger noted Judge Bass's big Studebaker rig sitting out front of the livery barn at the far end of town. As Sam and Tommy turned their horses to the hitch rail out front of the sheriff's office, Sam looked back along the boardwalk and watched the

three men move away from the barber pole. The three
ducked their heads away from the ranger and stepped
into their saddles, one of them stuffing the wanted
poster into his coat pocket.

"Looks like those three either know *you*," Rojo said
with a slight chuckle, "or else they're trying their best
not to."

"They know me. I know them too," Sam replied in
a lowered tone of voice, keeping a suspicious eye on
the three. "Hiding under your hat brim doesn't help
you, Carter Roby," he muttered, as if the man who'd
stuffed the poster into his pocket could hear him. "I'd
recognize that Circle T buckskin anywhere. Word is
he killed the man who owned that horse." He kept
an eye turned to the three men as they nudged their
horses into a trot and rode out of town.

Shaking his head, Rojo said to Sam as he stepped
down from his saddle, "I hope I'm not about to get a
bad reputation being seen riding with you, Ranger."
He hitched his reins, as well as those of Sealey's horse
beside it.

"Riding with me is about to come to an end for
you, Tommy Rojo," said Sam, also stepping down and
hitching his barb. "I can't say I enjoyed your company
much." He glanced at the swarm of flies dipping and
swirling around the black crusted-over bullet hole in
Sealey's head.

Rojo gave a taunting grin. "Aw, come on, Ranger.
You and me ought to become pals now that I'm becoming a bounty hunter instead of an outlaw—" He
stopped and corrected his words: "An *alleged* outlaw,
that is."

"Oh, you're a bounty hunter now?" Sam asked. "When did this happen?"

"All the way here I've been thinking it over," said Rojo. "I've been looking for a change in occupations. I believe this is it." He gestured a hand toward Sealey's body.

"Killing your pard from behind doesn't make you a manhunter," Sam said, "and becoming a bounty hunter doesn't put you right with the law. If I was you, I'd take my bounty money and clear out of the territory before your luck runs out. There's some men who won't allow you the advantage of shooting them when their back is turned."

"You sure have let this little back-shooting incident of mine get under your skin, Ranger," Rojo said, still grinning. "I've never seen what difference it makes, front or back." He shrugged. "Dead's still dead, no matter how it happens. Don't you think?"

"I think it's best you and me don't talk any more about it, Rojo," Sam said. He took off his dusty pearl gray sombrero and batted it against his leg. Stepping up onto the boardwalk as he slapped his gloves against his dusty shirt, Sam reached for the door handle to the sheriff's office just as the door opened. Judge Henry Edgar Bass stood staring at him in surprise.

"Morning, Judge Bass." Sam was not as surprised, having already seen the judge's big coach in town.

"Ra-ranger!" said Bass, trying to regain his composure. Sam's appearance in Sibley clearly caught him completely off guard. "Wha-what brings you to town?"

"Law business," said Sam.

"Oh . . ." The judge looked back and forth as if someone might be following the ranger. Seeing Rojo standing close behind Sam and seeing Sealey's body lying over the saddle, he said, "I'm not due to preside over any cases here for a few more weeks." He eyed the black bullet hole in the back of Sealey's head. His expression turned grim. "I'm afraid I'm here in Sibley as the result of a very personal tragedy." He stepped back and allowed Sam and Rojo to enter the office as he spoke.

"Yes, I heard about your brother's death," Sam said respectfully. "You have my condolences." Behind him, Rojo stepped inside and closed the door.

"Thank you, Ranger Burrack," the judge said, averting his eyes from the ranger in his grief. "I know you and I have had our differences in the past, but at times like these it's good to know that men on the same side of the law can be counted on to stick together." He raised his head and looked back and forth between Rojo and the ranger. "Now, what is your business here today, Ranger Burrack?"

"I have a man here who's claiming the reward for killing Dade Sealey, Your Honor," Sam said, gesturing Rojo up closer to the judge. "This is Tommy Rojo." To Rojo he said, "This is territorial judge Bass."

Neither of the two offered to shake hands.

"Indeed?" said the judge, taking on the same officious tone he'd used with Price and Frisco Phil earlier when it came time to talk about money. Scrutinizing Rojo closely, he said, "I take it you have proof that the person lying dead out there is Dade Sealey."

"I do, Your Honor," Rojo said confidently. "The

ranger here will identify him for you. He'll also tell you it was me—*I*, that is—who killed him. Right, Ranger?"

"That is true, Your Honor," Sam said, not mentioning how low he thought it was, Rojo shooting Sealey in the back of the head. "He killed Sealey for the bounty money. I am his witness."

Detecting something in the ranger's voice, the judge asked, "Is everything all right, Ranger Burrack?"

Sam eyed Rojo but said, "Yes, everything is all right, Your Honor."

"The ranger's got a knot in his tail because I shot Dade Sealey from behind, Your Honor," Rojo cut in. He gave his familiar grin. "Knowing Dade Sealey, I'd say he got as good as he gave. I hope you agree."

"It doesn't matter if I agree," said the judge. "You shot him, you get the reward." He paused, then asked, "Are you a professional manhunter, Mr. Rojo?"

"As a matter of fact, yes, I am," Rojo said, taking a step forward. Cutting Sam a glance he said, "To be honest, I have to admit that I have only recently come into the profession. But what I lack in experience I more than make up for in enthusiasm."

"This is his *first* bounty work, Your Honor," Sam offered.

"But it's not going to be my last," Rojo added quickly. "In fact, the more I think about it, the more I think I might try my hand at tracking down Texas Bob."

"I see," said the judge in contemplation. "That is most commendable of you." He gestured toward the front door. "Please excuse the ranger and me while we discuss a private matter. Feel free to go to one of the saloons and have yourself a drink while you wait for me to go to the bank and bring you the reward money."

"That's mighty courteous of you, Judge Bass," Rojo said with a smile, already on his way to the door. "I'll just ease my way over to the Bottoms Up and have myself a shot or two to cut the trail dust."

No sooner had Rojo stepped out the door and closed it behind himself than the judge turned to Sam. "Ranger Burrack, thank goodness you two have arrived," he said, speaking rapidly. "I need all the help I can get on this. Sheriff Thorn is away. I've got his deputy and another fellow on Bob's trail, and of course I've put up money of my own for bounty, one of the victims being my brother. Perhaps Mr. Rojo will—"

"Your Honor, Tommy Rojo is not a man I would put much faith in," Sam said, cutting him off. "He and Sealey knew one another. I doubt if he would have managed to get so close to him otherwise."

"But he's one more gun I'll have on Texas Bob's trail," Bass submitted. "While he and the others keep Texas Bob hounded, I expect you can find him and take care of this once and for all." Bass hadn't expected a territory ranger to come riding in so soon after his brother's death, especially one with a reputation like Sam Burrack's. The more guns the better, he decided. "I hope you meant what you said about helping me any way you can."

"Yes, Your Honor, of course I meant it," the ranger replied. "I'm going to talk to Lady Lucky if she's up to it."

"Speak to Lady Lucky?" Bass' expression changed only a little, but enough for Sam to notice. "I fail to understand how talking to her is going to hasten the capture of Texas Bob Krey." He shook his large head. "No, no, let's waste no time here in Sibley. I need you out there on the trail, where your skill in man-hunting will do some good."

Sam stared at him. "I don't waste time, Your Honor. I'll speak to her while my horse gets grained and rested. Then I'll get on Texas Bob's trail."

"I want you to realize that Lady Lucky is a friend of Texas Bob's," said Bass, agitation starting to show in his voice.

"Being Bob's friend doesn't make her a liar, Judge Bass," Sam said firmly. "I'd like to hear from her who was most at fault."

"I already know who was most at fault," said Bass, getting more irritated with the ranger. "What I need is for someone to ride out, find Texas Bob and ki— I mean bring him in for trial!"

"Which I will do," Sam said firmly, still giving him a flat stare, "as soon as I've talked to Lady Lucky." He also wanted to talk to Deputy Claude Price and ask him about paying Lepov to kill Texas Bob. But he wouldn't mention that until he had Price standing right in front of him so he could spring the question on him and see the look on his face when he tried to answer.

*   *   *

Three miles out of Sibley, Carter Roby brought his horse to a halt in a rise of dust. Behind him, the other two men, Ty Shenlin and Cinder Kane, did the same. Turning his horse and staring back toward Sibley, Roby said, "I know that blasted ranger recognized me. I can feel it in my bones."

Shenlin and Kane, two gunmen recently up from Missouri, looked at one another. Kane spit out a wad of tobacco he'd been chewing and wiped his hand across his mouth. "Let's ride back and kill him, then, if he's making you jittery."

"I've never been *jittery*, old man. Keep that in mind," Carter Roby said with a trace of a threat in his voice.

"Duly noted," said Kane, his wrists crossed on his saddle horn, his expression flat and unimpressed. "Yet, again I ask, 'Why don't we ride back and kill him, if his presence disturbs you in *any way*?' "

"*Disturbs* me?" Roby's face hardened. "Disturbed is something else I've never *been*."

"Now, fellows . . ." Ty Shenlin smiled thinly. Rubbing his horse's mane, he said to Roby, "You need to understand that my pal Cinder here ain't exactly one to mealymouth around. He'll call a thing the way it fits him and the rest of the world be damned." He stopped rubbing his horse's mane and added, "He doesn't mean it to be rude or overbearing. Do you, Cinder?"

"Not at all," said Kane, still wearing his same flat expression. Suddenly, as quick as a whip, his wrists uncrossed, his rifle came up from his saddle boot and he levered a round into the chamber before Roby had a chance to react. "You want him dead or not?" he asked, his expression unchanged.

Roby froze, uncertain if Kane was asking Shenlin about killing *him*, or asking *him* about killing the ranger.

"Well? It looks like it's up to you, Roby. You're the rod over this bunch," Shenlin said, smiling.

Roby felt a sense of relief. He was glad he hadn't gone for his holstered Colt. Looking at the rifle in Kane's hand, and the cool smile on Shenlin's rough beard-stubbled face, he knew he needed to show them both he was not a man to hesitate when it came to killing, lawman or otherwise. "Yeah, why not?" he said in a tough tone.

"Suits us," said Shenlin.

Drawing his rifle, Roby pointed it up at a cliff sixty feet above the trail. "From up there, we'll watch for him when he comes up off the flatlands." He started to gig his horse away from the trail and up a steep path through the rocky hillside. But when he looked back, he saw the two only staring at one another. "Well, what are you waiting for?" he asked.

"How do we know he's coming this way?" Shenlin called out to him. "Kane and I were talking about riding back to Sibley and cutting him down face-to-face in the middle of the street. Right, Kane?"

"Yeah," said Kane, with his same flat expression. "I never figured on ambushing him, three on one."

Damn it! Roby thought to himself, feeling his face redden. "Neither did I," he said. "I meant we could watch for him from up there, then ride down and face off with him, *if* he came this way. Save us riding all the way back to Sibley, eh?" As he spoke he backed his horse from the steep path and turned it onto the trail.

"Trouble with that is, if he *doesn't* come riding this way, we'll miss him altogether," said Shenlin, the thin mocking smile on his face. "I'm sure you've considered that?"

Without answering, Roby jerked his horse around on the trail in the direction of Sibley. "All right, then! You want to ride back to town and kill him face-to-face, let's do it!" He nailed his spurs to his horse's sides and raced away, waving his rifle for them to follow him.

Kane tapped his horse forward at a walk and said to Shenlin, "*Jittery*, I says."

"Yep," said Shenlin, gigging his horse along beside Kane's, "I believe you're right."

Before the two had ridden a mile back toward Sibley, they spotted a rise of dust coming toward them and stopped midtrail and waited until two riders came around the turn and stopped in surprise. "Whoa! Don't shoot!" said Frisco Phil, seeing three rifles pointed at him and Deputy Price. Both of their horses reared up. "What's got you jakes so spooked?" he asked as his horse touched down and circled nervously until he clenched in on his reins.

"Sorry, Frisco," said Roby. "We thought you was that crazy ranger and his partner riding us down."

"Jeez, Carter!" said Phil, settling his horse and re-adjusting his hat on his head. "You're getting plumb dangerous to be around!"

"He apologized, didn't he?" Kane said with his flat expression. "What more do you want?"

"*Nothing* more," said Phil. "When I said we'd meet you along the trail, I didn't mean we wanted to ride into your gun barrels." He gave Kane a hard stare.

"Easy, Frisco," said Shenlin, again having to speak for his pal, Kane. "He didn't mean no harm in what he said. Cinder is doing his best to get everybody's bark on today."

"Yeah? Well, he don't want to do that with me," Frisco said matter-of-factly. His stare cooled as he touched his hat brim respectfully toward the two men.

"What are these men doing here?" Price asked, trying to keep his words between himself and Frisco Phil.

"Meeting us," Frisco replied with a bemused look. "Ain't you been listening?"

"Meeting us *for what*?" Price asked, getting a bad feeling in the pit of his stomach.

"Carter Roby is an *old* friend of mine," said Frisco Phil, "and these two are some *new* friends of his. You know, like you're a *new* friend of mine?"

"I know what *new* and *old* means," said Price. "I'm asking what's the deal here."

"The deal is they're riding with us," said Frisco. "I figured five guns are better than two, hunting a bad man like Texas Bob." He grinned.

Price was having none of it. "Splitting a thousand dollars five ways. Uh-uh," he said with suspicion. "That's only two hundred each. That's not enough to make it worthwhile."

"But it's two hundred and fifty each if we kill you," Kane said bluntly.

Price bristled, but with a fearful look on his face. His hand clutched his gun butt.

"There you go again, Cinder." Shenlin chuckled. To Price he said, "Blow down, Deputy. It's just his way of funning with you. Right, Cinder?"

"Yeah, funning," said Cinder Kane with his same flat expression.

"You've got more in mind than killing Texas Bob, don't you?" said Price. "Let me remind you, I might be a blacksmith, but I'm also a sworn part-time lawman."

"Oh . . . come to think of it, we might have something more in mind at that," said Frisco, trying to sound cagey, "although killing Texas Bob *is* part of it." He looked Price up and down. "You need to calm yourself down and get acquainted with your new partners." He gestured a hand, taking in the endless rocky badlands. "You might have used to be a *part-time* lawman, but you're riding with some *full-time desperadoes* now."

Chapter 6

The ranger wasn't surprised when he talked to Lady Lucky. He found her propped up in a spare bed in the back room of the doctor's office, and she told him everything. Davin Bass had started the fight. He had fired first and he'd gone down after killing one player. There was no doubt in Lady's mind that he would have killed Texas Bob next.

"Are you going to be all right, Lady?" Sam asked as he fluffed up the pillow behind her head before taking his leave.

"The doctor says I am," Lady Lucky replied with a weak smile. "I feel better seeing you show up in the midst of all this. There'll be a lot of guns on Texas Bob's trail, wanting to collect that reward." She managed to grasp Sam's hand before he stepped away from her bed. "I know you'll see he gets a fair deal."

"You can count on it. Now get mended and get back on your feet, Lady," Sam said. Then he turned and left the room.

That's that. Texas Bob fired in self-defense, Sam told

himself as he stepped up into his saddle and reined his horse into the dirt street.

But no sooner had he nudged his horse along at a walk than Judge Bass hurried out from the sheriff's office and summoned him to a halt. "Not so fast, Ranger!" the judge called out. "I demand to hear what Lady Lucky had to say to you."

"You *demand*, Your Honor?" Sam replied in the coolest tone he could offer.

Seeing the impassive look on the ranger's face, the judge could tell Lady Lucky hadn't been sympathetic to him or his dead brother's position. "Yes, I *demand*, Ranger Burrack!" he said angrily, pointing a plump finger at Sam. "I *am* the territorial judge, this *is* my jurisdiction, and you *are* a servant of the law!"

Sam only stared at him, staying cool, watching the judge grow more excited as he spoke. Seeing the composed way in which the ranger stared down at him, the judge forced himself to take a breath before continuing. "Look, Ranger"—he paused, pulled a white handkerchief from inside his lapel and blotted his sweaty brow—"I've tried to be tactful with you about this matter. With anyone else I wouldn't have to spell things out this way. I want you to show some loyalty to our judicial system here. This is a situation out of the ordinary. In matters of this sort, one hand should wash the other. Don't you agree?"

"No." Sam shook his head slowly. "One hand doesn't have to wash the other if both hands are clean."

"Why, you ungrateful—" the judge fumed. His face reddened in anger and embarrassment. "I could have the badge ripped from your chest for talking to me in that manner," he said, his thick fists clenched tightly at his sides.

"I suppose you could." The ranger glanced down at the badge on his chest. Lowering his voice, he said, "But the best thing for you to do is let this thing simmer down some. You've put money on a man's head not because he's guilty of murder but because he killed your brother in self-defense."

But the judge would have none of it. "I asked you unofficially to bring this Texas Bob to justice. You refused to cooperate. So now, in an official capacity, I am ordering you to—"

"Careful, Judge Bass." Sam cautioned him. "You're turning this matter into a runaway coach. The farther it goes the faster it gets. You best get off now while you still can."

But the judge only glared at him. "Spare me your sage frontier advice, Burrack," he said with sarcasm. But he considered the ranger's words enough to rephrase what he had started to say. "I am not *officially ordering* you. But as one servant of the law to another, I am *strongly urging* you to bring Texas Bob in, *dead or alive*! Now, are you going to find him or not?"

"Yes indeed, Judge," Sam replied. "I'm going to look for Texas Bob, if for no other reason than to tell him about the price you've placed on his head and let him know that the law is *not* hunting for him."

"How dare you!" the judge growled as Sam touched his gloved fingertips to the brim of his sombrero and nudged his horse along the street. "You'll be finished when I'm through with you, Ranger! You might just as well take your badge off and throw it in the dirt!"

Sam didn't look back.

Watching the ranger ride away and seeing the faces of townsfolk turn toward the sound of his angry raised voice, the judge ducked his head slightly and walked rigidly back to the sheriff's office. From above the swinging doors of the Bottoms Up Saloon and Brothel, Tommy Rojo stared, grinning, licking a streak of beer foam from his upper lip. "Now that is one unhappy *Your Honor* going there," he said idly.

One of the Bottoms Up girls stepped up beside him and ran a slim finger along the edge of his ear. "Are we going upstairs now, or what, cowboy?" she purred.

Rojo jerked his head away roughly, without taking his eyes off the judge. "I'll tell you *when* and *if* we're going upstairs, Sugar Lou," he said, "and don't ever call me 'cowboy' again, understand?"

"I call everybody cowboy," said Sugar Lou.

"Not me, you don't," said Rojo, still watching the judge, seeing him slam the office door behind himself. "Now you've been warned. I ain't no stinkin' cowboy."

"Oh, I see," Sugar Lou said coldly. She backed up a step and threw a hand on her hip. "Then what are you, Mr. Better-than-Thou?"

"I'm a manhunter, Sugar," Rojo said, the smile leaving his face, replaced by a stern expression. "I hunt down dangerous men for the bounty on their heads."

"Oh my." Sugar Lou mockingly rolled her eyes

toward the ceiling. "All right, then, *bounty man*, are we going upstairs or not?"

"Not right now," said Rojo, still not looking at her as he drained the last sip from his beer mug and handed it sidelong to her. "Business is calling for me."

Rojo shoved his way through the bat-wing doors and walked across the street to the sheriff's office. Beside Sugar Lou, a pimp named Walter Truelock stepped up and said, "What happened with him? You were supposed to take him up."

Sugar Lou sighed and held out the empty beer mug on her crooked finger. "He said he's a bounty hunter. He saw the judge and took off after him—said it was business."

"Yeah?" Truelock stared after Rojo, watching him walk into the sheriff's office. "Every stiff who owns a gun is after that miserable reward the judge put out on Texas Bob." He scratched his chin in contemplation, then added, "I might ought to go after it myself. I could use the money, even though it ain't a lot."

Sugar Lou shook her head. "Everybody's going after Texas Bob. What are they going to do if they're unlucky enough to find him?"

"Yeah, you're right. That's a bad idea." Truelock let his tapping fingers fall away from the small ivory-handled derringer in his vest pocket.

Inside the sheriff's office, Judge Bass looked up from writing as Rojo closed the door behind himself. "There you are, Mr. Rojo. Good," said the judge. "I'm filling out the papers for you to draw your money from the bank right now."

"Obliged, Your Honor," said Rojo. Taking his hat from his head, he gestured with it toward the street. "I couldn't help but see the ranger and you having words out there . . ." He let his words trail off, then said, "Over your poor brother's murderer, no doubt?"

The judge only stared at him for a moment in contemplation. *All right, Ranger, if you can follow Price and Frisco Phil to Texas Bob's hideout, so can this bounty hunter,* he thought to himself. Then he said aloud to Rojo, "Let me ask you something, Mr. Rojo. Do you believe in the saying 'One hand washes the other'?"

"Like it's the gospel itself, Your Honor." Tommy Rojo grinned widely, holding up his hands and wiggling his fingers. "Now, you just tell me what you want done, and let's start washing."

Darkness had enfolded the rock canyons while Mary Alice and Texas Bob gathered the tin dinnerware, washed, dried it and put it away. While she wiped the tabletop with a damp cloth, she watched Bob kneel on a thick bearskin in front of the glowing hearth and take off his shirt. Raising the glow of an oil lamp, he looked closely at the bandage around his shoulder, relieved at finding no fresh blood since checking it that morning.

"I'm healing right along, thanks to your tender care and handling," he said to Mary Alice. He rounded his stiff shoulder as if to show her his improvement. At the edge of the hearth, the big dog, Plug, lay flat, his forepaws spread, his chin resting on the plank floor. He observed the man and woman curiously.

"You can't tell anything without taking off the bandage," Mary Alice said. She walked to the bearskin, wiping her hands on a clean dishcloth. "Here, let me take a look," she said, kneeling beside Bob.

Bob studied her eyes in the glow of the lamp and the flicker of fire in the hearth. She felt his gaze on her as she unwrapped the bandage enough to see the wound. "Don't look at me. I'm a mess," she said softly, giving a faint smile. Her forearm brushed aside a strand of loose hair from her cheek.

"You're an angel, you are," Bob said in a whisper. He slid a hand gently around her waist as she examined the wound closely for any unusual discoloration or swelling. Satisfied, she pressed the bandage back into place and rewrapped its tails around his shoulder.

"Was this just a trick to get me over here?" she said with the same faint smile, feeling his hand press her closer to him. She tucked in the ends of the bandage and patted his chest gently.

"Only three days here and you've seen through all my tricks?" Bob sighed and relaxed back onto a blanket-covered saddle he'd laid there the night they arrived.

"You've been easy to read, Tex," Mary Alice said. "But then, I am an expert at reading men." As she spoke she unbuttoned her dress, slipped it up over her shoulders and let it fall.

"*Shhh*, don't talk like that about yourself," Bob said, his hand still behind her waist, caressing her warm satiny skin. He nudged her gently, and she stretched out alongside him, careful as always of his mending wound. "I mean what I said," he whispered. "You are an angel."

"You bring that out of me," she whispered. Propped over him on her elbow, she looked down into his eyes. "It's easy with you." She brushed his hair from his forehead with her fingertips and leaned forward and kissed him long and deep. When the kiss ended she looked into his eyes, seeing no guile there, no deception, nothing that unsettled her, nothing that cautioned her against him.

"I wish . . ." He hesitated, then continued, "I wish it would have been like this with us before."

"You always were my favorite," she said. She wasn't going to ask if he'd felt the same. She wanted to know, but she wouldn't ask.

"Still, it was different," Bob said. "I can't say how, or why, but it was different then."

"I know," she said, and she kissed him again, tenderly, yet feeling an aching for him welling inside her as her lips lingered near his mouth even after the kiss had ended. "Different in every way," she whispered into his parted lips. "This feels like—" She stopped herself short. It wasn't that she thought he wouldn't believe her saying it felt like the first time. She felt she could say anything to him and he would understand.

"Like the first time?" Bob whispered, finishing her words for her.

Mary Alice did not attempt to reply. She smiled to herself and nodded against his cheek.

"Me too," he whispered; and she felt her emotions overpower her. Tears welled in her closed eyes. She knew that a man held himself to limits when he lay down with a woman he'd bought and paid for. She knew as well that she and the rest of the doves held those same limits when money changed hands. It had been a long time since a man had held her this way— a long time since she had allowed it.

She had admired Texas Bob those times when he'd come calling and chosen her over the rest of the girls. But these days with him, the two of them alone together, she loved him, she told herself. And she had to hold herself back to keep from saying the words aloud.

As if hearing her thoughts, he drew her closer against him. "I know," he whispered. "I feel the same."

At his spot at the corner of the hearth, the big dog raised his ears and eyes in curiosity, seeing the woman and man become one in the orange shadowy glow of firelight. Then he settled his chin back down on the floor, let out a breath and closed his eyes.

Later in the night, when the fire had burned down into a slowly crackling bed of embers, she awakened beneath a quilt he'd spread over her when he'd stepped up and dressed himself. Feeling the empty spot beside her, she looked up, almost startled by his absence, and saw him sitting at the table in a circle of lantern light. On the table lay his Colt, beside it a cloth and a tin of oil. She watched him hold the gun up close to his ear and click the cylinder slowly, listening for any imperfection down deep in the steel bowels of the weapon.

She waited until he lowered the Colt and began

loading it with six bullets standing in a row on the table like soldiers at attention. "You're—you're leaving?" she said quietly, hoping her voice didn't reveal her disappointment.

But it did, she realized, seeing him lift his eyes to her as he slipped another bullet into the Colt. "Come daylight, a little before," he said.

"Weren't you going to tell me?" she asked, knowing her voice wasn't hiding a thing.

"I was." He sighed. "I suppose I wanted to put it off long as I could."

She rose to her knees, naked, found her dress, pulled it on and stood up and straightened it. "Do you mean put off telling me or put off leaving?" she said, in an attempt to lighten the matter.

"One hurts as bad as the other," said Texas Bob, sliding the Colt into its holster. "But I've got to go. You know I've got to."

"Yes, I know," she said softly. She walked to the hearth and picked up the coffeepot from the stone mantel. "I'll boil some coffee."

Near her feet, the big dog raised his head and watched her, then stood and stretched and shook himself, and walked to the door. Mary Alice opened the door, let the dog out and stood staring out into the gray starlit darkness for a moment, composing herself. She knew the silence behind her lay waiting to hear from her. After a moment, when she trusted her voice again, she said aloud to Texas Bob, and to the darkness before her, "God, Tex, if something happens to you, I'll die . . . I just know I will."

"Don't say that, Mary Alice," she heard him say

behind her. She heard his footsteps approaching her and she turned in time for him to take her in his arms. "Nothing's going to happen to me. Nothing ever does."

"Tex." She sobbed against his chest. "I get a terrible feeling about this, about you leaving—"

"Shhh. You hush that now," he said gently but firmly. "I'm coming back here, to you, Mary Alice, if you'll have me." He held her tightly. "I give you my word. Nothing or *nobody* is keeping me away from you."

"Take me with you, Tex," she blurted out. "I'm so afraid."

"You're safe here, Mary Alice," he said. "Nobody knows about this place except you and me and ole Plug there." He nodded at the dog as it meandered around the dusty yard with its muzzle to the ground.

"I'm not afraid for myself, Tex," she said. "I'm afraid for *you*."

"You've got to stop being, Mary Alice," Texas Bob said firmly.

"I—I will, Tex," she stammered, getting herself under control. She offered a feigned smile. "What's wrong with me anyway? I'm never this foolish. Look how I'm shaking." She tried to be strong.

"Mary Alice," he said against her tear-moistened cheek. "It's been a long time since either of us felt this way toward anybody. I expect it's got us both a little spooked." He tried a slight chuckle. "But there's nothing says we're going to come to a bad end. Let's both show a little faith here."

"I'm trying," she said. "But I just feel so—"

He pulled his face back from hers and tipped her chin up to meet his gaze, cutting her off. "Look at me," he said with gentle finality. "I'm going to find Sheriff Thorn and tell him what happened. Then I'm coming right back here." He gestured toward his wounded shoulder. "This is nothing. I might wound easy enough, but I'm awfully hard to kill." He smiled at her. "Especially when I've given my word . . . Especially when I've got my very own angel waiting here for me."

PART 2

PART 2

Chapter 7

At dawn, Sheriff Mike Thorn crossed the dirt street
of Camp Verde through a raw whistling wind. He held
the brim of his Stetson bent down to shield his face
from the sharp cold dust. "Confounded wind," he
growled to himself beneath the batting of his long
loose duster tails. "This had better be good."

At the plank door of a half-adobe, half-pine-
timbered building, he hammered with his balled fist
until the door opened just enough for him to squeeze
inside. As he stepped sidelong, a black hand slammed
the door behind him and slipped an iron bolt into
place to hold it shut. "Mercy!" said the black man as
he stepped back from the door. "I never seen such a
wind in this river valley!" He grinned broadly. "In
Mississippi I seen it blow so long and hard, when it
stopped all at once all the cows fell over." He chuckled in a deep voice.

Sheriff Thorn stared at him coldly. "You summoned
me here to tell me that, Elmore?" he asked flatly.
" 'Cause if you did, I already heard it."

"No, sir, Sheriff," said Elmore Gant, turning more serious. He gestured a wide hand toward two men who sat huddled at a wooden table. "This is Dulsko, from the Big Daisy Mine project up on Cleopatra Hill—"

"I've met Mr. Dulsko," Thorn said briskly, taking off his Stetson and shaking dust from it.

"And this is Andrej Goran," said Elmore, swinging his hand from Dulsko to Goran. "We all call him Andy. He's more sober now than when he arrived. He drank his way from one town to the next till he got here. Seems he just got back today from Sibley."

"Oh?" Thorn's attention was piqued at hearing his town mentioned.

"Yes, sir, and he's got quite a tale to tell," said Elmore. "I thought you'd want to hear it right off."

"Yes, I do," said Thorn, looking the Croatian over good, seeing the dirty bandage on his forearm. "What happened to your arm?" he asked Goran.

Goran stared blankly.

"He got it burned in Sibley." Elmore interceded, a look of satisfaction coming to his eyes, having something of importance to say.

"Can't he talk?" Thorn asked sharply, staring down into Goran's dark bloodshot eyes.

"Not so's you and me would understand him," said Elmore. "That's why I brung Dulsko here when he started babbling something about a fire in Sibley, then about a gunfight." Elmore stared at the sheriff expectantly.

"Oh," said Thorn, realizing the Croatian spoke very

little English. To Dulsko he said, "Ask Andy here how he burnt his arm in Sibley."

Ernst Dulsko turned to Goran and spoke to him in their native tongue. After a moment of listening closely while Goran spoke, the translator turned to Thorn and told him everything.

Shaking his head slowly as he let the story sink in, Thorn finally said in a tone of regret, "I can't believe Texas Bob would do something like that, 'less of course it was in self-defense." He looked at Goran as he asked Dulsko, "Was Lady Lucky still alive when you left?"

Dulsko asked and Goran replied, nodding to the sheriff. To Thorn, Dulsko said, "Yes, as far as he knows. She was alive when he had his arm bandaged and left town. But he does not know what condition she was in."

"Well, thank God she's alive," said Thorn. He placed his Stetson back atop his head. "I'm headed back to Sibley anyway. I expect I'll speed it up some, maybe take some high ground and cut over through the ponderosas."

Elmore and Dulsko gave one another a wary look. Elmore said, "Sheriff, you best want to stick to the trails twixt this river valley and Sibley. There ain't nothing but trouble for a man out there—"

"I believe I know my way home as well as the next fellow, Elmore," Thorn said testily, cutting him short.

"Yes, sir, Sheriff, I know you do," Elmore said. Then he shut up and clenched his jaw as if to keep from saying anything more. But he could contain his silence for only a few seconds before saying, "What are you going to do if Texas Bob *is* in the wrong on this? What if he *did* shoot everybody down and set fire to the saloon?"

Thorn stared at him blankly. "I suppose I'll have to bring him in."

"Ha!" Elmore scoffed. "I know Texas Bob. He won't be taken no place he don't want to go."

Reaching for the bolt on the door, Thorn said in a sarcastic tone, "Then let's hope he's not wrong. Else I'd have to bring him somewhere he didn't want to be." He pulled the bolt to the side, opened the door and stepped out into a howling swirl of dust. "Blasted wind!" he shouted aloud. Bending his hat brim down over his face, he walked leaning sideways to the livery barn, where his horse stood grained and rested.

"I hope you filled him good, Oldham," Thorn said to the liveryman. "I don't want to stop till we've got up out of Verde River Valley and cleared this wind."

"He's fed better than you or me either one, Sheriff," said Oldham McCoy, rubbing a hand along the horse's flanks and patting his rump. "But if it's blowing this hard down here, what do you think it'll be like up on the desert flats and the rock lands?"

"I'm banking on it being blown out by then," said Thorn. Reaching for his reins he added, "It won't matter anyway. I've got to ride through it. Had a saloon burn down and some folks shot to death."

"Hmph," said Oldham. "I thought stuff like that never happened in your town, Sheriff."

Thorn stopped long enough to give him a hard stare. "Note that I wasn't *in my town* when it happened, livery keeper." He put a gold coin into the liveryman's outstretched hand, swung up into his saddle and turned the chestnut toward the front door.

Claude Price and Frisco Phil Page sat atop their horses a few yards ahead of Carter Roby, Ty Shenlin and Cinder Kane. After a three-hour wait, they finally watched the Cottonwood stagecoach lumber into sight on its weekly turnaround trip back from Flagstaff. Reaching up and drawing his hat string up tight beneath his chin, Frisco Phil said, "Here she hauls, pards. Better get ready. We're going to do it."

"Wait a minute! Do *what*?" said Deputy Price, holding his horse back, seeing Phil about to slap its rump with his gloved hand.

Frisco Phil held his hand ready, but gave Price a bemused look and said, "Why, rob this big fat stage coming here, Deputy. What did you think we've been waiting to do, dance to a fiddling band?"

Behind them the other three stifled their laughter. Price shot them a bristling glance, then said to Phil in a stern tone, "I thought we were waiting to see who's on the stage, not rob it!"

Frisco Phil took a deep breath as if trying to be patient with the part-time lawman. "We *are* going to see who's on it, Deputy," he said, "and of course if it's full of armed guards or soldiers, we're going to send it on about its business." He held up a gloved finger for emphasis. "But let's say there's no armed guards, other than the shotgun rider. Wouldn't it be foolish of us to *not* rob it? I mean, us being outlaws and all?" As he spoke he drew his Colt from his holster and cocked it threateningly. "Now get yourself out in front of us and let's get going."

"I'm doing it, but I don't like it," said Price. He drew his bandanna up across the bridge of his nose, masking his face.

Frisco Phil quickly reached up and jerked it back down. "Are you dim-witted, Deputy?" he asked. The men laughed. "You can't wear a mask! They won't stop!" he said.

Price looked confused.

"We want you out there on the trail with your badge on, so's they'll see it's you and rein down for us," Frisco said. He gave the men a look of disbelief, bringing more muffled laughter.

"But they'll recognize me!" Price protested.

"Let me and our pards take care of that," Frisco said gravely. "These folks ain't going to *recognize* nobody, I can tell you."

"I can't go along with that!" said Price, feeling sick all of a sudden at what he'd gotten into. "That's cold-blooded murder."

"Now you're disappointing everybody," Frisco said coolly. "Hear that, pards? I know you all had your hearts set on robbing this stage."

"I sure did," said Cinder, all three of them nudging their horses closer. "It's all I've thought about for days."

"Me too," said Ty Shenlin. "I owe some debts I wanted to take care of."

Rising in his saddle, Carter Roby said, "Whatever we're going to do, we best get to doing it. They're almost inside the canyon."

Frisco looked at Price with his gun cocked and pointed at his chest. "Can't you see what a good thing we've got here? We're working for the *judge*! No matter what we do out here, we can lay it on Texas Bob. We come upon a stage just in time to see him riding away. He robbed it and killed everybody. We got there just a minute too late to stop him."

"I don't know if that'll work," said Price, hoping to stall as long as he could. "What if Judge Bass won't believe Texas Bob robbed the stage?"

"Oh, he'll believe it," said Frisco. "He'll believe Texas Bob killed *you* too, if you don't get cracking." With no more on the matter, Frisco slapped the rump of Price's horse and sent it bolting toward the trail.

"Where did he ever find a lawman that stupid?" Carter Roby said to Shenlin and Kane. The three gigged their horses, but stayed back out of sight along a wall of rock while Price and Frisco Phil rode out into clear view of the oncoming stage.

Midway, Frisco said to Price, "Wave them down, Deputy! Make sure they see that tin badge."

"Oh, no," Price said with regret, raising a hand and waving it back and forth. "This is Teddy Ware and Norbert Block. They both know me."

Frisco gave a dark chuckle as the coach began to slow to a halt. To the three men hidden from sight he said sidelong, "See, pards? I told yas this was going to be sweet as a wedding cake."

"Whoaaa!" the stage driver, Norbert Block, shouted to the horses, pulling back hard on the traces and the long brake handle as the six big coach horses stopped six yards away.

"Dang, Deputy!" the shotgun rider, Teddy Ware, called out. "We almost didn't stop for you. What brings you out this far from town?"

Price seemed stuck for a reply. But Frisco called out, "We're hunting a killer for Judge Bass, a fellow by the name of Texas Bob Krey."

The two grizzled bearded stage men looked at one another. "Texas Bob, *a killer*?" said the driver. He looked at Price instead of Frisco Phil. "That's a hard thing to believe, Deputy."

"Hard but true," said Frisco, sidling closer to Price in case Price did something to warn the stage men.

The driver looked away from Price to Frisco Phil. "Don't I know you? Ain't you the one who slings whiskey at that pigsty in Sibley?"

"If you mean Vinten Kriek's Rambling Dutchman," said Frisco, "yeah, I used to. What of it?"

"Nothing of it," the shotgun rider cut in, his sawed-off double-barrel in his fringe-gloved hand. "We're just both wondering why you're doing the talking is all." He said to Price without taking his wary eyes off of Frisco Phil, "Cat got your tongue, Claude?"

"No," Price said quickly, sounding almost startled by the question. "What Phil says is true. We're hunting for Texas Bob. He shot Judge Bass's brother, Davin, maybe killed a couple more, and burned down a saloon."

"Burned a saloon in Sibley, huh?" The driver gave a sharp little grin. "That's one down and thirty to go, far as I'm concerned."

"Anyway, that's why I stopped you," said Price. His

face was sick and nervous. "We want to know if you've seen any riders headed out across—"

"We're going to have to search your stage," Frisco called out, cutting Price off.

"Search our stage?" said Ware. His finger slipped inside the trigger guard of the shotgun. "You must be a lunatic, bartender." The shotgun rider began to rise up from his seat, his weapon coming up to his shoulder.

"Pards!" Frisco called out over his shoulder, summoning the three riders hidden behind the large rock. As the three nudged their horses into sight, their guns drawn, cocked and pointed, Frisco demanded, "Drop the scattergun and sit your ass back down! Throw down the strongbox!"

But the shotgun rider would have none of it. "Price, *you skunk*!" he bellowed at the deputy. At the same time he swung the shotgun toward the other three men and fired both barrels. The impact of the double blasts angled down onto Carter Roby, hammering both horse and rider into the dirt. Ware, seeing that the two blasts were all he would get, shouted, "Go!" at the stunned driver.

Block started to lash the traces against the six coach horses' backs, but before the animals could make a lunge and get the heavy coach moving, a hail of pistol fire sliced through the two men and left them lying dead on the coach seat. Bolting to the coach, Frisco leapt up from his saddle onto the seat, grabbed the fallen reins and leaned back into them, drawing the frightened horses to a halt and holding them there until they settled.

In the dirt, Roby's big buckskin lay dead. But Roby had struggled to his feet, his chest pumping blood from countless buckshot holes, his face and forehead chewed and maimed beyond recognition. "Oh God, where's my hat!" he shrieked, staggering and trembling. "Where's my hat! My hat!"

"I got it," said Cinder Kane, swinging down from his saddle. In one motion he picked up Roby's buckshot-riddled hat from the dirt, held it in front of the blind, bloody face and fired two shots through it. "I didn't think he'd ever shut up," Kane said, looking down at Roby's body lying across the dead buckskin.

"Oh, Lord," Price whispered, looking first at Roby, then at the two dead coachmen.

Seated on his mount beside Price, Ty Shenlin reached out and held the deputy's horse by its bridle, keeping Price from going anywhere.

"He was as good as dead anyway, Deputy," said Shenlin, giving a cruel grin. He nodded at the coachmen. "So was they, once they stopped to see what you wanted."

The others grinned slyly. From atop the coach Frisco Phil said, "See how valuable you and that tin badge are in the right hands, *Deputy*? You're going to be our sugar teat. We're going to suck on you and that badge as long as we can." He chuckled as he hefted a strongbox from atop the stage and heaved it to the ground.

"I came out here to get Texas Bob," Price protested. "I never counted on getting involved in something like this."

"Shoot it open, pards," said Frisco, nodding down

at the iron strongbox. To Price he said, "Use your head, Deputy. The more stuff like this we pin on Texas Bob, the better it's going to look on you when you bring him in shot full of holes."

"That's all well and good," said Price, watching as the others cocked their guns and aimed at the strongbox, "but I didn't see us getting any closer to Texas Bob."

"Pay attention, *Dep*," Frisco said, shortening Price's official title to a mere nickname. "It's all going to work out fine. Texas Bob is just one small splinter on a whole big board."

Frisco and the men laughed, then fired a volley of shots at the strongbox.

Chapter 8

It took four volleys of shots before the battered brass Hadley lock fell open and dangled on the side of the strongbox. Fanning a thick cloud of gun smoke, Frisco Phil jumped down from atop the stage, walked over to the bullet-scarred container and flipped the heavy lid open.

"If this baby was shooting back at us we'd all be dead," Cinder Kane said cynically, reloading his smoking revolver. "I never seen a lock so hard to bust."

"Whoo-eee!" As the three men gathered closer, Frisco picked up a thick bundle of money and shook it vigorously. "This will more than pay for any bullets you've wasted." He threw the bundle to Kane, who caught it and hefted it on his palm.

"It'll help," he grinned, tossing the bundle on to Shenlin.

"A lot," Ty Shenlin agreed.

Price looked on expectantly. In spite of his position against robbing the stage, he stood ready to catch the bundle when Shenlin tossed it to him. But to his disappointment, he saw the hard-faced outlaw kiss the money and pitch it back to Frisco Phil.

Seeing the look on Price's face, Frisco said, "Look at ole Dep here. You'd think somebody spit in his whiskey. Don't worry, Dep, you're gonna get yours." He grinned and added, "I'll see to it everybody here gets what he deserves when the time comes. Right, pards?"

"It goes down good with me," said Kane.

"Me too," said Shenlin. He tweaked his thumb and finger together. "So long as you cut me a little taste to pass across the bar and along to the ladies when we go through a town."

"I've got you covered," said Frisco. "Just remember this is only a start. There's more coming."

"Coming from where?" Kane asked.

Before answering, Frisco said to Price, "Dep, go stick Roby and the stage men into the coach and give the horses a whack."

Price couldn't miss seeing that Frisco didn't want to talk business in front of him. But he wasn't going to mention it now. He realized he stood in a bad spot with these men. He'd have to work himself out of it carefully somehow, if he wanted to stay alive. All this, he chastised himself, because he'd been jealous of the doves in Sibley showing favor to Texas Bob.

On his way to shove the bodies into the coach, he heard Frisco Phil say to the other two, "Pards, I'm telling you, ole Dep and that badge of his will stop any stagecoach in these parts."

"Yeah," said Kane, giving a glance in Price's direction, "so long as we don't leave any living witnesses behind."

"Is leaving living witnesses a problem for you?" Frisco asked.

"Not as much as it is for *them*," Kane chuckled. "I never cared much for living witnesses anyway."

"All right then. Listen up," said Frisco. His voice fell too low for the deputy to hear as he continued speaking to the other two.

So be it, Price grumbled sullenly under his breath. He jerked the stagecoach doors open, dragged each of the three bloody bodies over in turn and pulled it up inside. Before he stepped down out of the stage he spotted a watch that had slipped out of Teddy Ware's vest pocket. For years he had admired the watch, knowing that the other end of the fob was attached to the crooked trigger finger of a long-deceased California outlaw named Jeuto Vargas.

Looking out first to make sure no one saw him, Price whispered, "Sorry, Teddy, but I ought to get something out of this deal." He quickly snatched the finger out of the vest pocket and stuffed the fob, chain, watch and all into his trouser pocket. The others didn't need to know about this, he told himself. Smoothing his trouser pocket and taking a deep breath, he walked to the rear end of the lead coach horse and gave the big animal a solid slap with his glove. *"Hiiiyiii!"* he shouted loudly, sending the coach rambling off along the trail in a fresh rise of dust.

Hearing Price, and seeing the driverless coach pick up speed as it rolled away, Frisco Phil said to the other two, "Wait a minute." He turned to Price and called out in a somber tone, "Dep, I hope you checked and made sure everybody was dead first."

"Yep, of course I did," Price lied, not wanting to look bad to the others.

Frisco gave the other two a dubious look, then said to Price, "You cut their throats to make sure?"

"No, I didn't," said Price, seething, knowing Frisco was mocking him in front of Shenlin and Kane. "But they're dead as dirt. No question about it." He added smugly, "I can tell when a person's dead or alive."

"Oh, I see." Giving the other two a guarded wink, Frisco said, "Hear that, pards? Dep here can tell if a person is dead or alive." He stepped over menacingly close to Price and said, "Would you stake your life on it, Dep? Because this is no game for weak players. Let a man get away alive, and he'll come back to reckon with you every time."

"I said they're dead, Frisco," Price said firmly, not wanting to look small in front of these men. "If you don't believe me let's chase that stage down and you can check for yourself."

Frisco gave him a harsh stare, but after a moment let himself chuckle under his breath. "All right, Dep. That's what I like to hear—a man who knows his ground and stands it. If you say they're dead, by thunder they're dead."

"What about this money, Frisco?" Kane called out, holding up a bundle of bills in either hand.

"Feed-sack it," said Frisco. He stepped over to his horse, jerked a feed sack from his saddlebags and tossed it to Kane and Shenlin. "Hurry it up. I want to get back to Sibley and let the good judge know what kind of hell Texas Bob is raising out here." He grinned at Price. "What do you say, Dep?" Behind him Shenlin and Kane hurriedly stuffed the money into the feed sack and carried it to Frisco's horse.

"I say that's pushing things," Price replied. "If anything goes wrong we're going to be—"

"Aw, come on, Dep," said Price, cutting him off. "Why can't you relax and take it easy? We're riding a winning horse here."

Watching the two other outlaws tie the feed sack behind Frisco's saddle, Price settled himself, realizing that to be disagreeable with these three wasn't a wise position for him to take right now. "You're right, Frisco," he said, tugging his hat onto his head. "I've been wearing this badge so long it's starting to twist my mind up. Sure, let's ride into Sibley. What's the worst can happen? Nobody but us knows what's gone on here, right?" He looked all around from face to face.

"There you go, Dep," said Frisco, grinning. "Now you're showing me something." As he spoke he walked sidelong to his horse and swung up into the saddle. "I thought I was going to have to pistol-whip you in front of our pards here to get your thinking straight."

"My thinking *is* straight, fellows," said Price. He stepped over to his horse, ignoring what he knew was an overbearing threat any way he looked at it. Swinging up into the saddle, he gigged his mount forward and reined it alongside Frisco. He knew the other two were going to form a half circle around him, keeping him well within their reach.

Sheriff Mike Thorn rode up out of the shelter of the rock land and stared out across the rolling stretch of cactus and creosote swaying before him. From left to right, ragged balls of tumbleweed bounced and swirled and continued on, like apparitions blown into being on the raw wind. He'd had two days out of the wind. That was as much as he'd get for the time being.

Thorn sighed, raised his collar and rode on, concentrating on the jagged purple hill line lying in the distance. On a calm day, with the right cayuse beneath him, this would have been a time for him to doze in the saddle and let the animal make the crossing on its own. Not today, though—not in this wind, he reminded himself, nudging the horse forward.

But before he'd ridden a mile, he felt a rumble of hooves and saw the big stagecoach rise up from the earth before him in a windswept flurry of dust and weed, its canvas back loose and flapping sidelong as it barreled toward him. "Whoa, Jim!" he said to his horse, pulling it to a sliding halt for a moment while he scrutinized the matter. "What the blazes is a stage doing out here?" he said to himself.

Knowing that any answer to his question would have to come from the stage, he gigged his horse forward, swinging out in a half circle to get out of the speeding coach's path. Waving his hat to no avail, he watched the coach grow closer until he saw it wasn't going to even slow down, let alone stop for him. "By thunder, you *will* stop!" he muttered with determination.

He nailed his spurs to the horse's sides and put the big animal into a full run. When he arrived full speed up alongside the coach he looked up through the dust and wind. Recognizing the driver, he shouted, "Teddy Ware, pull up! Pull up! Do you hear me?"

But upon seeing the seasoned old shotgun rider staring blankly ahead, his chest, face and hands black with blood, Thorn sped his horse's pace up, pulled over close to the lead stage horse and crawled over onto it from his saddle. Feeling his hat blow away, he gathered the long traces to the lead team and lay back on them steadily until the winded horses slowed to a halt.

"Lord, I don't want no more of that!" Thorn said aloud, panting. He climbed down and ran his hand along his bare head. Hurrying back through the dusty wind, he didn't bother calling out to the slumped driver. He knew Teddy Ware was in no shape to answer him. But once he'd climbed up into the driver's seat and turned Ware toward him, he said to the half-conscious man, "Teddy! Where's Norbert? What's happened? Who did this?"

"He . . . he stole . . . my watch," Ware rasped, fresh blood running down across the dried blood on his chest.

"Who did, Teddy?" the sheriff asked urgently. "Who stole your watch? The man who robbed you? Who was it?"

"My watch . . ." he murmured in a trailing voice.

"Who, Teddy! Who did this?" Thorn insisted, shaking the man as if it would awaken him. Realizing the old shotgun driver had said his last words, Thorn eased him back into his seat and patted his dusty shoulder. "Don't worry, Teddy. I'll find out who did this."

He saw a streak of blood where Ware had climbed from the stage to the driver's seat. He set the brake, wrapped the traces around the long handle, then stepped down and looked inside. Wincing at the sight of Norbert Block's body and the gory half-face of the dead outlaw, Carter Roby, he stepped back for a minute as if to prepare himself. Then he swung the stage door open and took a deep breath.

Three hundred yards away on a sandy low rise, Frisco Phil's Winchester rifle reached out and caught Thorn's tumbling Stetson on the tip of its barrel. "So there's the sheriff, and here's his hat." Frisco gave Shenlin and Kane a curious look, then turned a dark stare to Price, Thorn's hat hanging on his rifle barrel. "You better tell me quick, Dep. How do you suppose that stage got headed in this direction—toward Sibley, without a driver turning it this way?"

"I don't know, Frisco," said Price, standing his ground, but shakily. "I can't tell you what a loose team of horses is apt to do. Nobody can."

Kane and Shenlin stared out at the stagecoach. "The question is, what are we going to do about this sheriff snooping around, maybe backtracking and figuring things out?"

"What do you say we ought to do, Dep?" Frisco

asked coolly, sticking his rifle up high enough for the wind to lift the battered Stetson and send it skittering away.

Price kept calm. "I say we circle wide of him and go on to Sibley. What can he say? He didn't see us do anything."

"Yeah, maybe," said Frisco. "Or, how about this? We ride in, tell him we're out here searching for Texas Bob, and feel him out, see if he thinks anything suspicious about us."

"But no killing?" Price asked, as if looking for reassurance.

Without answering him Frisco looked at the other two, grinned and said to Price, "You're going to lead us in. He'll trust his faithful deputy riding in, bringing a posse with him to help uphold the law. Right, pards?"

Shenlin and Kane nodded in agreement. "Let's get it done and get out of this wind," Kane growled.

"Uh-uh," said Price, shaking his head. "I won't lead you in to him if you're going to kill him."

"Won't?" Frisco said calmly. Stepping in close, he quickly reached out, jerked Price's Colt from his holster, smacked him across the side of his head with the barrel and stepped back. Price's legs buckled; he dropped to his knees. He held his throbbing head.

"Get up, Dep," said Frisco. "You weak piece of sow meat!" He grabbed Price and dragged him staggering to his feet. "Shoot this fool," he ordered Kane and Shenlin. "I'm tired of his mouth."

Kane and Shenlin drew their pistols, cocked them and pointed them at Price's chest.

"Wait! Please!" said Price. He could see that this was no bluff, that these two were going to leave him lying dead on the sandy ground. "I'm not saying I *won't* ride down there with you!"

"It sure sounded like it to me." Frisco gave him a look. "What about it, pards?"

"Yep, I coulda swore that was what he said," Kane replied, gun in hand.

"His very words," said Shenlin. The two stared coldly at Price, who looked back and forth wild-eyed.

"What I meant was, I didn't want to kill him. He doesn't know anything! But I'll lead us down there—of course I will. I'm a part of this as much as the rest of yas! Don't shoot!" he pleaded.

Frisco raised a hand toward Shenlin and Kane. "All right, pards, once *again* our *deputy* here has had a change of heart." He glared at Price as he backed away, shoving Price's gun down in his belt for safe-keeping. He lifted the feed sack of money from behind his saddle and carried it over and dropped it on the ground, not wanting the sheriff to see it. "Get your saddle under you, Dep," he said. "Don't ever again tell me what you *won't* do. I'll pistol-whip you like you're a woman."

Chapter 9

The wind had died down some by the time Sheriff Thorn had dragged Teddy Ware from the driver's seat of the stagecoach and pulled him inside with the other two. He'd taken his canteen from his saddle horn, uncapped it and had a long swallow of tepid water when he caught sight of the four riders atop the same low rise where he'd first seen the stage.

"Easy, Jim," he whispered to his horse, although the animal had shown no sign of wariness, other than pricking its ears toward the strange horses. Thorn slipped his rifle from its saddle boot, levered a round into the chamber and led the horse around to the corner of the stage.

Seeing the sheriff take a defensive position, Price called out from twenty yards away, "Sheriff Thorn, it's me, Claude Price. Your deputy." He swung an arm back and forth above his head.

Recognizing Price, Thorn took a breath of relief. But he kept himself at the edge of the coach instead of stepping out away from any cover. "Price, who's that riding with you?" he called out. He let the riders see his rifle come up against his shoulder.

"We're a posse, Sheriff," Price called out. "Judge Bass sent us out searching for Texas Bob Krey."

"You don't say," said Thorn, seeming unmoved by the mention of the territorial judge. He cocked the rifle hammer, seeing the four continue to ride closer. "Why don't all of you stop right there. Introduce us, Deputy."

"Slow down, pards," Frisco said quietly, seeing that he had underestimated the sheriff.

"This is what I was afraid of," Price said, barely above a whisper.

"Get us in there, Dep, damn it!" Price growled, jerking his horse into a short circle and not letting it stop long enough for the sheriff to get a tight aim on him. But it was a move the seasoned old lawman saw through right away.

"Hold your horses still, all of you," Price warned in a low voice. "Thorn is no fool."

The four settled their horses, but it was too late. Thorn had already drawn an impression of the men.

"Sheriff," Price called out, "this is Phil Page, Mr. Kane and Mr. Shenlin. Like I said, Judge Bass sent us looking for Texas Bob. There's been a lot happen while you were gone." He shook his head. "We had a terrible shooting. Texas Bob went on a wild killing spree. He even burnt down a saloon."

"So I heard," said Thorn, keeping his eyes on Frisco and the other two. "Phil Page, huh?" He looked Frisco up and down. "I've seen you slinging whiskey at the Rambling Dutchman."

"I was— That is, I *am* a bartender there, it's true," said Frisco. "The judge asked for my help and I felt it my civil du—"

"Make up your mind, Phil Page," the sheriff said, cutting him off. "Are you still a bartender, or has something else caught your interest?"

"This is as close as we're going to get," Frisco whispered under his breath. "He's going to be a hardhead about this. I can see that already." He gigged his horse into another short circle. Jerking his big Colt from his holster as he nailed his spurs to the animal's sides, he shouted, "Kill him, pards!"

The men charged the sheriff's position, pistols firing. "You too, Dep!" Frisco shouted, slapping Price's horse on the rump to make sure Price stayed with them.

But as the riders made their attack, Thorn's rifle went to work. His first shot sliced through Kane's upper arm, almost knocking him from his saddle. His second missed, but lifted Shenlin's hat from his head and sent it spinning away. Riding beside Price, Frisco saw the two veer their horses away and flee for cover. "Cowards!" he screamed. But before the word had left his mouth, a bullet ripped through the air an inch from his ear and caused him to duck low in his saddle as he and Price turned and fled behind Kane and Shenlin.

Thirty yards away, over a sheltering low rise of sand, Frisco and Price slid their horses to a halt as another rifle shot whined through the air behind them. "I've never seen a man fire a rifle that fast!" Frisco said, jumping from his saddle.

Price sat silent, knowing that anything he had to say wouldn't be welcome. As far as he was concerned, now that Thorn had seen him, he had to make sure the lawman never made it back to Sibley alive. This was where his envy of Texas Bob had brought him, he told himself, looking at his unsavory companions.

"I'm shot!" Kane said, unwrapping his hand from his upper arm, revealing the rip Thorn's bullet had made in his bloody shirtsleeve.

"It's just a flesh wound," said Frisco, trying to dismiss the matter.

"Hell yes, it's a flesh wound," said Kane, glaring at him, "but that's because it's *my* flesh! What would it be if it was yours?"

"Take it easy, pard. This is no time to argue," said Frisco. He turned a heated stare on Price. "Why didn't you warn us this sheriff would put up such a fight?"

Price stared at him. "You're right. This is no time to argue. We've got to kill him and get out of here before somebody shows up."

"Kill him how?" said Shenlin, the hair on his bare head standing sidelong on the wind. "The man's a crack shot!"

"If he was a crack shot, you'd both be dead!" Frisco growled. "Dep is right. We've got to kill him, else everything we've done is going to hang right around our necks." He looked at Price. "What have you got in mind, Dep?"

Price couldn't believe he stood there talking about murdering the lawman he worked for, the man who had held the Bible he'd sworn an oath on to uphold the law. He took a breath and said, "There's four of us. We've got to split up and hit him from all four directions at once."

"I'm wounded!" Kane shouted, holding up his bloody hand. "Or maybe you didn't hear!"

"I'm near wounded myself," said Shenlin, running a hand back over his bare head. "I say we surround him and wait him out."

"Wait him out?" Frisco gave him an angry look. "What does that mean—*wait him out*?"

Shenlin replied, "It means that sooner or later he'll run out of food and water and have to—"

"So would *we*, Shenlin," Price said, cutting him off with a tone of disgust.

"Not if yas held him pinned down while I rode somewhere and brought back enough food and—"

"Shut up," said Frisco, his Colt coming up cocked and pointed at Shenlin's chest. "Get on your horses, both of you! You heard Dep. We've got to get this thing done and get out of here!"

Texas Bob had come upon the wagon tracks earlier and followed them for over a mile, veering away only when he'd first heard the sound of gunfire and had ridden to higher ground for a better look. But the shooting had stopped by the time he reached the low rise where Frisco had left the feed sack full of stolen stage money. Seeing the feed bag lying in the dirt, Bob slipped from his saddle, opened it and looked inside. Then he looked down at the stagecoach, recognizing Thorn and seeing the sheriff hastily pulling small packages and wooden crates out from the rear freight hold of the coach and stacking them in front of himself and his big black and white paint horse for protection.

"Just the man I'm looking for," said Texas Bob, closing the feed sack and standing up with it in his hand. "What have you gotten yourself into, Sheriff?" Bob asked himself quietly, seeing the four riders slip out across the sand in four directions. Hurrying, he walked away with the bag of money toward the lip of a flat rock lying on the sandy ground.

At the stagecoach, Sheriff Thorn knew he didn't have much time before the men made another run at him. There wasn't a doubt in his mind what Price and his newfound friends intended to do. Price couldn't allow him to make it to Sibley alive. Price was not a hard case, certainly no cold-blooded killer. In fact Thorn doubted the blacksmith had ever even shot at a man, let alone killed one.

But it made no difference now. Price had been up to no good with these men. Whatever he and his three accomplices had done—he'd bet they were the ones who'd robbed the stage and killed Block and Ware—now that Thorn had seen him, he knew his part-time deputy was desperate to cover his tracks.

"It looks like we're fixin' to get on with it, ole hoss," Thorn said to the paint, seeing the dust of the four riders as they slipped along just out of sight over the low, rolling terrain. "I wish you was smart enough to keep your head down."

As he spoke he checked his rifle, took out his Colt and a small-caliber hideaway gun and laid them side by side on one of the wooden crates. "I expect an old lawman like me can't ask for much better than this."

He looked at the horse and grinned. "Think of what a story it'll make if I get through this and leave all four of them hanging out to dry."

No sooner had he spoken than a shot rang out and a bullet thumped into a wooden crate. He ducked down and came up with his rifle to his shoulder, scanning back and forth for a target through a renewed swirl of dusty wind. Before he took tight aim toward the distant rider far to his left, a shot came from the rider to his right.

Splinters from a crate stung the side of his face. He fired, but his shot fell short, raising a spray of dirt and pieces of an exploding barrel cactus. Crouching down beneath the coach, he looked all around, then dropped onto his belly, seeing the riders advance from all four directions, their guns firing. He shouted as he fired from under the coach, "Come get me, you sonsabit—!" His words stopped short as he heard round after round of powerful rifle shots resound above the cacophony of six-shooters.

"Who in blazes is out there?" he said aloud to himself, noting that the pistol fire began to wane under the heavy pounding of a repeating rifle. Levering another round into his rifle, he got off a quick shot at the outline of the rider to his left before the man turned his horse sharply and raced away into the thick billowing dust. A rifle shot from out in the dusty wind produced a painful-sounding scream from one of the unseen gunmen.

"Whoever you are out there, thank God for you!" the sheriff said, feeling relieved now the odds had been evened a bit. He fired to his right and levered another round, searching the dusty wind for a target. From the direction of the mysterious rifle fire he saw the grainy outline of a lone rider coming toward him from within the dusty swirl. "Thorn! It's me, Bob Krey!" a familiar voice called out. "Don't shoot. I'm coming in!"

"Texas Bob?" Thorn cried out. "Lord, yes, man! Get on in here, while these rats are running for their holes!" He shouted in a louder tone, hoping Price and his three partners could hear him.

A moment later Texas Bob slid his horse to a halt, jumped down from his saddle and hurried in behind the stage cargo. "Are you all right, Sheriff?" he asked, rifle up as he scanned back and forth, watching the wind subside enough to give him a better view of the barren rolling land.

"I've been better," Thorn said, crawling up from beneath the coach. "But it's good to see a friendly face out here, things being as they are." He also scanned back and forth with his rifle. "Now that I've got an extra gun, maybe we ought to tie off these horses behind the stage and ride it out of here fast as it'll carry us, before these owlhoots get their courage up and come back at us again."

"Bad news, Sheriff," said Bob. "The lead stage horse is dead in his harness. I saw him down when I rode in. I can crawl out there and cut him loose if you really want to make a run for it."

Thorn thought about it, realizing the shooting had stopped altogether, for the time being at least. "Let's wait and see what they've got up their sleeves. One of them is my deputy, Claude Price, so I'm not expecting anything too smart from them."

"Claude Price is trying to kill you?" Bob said, surprised.

"Yep," said Thorn. "He rode in saying him and the other three were carrying out Judge Bass's orders, hunting you down."

"I'm not surprised, Sheriff," said Bob. "He gave me a bad time in Sibley. I left town because of him. I expect you heard all about the shooting over there."

"Heard it. Didn't believe it," said Thorn. He glanced sidelong at Bob without lowering his rifle. "Leastwise, I didn't believe you gunned everybody down and burnt the saloon on your way out of town."

"That's what the story has grown into?"

"Yep," said Thorn. "That's the grapevine talking. I figured I best find you and hear what really happened." He turned his face toward Bob long enough to look him up and down. "What had you planned to do, run and hide from the law?" Thorn asked.

"No," said Bob. "Believe it or not, you're the man I was searching for when I found this ambushed stage and ran into these knuckleheads."

"What *did* happen?" the sheriff asked. "Tell me everything."

"Gladly, Sheriff," said Bob, still searching all around for the vanished riders. "First of all, how's Lady Lucky doing?"

"I can't tell you, Bob," said Thorn. "I haven't made it back to Sibley yet. I got under way soon as I heard everything from a Croatian miner from over near Jerome. He said he was there. He's got a burnt arm to prove it. He says you carried him out of there, saved his life."

"He was on my way," Bob said, playing it down. He offered a tight grin. "I hope you'll believe me when I tell you the shooting was in self-defense."

"I've never known you to lie, and I've never known you to start a fight, Bob," said Thorn. "Now, out with it, so I can say I've heard your side when we get to Sibley."

"Here goes," said Bob. Without lowering his rifle, he told the sheriff about that fateful night in Sibley when he shot the judge's brother.

Chapter 10

———

At the same windblown rise from which the four riders had first charged down at Thorn, Frisco Phil stomped back and forth in the dirt, his fists clenched tight at his sides, the rising wind licking at his duster tails.

"Are we going back, Frisco?" Shenlin asked above the wind, wiping the sweat from his forehead with a bandanna.

"No, we're not going back," said Frisco. "We're not fool enough to ride into *two* rifles." He jerked his dusty hat from his head and slapped it against his leg in anger. "Of all damned people to show up—Texas Bob Krey himself! I can't believe this kind of rotten luck!" He kicked the yellow-flowered tip off of a low barrel cactus.

Hurrying back from a few yards away, where Frisco had laid the feed bag of money, Price said, "You want to hear *bad luck*? The money is gone!"

"Gone?" Frisco stared at him. "What do you mean, it's gone? How can it be gone?"

Price pointed at the single set of hoofprints left by Texas Bob's horse, the wind having all but covered them from sight. "It's gone because Texas Bob took it! That's my guess."

"That's my guess too," Frisco said, settling himself, staring through the dusty wind in the direction of the stagecoach. "All right, Texas Bob. You've got our money, but let's see how long you can keep it." He spat onto the ground.

Shenlin and Kane looked at each another; both of them seemed worried. "You said we wasn't foolish enough to go riding up against two rifles, Frisco," Shenlin said in a fearful tone.

"Don't soil yourself, Shenlin," Frisco said with contempt. "We're not going to ride in like bats out of hell, if that's what you think." He held down his hat brim against a hard surge of wind. "We're going to ride on ahead and set a trap for them."

"An ambush." Shenlin nodded. "Now that makes more sense than anything."

"Yes, an ambush it will be," said Frisco, "and I know just the place to do it."

"Whatever we're going to do, we best get to doing it," Price cut in restlessly above the whirring wind. "Thorn can't be allowed to return to Sibley alive. He's got to die, even if I have to kill him with my bare hands."

Frisco looked at him, a sarcastic half smile coming to his face. "My, my, how violent you've become all of a sudden! And to think, you was the one who didn't want to kill the good sheriff only an hour ago."

"I'm in a bad spot here, Frisco," said Price. "We shoulda left well enough alone, took the money and gone on to Mexico. But *nooo*! Look at us now—the money's gone, Thorn sees through our scheme, Texas Bob Krey is still free as a bird, and he's shooting at us, with the law on *his side*!"

"Don't tell me what we should have done!" Frisco said angrily. "What's done is done. Now we've got to play this hand on out the way it's been dealt to us!" He turned to Shenlin and Kane. "You two, get up and in your saddles. We've got to get ahead of the sheriff and Texas Bob and stay ahead." Frisco and Price both swung up into their saddles, a blast of wind whipping their duster tails out behind them.

Groaning, the other two outlaws rose and climbed atop their horses, the wind whistling and roaring past them. "I didn't bargain on getting shot at," Shenlin grumbled.

"Nor did I," said Kane, between the two of them. "But that money we stole is rightfully ours, and I'll do what we have to to get it back." They turned their horses into the wind and followed Frisco and Price.

At the stagecoach, Texas Bob had used the renewed wind as cover while he crawled out and cut the harness and traces from the dead horse. The five remaining coach horses stood with their heads bowed, leaning, their manes and tails sidelong on the whirring wind.

When Bob arrived back at the coach, where Sheriff Thorn stood crouched at the front wheel, he crouched himself and said, "So far, so good, Sheriff. This wind came back at the right time."

Thorn cursed the wind under his breath and shouted

above it, saying, "A lot of good I would have been. I can't even *see* the front horse in all this dust."

"That means Price and his pals can't see us either," said Bob. "This is our best chance at getting off this open land."

"I know it," said Thorn. "I'm ready to go when you are."

With their two horses hitched to the rear of the stagecoach, they climbed aboard the big rig and moved along slowly and steadily through the dusty wind, Thorn driving the five coach horses, Texas Bob beside him, his rifle in hand and Teddy Ware's shotgun lying across his lap. When an hour had passed and the wind had lessened in its intensity, Thorn looked across the rolling land and said, "It would be a stroke of luck if they decided to take off with their plunder and let us be."

"I wouldn't count on it, Sheriff," said Texas Bob. "I found a feed sack full of money lying where they left it. They won't ride off without it is my guess."

"They left it there so I wouldn't see it on them. Those rats intended to leave me laying dead with these other three sure enough." He gave a dark chuckle under his breath and said, "Way to go, Tex."

Tex nodded. "I would have brought it, but I didn't know what I would find down here. On top of all my other trouble, I didn't want to be caught out here with a shot-up stage and me holding a bag full of stolen money. So I hid it."

"Good thinking," said Thorn. "I hope you marked your spot well. It'll be hard to find after this big blow."

"It's under a flat rock, no more than ten yards from a bed of yellow barrel cactus along the rise back there." He looked at Thorn and added, "I figured I better tell you, in case you make it back to Sibley but I don't."

"We'll both make it to Sibley," said Thorn, "so don't give that any more thought."

"I won't," said Texas Bob, "but I thought I ought to tell you anyway."

"Good enough," said the sheriff. "I'll remember it."

He gazed along the distant rolling land, seeing the dust had settled greatly since the wind subsided. "If they come now, we'll be able to see them from a long ways off."

"Yeah," said Thorn. "That's why I'm thinking we won't see no more of them until we reach the hills up ahead." He nodded toward a long stretch of rocky hills that had risen out of the dust along the edge of the horizon. "We could have a real dogfight on our hands once we get inside there." Without looking at Texas Bob, he said, "I'm glad it's you here with me, and not some I can think of."

"Same here, Sheriff Thorn," Bob replied, also without facing the sheriff. After a pause, Bob added, "I want you to know that I feel lots better now that I've told you what happened in Sibley."

"So do I." Thorn nodded. "We'll get it straightened out first thing, Bob. You can count on it."

"I never would have left town the way I did had it not been for Price trying to kill me in my cell. He would have done it too, if Mary Alice didn't come along when she did."

Considering it, Thorn said, "Well, fortunately, we see the kind of man Price is now. Once we tell the judge and the town how he is, they'll understand, and they'll not only exonerate you, they'll commend you for coming in to help me out back there." He nodded over his shoulder. Then he gave a tap on the traces in his hands, not speeding the five big team horses up but keeping them attending to their same steady pace.

"The townsfolk will," Bob said. "But what about Judge Bass? Is he going to be able to understand what I did, shooting his brother, even though it was self-defense?"

"He'll have to, Tex," said Thorn. "I know he appears to have flown off the handle. But when he hears what happened at the jail, he'll have to understand why you cut out the way you did. When he hears what Price and these others did out here, he'll have to realize that Price is not a man whose word can be trusted." He glanced at Texas Bob, then added, "Don't forget, Mary Alice can testify to what happened in the jail. Lady Lucky can testify to what happened at the shooting too."

"Lady Lucky is a gambler. Mary Alice is a dove, Sheriff. That is, she was. Now that her and I are together, she's out of that business. But will the judge take their word for anything?"

"He might not if there was anybody to dispute them. But there's not." He offered a tired smile. "Besides, doves, gamblers and rowdies are the usual witnesses to gunfights. I've never once had a preacher come forward and say he saw a shooting in a place like the Sky High Saloon." His thin smile widened. "I'm sure there's been some who *could* have come forward."

"I see what you mean," said Texas Bob, contemplating the matter. After a moment he said, "Then I just have to go to Sibley and get this over with."

"That's right," said Thorn. "When we get to Sibley, you're going to let me handle this. I'll talk to Bass. He's a judge. He'll have to abide by the law whether he likes it or not."

"Sheriff, I'm obliged to you," said Bob, relaxing a bit on the wooden seat. "I have to admit I was worried about what this might turn into."

"Don't be," said Thorn. "You've got everything on your side." He tapped the traces again. They rolled on.

Overlooking the flatlands, Raul Lepov smiled to himself. He lay stretched out on a lip of rocky ground, using his hands to shield his eyes from the glare of the low evening sun. Beside him lay his repeating rifle, the long sights already raised into position. He had been following the stage from a safe distance for the past two hours, since recognizing Texas Bob. Now that the stage had reached the lower edge of the hill line, he'd ridden on and gotten above it. This was the place for him to make his move, he'd told himself. He hid his horse among the rocks and crawled forward on the rough ground.

Watching Thorn step down from the stage after stopping the horses and setting the brake handle, Lepov smiled and said under his breath, as if Thorn might hear him, "I only wish that you were that *loath-some* ranger, so I could kill two *chicky-birds* right here, for good reason. As it is, I must kill *you* just for being here with *Cawboy* Bob." He shrugged in mock sadness. "But such is the way of this world."

He turned his eyes toward Texas Bob as Bob stepped down on the other side of the coach, his rifle in hand. Watching Bob stretch and slap dust from himself with his hat, Lepov reached around to his side, picked up his own rifle and raised it to his shoulder. "And you, *Cawboy* Bob. You I must shoot for the best reason in the world—because *imbecile* deputy has paid me to do it." He grinned. "I will force him to pay me more when I roll *Cawboy* Bob's head across the floor to him." He kept his eyes on Texas Bob as he peeled his fingerless black gloves from his hands and laid them out neatly in the dirt beside him.

On the last stretch of upward sloping flatlands, Texas Bob gazed all around, then looked at Thorn as the sheriff stepped out from the far side of the stage, his rifle in hand. "From here on in, it looks like nothing but good ambush country," he said.

"It's all treacherous ground up there," said Thorn, nodding toward the sloping trail. "But the spot I've got in mind is halfway through these hills. Once we're in there we're trapped. Out here, we can make a run for it if we have to." He gestured toward the rocky hillsides. "In there, they can cut us off from both directions. We'll have to stand and make a fight"—he looked at Texas Bob with his thin smile coming to his face—"just the way we like it." His words ended with a hard cough. His arms flew out beside him.

"Sheriff!" Bob said, seeing a strange look come to Thorn's face and feeling something warm and wet splatter on his own face. But before Bob's words were out of his mouth, the rifle shot resounded from up the hillside as the sheriff stumbled toward him and collapsed into his arms.

Caught by surprise, Texas Bob acted instinctively. He fell to the ground and dragged the limp sheriff under the stagecoach, feeling the spooked horses rock the coach back and forth violently, then yield to the firmly set brake.

"Sheriff, hang on! Don't you die on me!" he shouted, but at the same time he saw the gaping hole in Thorn's chest and the blank look in his eyes and realized that the old lawman had died in his arms.

From his rocky perch, Lepov grinned and levered another round into his rifle chamber. Looking down at the bloody smear across the dirt leading under the coach, he sang to himself in a cheery, melodious voice, "Come out, come out, *Cawboy* Bob, so that I can shoot a hole in you too!"

Nothing could be done for Sheriff Thorn. Bob wiped the dead sheriff's blood from his face, then reached out quickly, grabbed his rifle and jerked it back under the stage. Not one to shrink away from a fight, he crawled out on the other side, stayed in a crouch and hurried to the rear corner of the coach for a look up among the rocks.

Within a second another shot sounded; this time the bullet thumped into the wooden coach frame only inches from Bob's head. He ducked back quickly, but as he did so he managed to catch a glimpse of gray smoke above the lip of rock protruding from the hillside.

"All right, Price! Come and get me!" Bob shouted, slipping his rifle barrel around the corner of the stage and firing a shot. "Thorn is dead! You and your friends are going to hang for it. You've got nothing to lose!" He levered another round into his rifle chamber and called out, "I've got the bag of money! What are you cowards going to do about it?"

Price? A bag of money? On his lofty rock perch, Lepov gave a curious look, followed by a crafty smile. Texas Bob had mistaken him for Claude Price. "If that *imbecile* deputy had a bag of money I would take it away from him," he said aloud to himself. He raised his head as if prepared to call out a reply. But as he did so, two rifle shots were fired close together, both ricocheting off the rock near his face.

"Ah, *Cowboy* Bob is quick with a rifle, eh," he chuckled to himself, touching his cheek where chips of rock had struck him. "Now I see that I must slip down close, like a serpent, and make my final strike." But as he spoke his attention went to a lone rider who had just appeared over the far edge of the flatlands, coming from the same direction as the stagecoach. He looked back at the stagecoach, then at the lone rider again.

Recognizing the ranger, Lepov smiled. "Fate is kind to me on this day." He lightly kissed the tip of his rifle barrel, took close aim on the ranger and squeezed off his shot. But upon seeing his shot fall short and to the ranger's right, he reconsidered his situation. Watching the ranger's horse pound closer, taking a

zigzag path toward him across the rough land un-
nerved him.

Looking back down at the stagecoach he said under
his breath, "This is truly your lucky day, *Cawboy* Bob.
Enjoy it." He touched his fingers to his wide hat brim
as if commending Bob's good fortune. Then he quickly
gathered his rifle, his fingerless gloves and spare am-
munition, and scooted backward away from the rock
edge and hurried to his waiting horse.

Chapter 11

The ranger had seen the rifle shot kick up sand ten yards ahead of him. But even with the suddenness of the shot, he had managed to pinpoint where it had come from. It wasn't from the stagecoach, Sam told himself, keeping an eye on the rising hillsides to his right as he drew his rifle from its saddle boot.

At the coach, Texas Bob also spotted the lone rider coming toward him. His first thought was that Price and his pals had split up again, the same tactic they'd used against Thorn earlier, before he'd shown up to help. Having just fired a shot up at the rock edge, he levered another round into the rifle chamber, squatted down and braced his barrel against the rear coach wheel to steady the shot.

"I won't have to worry about you anymore," he murmured to the zigzagging rider, taking close aim and waiting for him to ride back into sight after disappearing down into the roll of the land. But after a long wait with his whole body tensed and ready, his finger poised to squeeze the trigger, he realized that the rider must have seen him and stopped short or taken another direction.

Texas Bob swung back and forth, scanning the land around him. The rise and fall of the rough, rolling hills offered a rider a chance to move in close on his prey if he knew how to use the terrain to his advantage. This rider knew, Bob told himself.

Seventy-five yards away, out of sight, the ranger led his horse around the low belly of a dry creek bed, able only to estimate what gain he had made for himself until he dropped his horse's reins and walked up, rifle in hand, to the crest of the rise. There, lying flat, he held a battered army telescope to his eye and looked out at the stagecoach, recognizing the lone figure with the poised rifle and a look of determination on his face.

After looking the stage over closely and making sure Bob was by himself, Sam lowered the lens, pulled himself back a foot from the edge and called out, "Texas Bob Krey, this is Arizona Territory ranger Sam Burrack." He waited for a second, his rifle ready in his hand, then called out, "I've been following the stage tracks. Drop the rifle and raise your hands. I'm coming in."

A moment passed while Bob thought it over. Sam knew the answer almost before it came. "I'm not dropping my rifle until I see for sure who you are," Bob called out, thinking the ranger's voice sounded familiar, but not yet willing to bet his life on it.

"I've been looking for you, Bob," Sam called out. "I know about the shooting in Sibley. Lady Lucky says it wasn't your fault."

"That's right. It wasn't my fault," said Texas Bob,

listening closely, not about to be tricked by Price and his pals. "So why are you on my trail?"

"To tell you so myself, before you got yourself into trouble," Sam called out. "Bass has men out to get you, for a reward he's put on you. I'm trying to be on your side, Bob, if you'll let me."

"Then don't ask me to throw down my rifle, if you're on my side," Bob replied, sounding dubious and still not convinced—at least not enough to disarm. Even if this was the ranger talking to him, Bob had to wonder if this was just his way of taking him into custody.

"I know what you're thinking, Bob," said Sam. "But you've got to trust me. I've tracked down a stolen stagecoach and found you standing beside it."

"That's just part of it," said Bob. "I've got Sheriff Thorn lying dead under this rig. I've got three more bodies inside it. See why I feel better holding this rifle?"

Sam winced at hearing about Thorn, but he replied sharply, "I'll listen to whatever you've got to say, but there's only one way this is going to go. Now drop the rifle and raise your hands," he repeated firmly. "I'm coming in."

"I'm not dropping it," said Bob. "Come in one-handed. I'll meet you the same way."

Sam eased up enough to take a look toward the stage and up past it into the rocky hillside. Halfway up the hill he saw a drift of trail dust that Lepov's horse had raised in the Frenchman's hasty getaway. "I hope you're not too hardheaded for me to help you, Bob," Sam called out.

"I hope you don't think I'm stupid enough to throw down my rifle when people have been out to kill me ever since I left Sibley, Ranger," Bob replied.

Sam saw his point. Even as he'd spoken, he'd stood up and stepped to the top of the rise, holding his rifle out in his right hand. His left hand out to his side, clearly empty, he took a step forward. "If I didn't hold you in high regard, Texas Bob," he said, "you wouldn't be standing there." He took another step forward. "Don't disappoint me."

Seeing that it was in fact the ranger, Texas Bob felt a little relieved. But as he took a step forward with his rifle held out in the same manner, he glanced back over his shoulder toward the rocky hillside and noted the same rise of dust. "If I didn't trust your word, Ranger, we'd never have gotten this far along," he said, now that he could watch Sam's eyes and judge his intentions. "Are you going to try to take me in?"

"You have my word, I'm not taking you anywhere you don't want to go, unless you had something to do with this," said Sam, seeing the splatter of blood on Bob's shirt, and the smear of red across his cheek.

"You've got my word I didn't," said Bob. He lowered his rifle an inch, watching the ranger to see if he did the same.

Sam nodded and followed suit, lowering his rifle until the barrel pointed at the ground.

"Thorn's deputy, Claude Price, and three other dry-gulchers were dogging him. I figure they did this. I came upon him and tried to help." He gave a sidelong nod toward the ground beneath the coach. "They waited here for us. They killed him all the same."

As Bob spoke, Sam stepped over and opened the stagecoach door.

"The driver, Norbert Block, his guard, Teddy Ware. And the third one there must have been a passenger, I suppose," said Bob.

Seeing Carter Roby's dead face, Sam said with a grim expression, "This is Carter Roby, one of the thieves, if I had to speculate. He likely got himself killed by the shotgun rider, judging from the buckshot in the face."

Texas Bob looked at him, more relieved. "So you do believe I had nothing to do with this?"

"Yes, I believe you," said Sam. "I also believe what Lady Lucky said about the shooting in Sibley being self-defense." He looked at Bob. "Now what we've got to do is get to Sibley before more shooters show up looking to claim a reward. Looking over your shoulder long enough can turn a man into a killer."

"Thorn said he could make the judge listen to reason and abide by the law," Bob said. "Now that he's dead, where does that leave me?"

"In the same place," said Sam. "Bass is not above the law just because he's a judge. You'll have to go in under my custody, for your own safety, in case any more guns start pointing at you. There's a fellow named Rojo who is a straight-up back-shooter. We've got him, and a Frenchman named Lepov, the deputy and his men, and who knows how many others to look out for until we get to Sibley." He nodded at the rifle in Bob's hand. "So you can keep your rifle until we get into town. Then you'll have to turn it over to me. That'll make everything official until we get Bass to drop this bounty and get the word out that you're not wanted."

"I hope you know what you're talking about, Ranger," said Texas Bob. "I came looking for Thorn to clear this up. Once he went down it hit me that the best thing for me to do was get out of here. I could've gone to my place, taken Mary Alice and headed for Mexico. Nobody would have seen me again." He paused for a moment of serious consideration and said, "Maybe that's *still* the best thing to do"

"I won't tell you what you ought to do, Bob," said the ranger. "But if it was me, I'd want to get this straightened out and clear my name before I went anywhere." He gestured toward the stagecoach. "Why run from the law? You're innocent."

"You have a lot more faith in the law around here than I do, Ranger," said Bob. "Don't forget, it was the law that jackpotted me in the first place."

"Price is no lawman," said Sam. "He could have been if he'd walked straight. But when it came to testing, he first abused the power of being a lawman by taking a personal grudge against you. Now look what he's sank to, robbing, murdering." He shook his head. "Don't even mention him and the law in the same breath. We'll get this thing straightened out. You've got my word."

"I'm going to have to trust somebody wearing a badge, Ranger," Texas Bob said. "Looks like you're the one."

Lepov rode hard, not resting his tired horse until he'd reached a place where the high trail meandered through a long deep ravine. There, looking back over his shoulder, he stepped down from his saddle and led his horse as he wiped dust and sweat from his face with a black bandanna. When the exhausted animal stumbled and faltered behind him, the impatient Frenchman yanked hard on the reins and cursed and threatened, "Keep up with me, you lazy beast, or I will have you for my dinner this evening!"

The animal struggled to right itself and trudged forward. But not more than fifty yards along the trail between two high-reaching rock walls, Lepov let out a tired breath and plopped down on a broken boulder. *"Cawboy* Bob can go to Hades for all I care," he grumbled, staring back in the direction of the stagecoach. "He can take the ranger with him!" His voice grew louder and more angry as he spoke. He heard it echo out along the ravine and fade upward and away. But almost before the echo had died, he heard a spill of rocks rattle down the wall across from him and, looking up, he saw two men pointing rifles down at him.

"Don't move, Frenchy," Frisco called out, "or I'll shoot your eyes out!"

Lepov's eyes widened in alarm; he raised his hands instinctively. But when he recognized the other rifleman as Claude Price, he lowered his hands and said, "Instruct your friend not to point his gun at me, *imbecile.* I am too tired for your foolish games."

"What did he call you?" Frisco asked Price, cocking his head with a bemused look.

"Never mind," said Price. "He's got some peculiar ways."

"I see," said Frisco. "Is this the French bounty man you told me about?"

The two began working their way down to the trail, step after careful step. Across from them, above Lepov, Shenlin and Kane started doing the same, making their descent to the winding trail.

"Yeah, that's him," Price said with a bit of contempt in his voice. "We've got to get rid of him before that stage comes rolling through here."

"Uh, uh, uh," said Lepov, wagging a bare finger back and forth in his cropped black glove. "I hear you talking about me. That is not polite." He gave Price a strange taunting grin. Then he slumped as if settling himself in for a long stay and said, "I refuse to go anywhere. My horse is tired and so am I."

"Get rid of this fool, or else kill him," Frisco whispered sidelong to Price.

"I'll handle it," said Price, not bothering to lower his voice as he stepped clear of the rock wall and walked toward Lepov. "All right, Mr. Lepov, did you kill Texas Bob the way I paid you to do? I know you had to see him along the trail back there."

"Yes, I saw him. No, I did not kill him," said Lepov. "I had him in my sights, but a nosy ranger arrived and diverted me." He shrugged. "I killed Sheriff Thorn, who was with him, though."

"Oh, you killed Thorn?" Price and Frisco looked at one another. "Are you sure?"

Lepov looked incensed. "Of course I am sure, *imbecile*. I am always sure who I kill and who I do not kill." He looked all around at Frisco, Shenlin and Kane as they pressed closer in a half circle around him.

"So, you didn't kill Texas Bob," said Price. "I take it you didn't kill the dove, Mary Alice, either?"

"No, I have not found her yet." He shrugged. "But I am in no hurry. We did not say when I must kill them."

"Give me my money back," Price said bluntly.

"Don't be absurd, *imbecile*," said Lepov. "It is not my policy to give back money once I have accepted it."

"Don't call me imbecile again." Price bristled, knowing how it looked, his allowing this man to call him such a name and his doing nothing about it.

Lepov smiled and shrugged again. "Don't be such an American sorehead. I told you I call you *imbecile* because I like you, nothing more."

"Give me my money back," Price insisted.

Friso, Shenlin and Kane watched intently.

"I have explained my policy to you," said Lepov. "If you have difficulty understanding it, I advise you to seek someone who can explain things to an *imbecile*." He looked back and forth at the gunmen and chuckled lightheartedly. Then, seeing Price's grim expression, he made a frightened face and said, "*Uhhh*, I am scared." Settling down, he said, "What are you going to do, *imbecile*? Shoot me? Because, let me warn you, if you do, the shot will echo off these rocks and be heard all the way back across th—"

Price's bullet cut him off, striking him just beneath his right eye and flipping him backward, his blood and bone fragments splattering on the rocks behind him.

Shenlin, Kane and Frisco looked at one another without saying a word as Price stepped forward, shoving his Colt back into its holster. Silently he went through the dead Frenchman's clothes until he came out with a roll of bills, riffled through them and stuck them in his shirt pocket.

"You paid him *up ahead* to kill Texas Bob?" Frisco asked as Price turned around and stepped away from the body on the ground.

Price lifted his Colt from its holster again and said in a tight raw voice, "Yeah. What about it?"

"Nothing," said Frisco, taking a step back, then seeing Price flip out the empty cartridge shell from his Colt and replace it with a fresh round. "Just being curious, is all."

Price looked back and forth among the three, the Colt still in hand. "I know it was a dumb thing to do, paying first. But that didn't make me an imbecile, did it?"

"Not in my book," said Kane solemnly.

"Mine neither," said Shenlin with a flat expression.

"Do you think it's true, him killing the sheriff?" Frisco asked, changing the subject.

"I hope so. I expect we'll know when that stage gets here," Price said. "If Thorn is dead, I get to start all over, free as a bird. We all do. Everybody will have to take our word for what happened out here."

"Yeah." Frisco said. "And our word is as good as gold, especially with the territorial judge acting in our favor." He grinned and watched Price shove his Colt back into its holster. "All we've got to do is kill Texas Bob and whoever is with him, take our money and drive that stage on into Sibley, bold as brass. Far as I'm concerned, we killed the men who robbed it."

"Yes, the same men who murdered Sheriff Thorn, don't forget," said Price.

"*Forget* that he killed our beloved sheriff?" said Frisco in mock astonishment. "How could I ever forget something like that?" The four laughed heartily among themselves.

Chapter 12

When the ranger and Texas Bob reached the hills without incident, they gave one another a wary look as they traveled slowly up the rocky trail. The question was not *if* they would be set upon by Price and the other gunmen—the real question was *when*, Sam told himself. On their way across the open land, Bob had told him about the hidden bag of money lying under the rock. The ranger knew that men like these weren't about to let that money slip through their fingers, no matter how many people they had to kill.

For the next hour they traveled upward, following the twisting trail deeper into the rocky hillsides, prepared for trouble at any second. As they reached a short flat stretch of trail they both spotted the abandoned horse at the same time. Off the trail a few yards from the horse they saw Lepov's black cape flutter on a breeze.

"I see it," Sam said, feeling Bob nudge him with his elbow. Stopping the stage and setting the brake, both he and Texas Bob climbed down and walked forward cautiously.

Bob stayed back a few feet and kept his eyes on the rocks above them, his rifle poised and ready, while the ranger stooped down beside Lepov's body and turned him over. "Here's one who won't be hunting for you anymore," he said quietly, seeing the bullet hole in the Frenchman's face, the splatter of blood on the rock wall. "It's the French bounty hunter, the one who first told me about what happened in Sibley. Price hired him to kill you."

Without taking his eyes from scanning the rocks above them, Texas Bob replied, "Yes, and like as not it was Price who put that bullet in him." He shook his head. "No wonder Price wanted Thorn dead."

"He's got a lot to answer for," Sam said under his breath, turning loose of Lepov and letting him flop back over on his face. Without setting his rifle aside, he took the Frenchman by one wrist and dragged him facedown to the stage. Opening the stage door and shoving the body inside, the ranger stepped back down and walked over to the tired horse.

As he helped Texas Bob keep watch on the rocky hillsides, he loosened the horse's saddle one-handed and let it drop to the ground. Loosening and dropping its bridle as well, he said, "They didn't even bother hiding the body or chasing this horse away. They knew we had to come this way to get the stage to Sibley."

"Yes," Bob agreed, "and they know they've got another five miles of this kind of cover to their advantage." As he spoke he backed toward the stage. He waited until the ranger was back on the driver's seat, and then he climbed up and seated himself.

"There's a place up ahead where the trail turns out of the sunlight and runs under a deep cliff overhang," Sam said almost in a whisper. "I'll be getting off there."

"Right," said Bob, still watching the upper edges of the rock wall.

Atop the rugged wall, Price and Frisco kept a guarded watch on the big coach as it rolled slowly on along the trail. "I say they never even heard the gunshot a while ago," said Price. "Even if they did, so what? We're here, they know it. Let's get this thing over with. The quicker they're dead, the better I like it."

"Relax, Dep— I mean *Price*," said Frisco, taking the ex-deputy more seriously now that he'd seen a dark, hardened change come over him. "The deeper we lead them along this trail, the less chance of them ever getting out alive." He grinned and gestured toward their horses and the other two men standing nearby. "Let's give them another half mile. There's a path that runs down there. It'll be easier carrying the money back up."

On the trail, when the stage had gone a hundred yards farther along, Texas Bob swung his rifle sidelong suddenly, only to see Lepov's tired horse moping alongside them. "This trail is getting me coiled tighter than a rattlesnake." He let out a breath, but kept his rifle up and his eyes on the high rocky edge a hundred feet above the trail.

Looking ahead to where the trail lay in a dark

shadow beneath a cliff overhang for thirty yards, Sam said under his breath, "Past there is where I figure they'll hit us, while we're riding out of the darkness back into sight."

"Let me know what you need me to do," said Bob, scanning upward.

"I want you to climb down out of sight, inside the coach," Sam said. "Tie the traces off snug and let the horses have their way until it's safe to come out."

Bob looked at him. "The horses will do all right. But I can't give you much help from inside there."

"If this works I won't need much help," said Sam, checking his rifle as he spoke.

"And if it doesn't work?" Bob asked flatly.

"Then it won't matter, will it?" Sam said. "You'll have to make a run for it on your own."

"Uh-uh," said Bob. "I'm not making a run for it without you. We both ride out of here together, or we stay here for keeps. I'm tired of everybody who's on my side getting killed."

"Fair enough," Sam nodded, watching the stage roll closer to the deep shaded overhang.

Atop the rocky edge, Frisco Phil and Price watched from the side of the trail while Kane and Shenlin climbed into place across from them. Looking down as the stage disappeared into the darkness, Frisco said to Price, "There they go, pard. As soon as they roll into sight, the three of yas let them have it."

"What do you mean the three of us?" Price gave him a questioning look. "What are *you* going to be doing?"

"I'll be doing my *share*, pard," said Frisco. "I'm

heading down to the trail." He added in a bit of a sarcastic tone, "That is, if it's all right with you."

Price just stared at him, but his expression demanded more of an explanation.

"I'll be ready to grab the money in case the gunfire spooks those stage horses and they make a run for it," Frisco said. "We don't want the stage running off this trail, and our money scattered all over the hillsides, do we?"

"All right, go ahead," Price said, relenting, seeing Frisco's point.

"Much obliged," Frisco said in his same sarcastic tone. Not wanting to discuss it any further, he pulled his bandanna up over the bridge of his nose, turned and slipped away into the rocks and down toward the trail.

Looking out over the trail to the other steep hillside, Price watched Shenlin and Kane slip along through the rocks in a crouch until they reached a point almost directly across from him. He acknowledged them with a guarded wave of his gloved hand. Then he stooped down out of sight and waited, cursing himself silently. All this out of his raw bitter spite for Texas Bob Krey.

"Damn fool," he grumbled crossly to himself. But he realized there was nothing he could do now but see this thing through no matter what the outcome. Once this was over, he promised himself, he'd walk the straight and narrow from now on. *You've got my word on that,* he thought to himself, not even realizing exactly who he'd made his promise to. God? Himself? He didn't know; he didn't care. For now he needed to concentrate on the killing at hand. He cleared his mind and waited tensely.

Moments later, as the stagecoach rolled into clearer sight out from under the cliff overhang, Price gave a quick glance toward Shenlin and Kane's position and levered a round into his rifle chamber. He rested his left elbow and gun barrel atop a rock for a close steady aim. But upon seeing the empty seat on the coach he quickly dropped back down out of sight. "They've left the stage! It's a trick!" he gasped aloud to himself, realizing Texas Bob and the ranger could be anywhere.

Straight across from Price, Shenlin shouted, "There they are! Kill them!"

Firing began, back and forth heavily on the other hillside. Crouched down behind a rock, Price clenched his rifle tightly and squeezed his eyes shut for a moment as if hoping it would cause this whole terrible matter to go away. But knowing that it wouldn't, he opened his eyes, steadied himself and belly-crawled a few yards to where he could take a better look without being seen.

From between two rocks at ground level, lying flat, with the smell of warm earth only an inch beneath his nose, Price saw the ranger and Texas Bob spring straight up from behind a rock as bullets from Shenlin's and Kane's rifles whistled past them. *My God, they're crazy!* he thought to himself. He couldn't fight crazy men!

So far, Shenlin and Kane had done most of the firing while Texas Bob and the ranger worked their way closer along the rocky hillside. Now, seeing the ranger and Bob side by side, Price watched and heard the single well-aimed shot explode from Bob's rifle just as Shenlin levered another round and raised his rifle for another wild shot.

No, Shenlin! Price wanted to shout, and let the gunman know that this was not the way to fight. He needed to settle down, take aim, make his every shot count—

Whatever advice Price had for the outlaw was of no use now, he thought. Texas Bob's bullet lifted Shenlin out of his poised crouch, straightened him with a snap and sent him flying backward, a spray of blood seeming to loom in the air. *I've got to get out of here!* Price told himself, scooting back from his hidden position.

But before he could take his eyes away from the gunfight, he heard Kane scream like some injured wildcat, "You sonsa—"

Kane's words stopped short as he jumped to his feet and fired repeatedly, only to catch a well-placed bullet in his chest from the ranger's rifle. "No! No! No!" Price whispered to himself as he crawled frantically down a grown-over path toward his and Frisco's horses.

The ranger looked all around the hillside, his rifle smoking. "That's two down," he said quietly "There's two to go."

Facing the opposite direction, scanning the hillside himself, Texas Bob replied, "Think Price and the other fellow's nerve didn't hold up?"

Sam said in a lowered tone, "Maybe, but let's not

count them out." He continued scanning back and forth, running his eyes down to the stage as the big horses moved along at an undaunted walk on the trail below. No sooner had he spoken than he spotted Frisco Phil crouched and running away from the stage, rifle in hand, toward his and Texas Bob's horses as the two animals tagged along a few yards behind.

"Got one wearing a mask," Sam said, raising his rifle quickly to his shoulder. But on the trail, Frisco glanced back and up in time to see the ranger taking aim, and he swerved away and dove off the trail into a stretch of mesquite brush and a thick bed of cholla cactus before the ranger took his shot. Hearing the masked man scream and seeing the thrashing going on in the mesquite brush, Sam winced and shook his head slowly. "He's got plenty to keep him busy for a while," he said, lowering his rifle.

Looking back along the trail, then forward and out across the opposite hillside, Texas Bob said, "I don't see Price anywhere." He looked back along the trail again and took on a concerned look. "I don't know if that's good news or bad, Ranger," he said.

"For now it's good," said Sam, nodding toward the end of the hills and the start of wide-open flatlands toward Sibley. "Once we get down from here, it'll be hard for them to slip up on us. Especially now that there's only the two of them."

Texas Bob lowered his rifle and looked over at the bodies of Kane and Shenlin lying sprawled and bloody on the rocks. Taking a deep breath, Bob said, "If you'll cover me, I'll drag these two down to the stage."

Across the trail, staggering away from the bed of

cholla cactus, Frisco whined under his breath and picked long spines from his chest and forearms as he looked back fearfully. He'd lost his rifle and hat in his wild gyrations trying to free himself from the painful thornlike cactus spines, one of which—longer than a lady's hatpin—had stabbed all the way through his left hand.

"Frisco! Over here," Price called out in a raspy whisper, seeing him from behind the cover of a brittle downed scrub piñon tree.

Frisco jerked his face forward, his right hand snatching his pistol from his holster and waving it back and forth wildly. "Where are you?" he said, having enough control to keep his voice lowered.

"Don't shoot! I'm over here," Price called out in a hushed voice, waving a hand back and forth.

Recognizing Price, Frisco staggered forward, plucking a long cactus spine from his neck just beneath his ear. Blood trickled. "I never had *anything* hurt this bad!" he said, keeping himself from sobbing as he climbed over the downed piñon and remained in a stooped position until he picked more barbs from his behind and his back. "I hope I'm not going to fester."

"You're stuck all over!" said Price, helping to pluck out the sharp spines along with him. "Shenlin and Kane are both dead," he offered.

"I know. I saw them fall," said Frisco. "I never seen two men go down that fast in my life. I couldn't believe it!"

"Well, you can believe it now," said Price, recovering from his panic as he helped pick out more long sharp spines. "What about the money?"

Frisco shook his head. "It's not there."

"It's not there?" Price stopped picking out spines and stared at him.

"That's what I said, didn't I?" Frisco snapped. "It's not in the stage. They've hidden it somewhere back there."

"That tears it," said Price. He blew out a frustrated breath. "I'm cutting out. I'm through with it."

"Oh?" Now Frisco stared at him. "Mexico, huh?"

"Yeah, Mexico," said Price. "What about you?"

"I'm going on to Sibley," Frisco said with determination. "I've got a judge on my side. I figure I'm going make out all right on this whichever way it goes." He studied Price's face for a moment to make sure he was paying attention. "The only question is whether or not you want me to tell him you're dead."

Price thought about it, tempted to say, *Yes, tell him I'm dead!* Yet, considering it, he finally asked, "Do you really think the judge will go along with anything we tell him?"

"Sure he will. He caused every bit of this," said Frisco. "If you were Judge Bass, what would you do when you heard all this—Texas Bob robbing the stage, killing the crew? He's out for Bob's blood anyway."

After another moment of careful consideration, Price forgot the promise he'd made to himself or whoever it was he'd made it to. "All right," he said finally. "We forget the money for now and get on into Sibley. We'll tell our side to the judge and get a feel for how he'll handle it. If it starts looking bad, we'll skin out of there before these two come riding in with the stage." He looked off toward the hillside where Bob and the ranger had started climbing down toward the trail. "I have to admit, I'd give anything to cut Texas Bob down a notch or two."

"Now you're talking," said Frisco, picking nail-sized cactus spines from the back of his bare head.

Chapter 13

Tommy Rojo sat perched on a spur of rock looming high above the trail leading to Texas Bob's hideout in the rugged hills. He'd followed the tracks of the bartender's and the part-time deputy's horses all the way from the livery barn doors. When the two sets of tracks had turned away, he had gone on, following the tracks of Texas Bob and Mary Alice into the rough rocky hills. He didn't know, nor did he care, why the deputy and the bartender had turned off the trail.

The pair had probably gotten afraid now that they'd grown closer to Texas Bob and had to face the prospect of shooting it out with him. Rojo grinned. Not him, though. With his method of fighting, he feared no man, not so long as he could slip up behind him. But he wasn't about to ride into a gunfight with Texas Bob, not when one good bullet in the back would take care of things.

After following the tracks as far as he could without Bob's big dog raising a fuss or without ending up in sight of the secluded cabin, he'd found this spot and

decided to wait it out. That had been three days ago.
He'd checked all around and decided that whenever
Texas Bob *did* come riding out, he would have to do
so on the trail lying below him. *Then he's mine.* Rojo
grinned to himself. He didn't care if he had to wait a
month. He gripped the rifle in his hand.

Rojo realized that there were all sorts of men out
hunting for Texas Bob by now. But he was the only
one who had used his head, kept his mouth shut and
followed the hoofprints. It was only fitting that he be
the one to reap the reward. Nodding to himself, he
stared intently at the trail below and imagined how it
would be when he delivered Texas Bob's cold stiff
body to the judge in Sibley. He was certain the judge
would see how good he was at man-hunting and insist
that he do all the bounty work for the territorial court
from now on.

Ten yards behind Rojo, two men, Trigger Leonard
Heebs and Mitchell Smith, slipped up quietly and
stopped beside a gnarled bare-limbed piñon. They
stood staring for a moment, watching the ambusher
nod his head as if carrying on a conversation with
some unseen entity.

"I always said he's a stone-cold idiot," Mitchell
Smith whispered sidelong to Trigger Heebs.

"I never argued the point with you," Heebs whispered in reply. He motioned them both forward,
silently.

The thing is, Judge . . . , Rojo said, a conversation
having started inside his head between Bass and himself. He used his free hand in a gesturing manner as
his eyes stayed fixed on the trail below. He'd begun

to imagine himself and Judge Bass discussing his next assignment, the amount of money he would receive. But the imaginary conversation was cut short as he felt a heavy boot clamp down on the small of his back.

"Whoa! Lookee here, Trig!" said Smith, keeping his boot clamped firmly. "I believe I've gone and stepped on a sidewinder!"

Trigger Leonard wrenched Rojo's rifle from his hand and snatched his Colt from his holster just before Rojo's hand reached for it. "Yep, you sure have, Mitch," said Leonard. "Expect we ought to smash its head?"

"That would be my thinking," Smith replied. Both men's voices sounded serious.

Rojo submitted, letting out a breath. "Dang, Trigger, you could get yourself killed sneaking up on a fellow like that."

"Oh?" Trigger Leonard looked at Rojo lying unarmed beneath Smith's boot. Grinning at Smith, he said, "Obliged, Tommy. I'll try to remember that."

"All right, you got me cold." Rojo looked humiliated. "I'm just saying in some cases you *would*."

"I see," said Leonard. "In some cases."

Smith moved his boot away, reached down and pulled Rojo up by the back of his coat. Rojo stumbled to his feet and brushed dirt from himself. Not wanting to be seen from the trail below, he guided them away from the edge until he was certain they were out of sight. "Where have you two been anyways? Me and Dade gave up on yas."

"So we noticed," said Leonard, handing Rojo his pistol butt first, then his rifle. "We passed through a dry mining town, saw where somebody got their brains spilled." He stared at Rojo. "Want to tell us about it?"

Rojo knew better than to try and stall these two. He winced and said, "It was terrible, what happened back there, to old Dade. A ranger blew his head half off! I was just lucky he didn't do the same to me!"

The two looked unmoved and unbelieving. "Tell us more," said Trigger Leonard, his hand resting loosely on the butt of the walnut-handled Colt holstered low on his hip.

"It's that same ranger who killed Junior Lake, his pa and his whole gang," said Rojo. Thinking of anything he could say to get the story going in the right direction, he added, "And he said he's looking for you, Trigger. That's the main message I wanted to be sure to get to you."

"So, you've been looking real hard for me?" said Trigger Leonard. "I mean, wanting to make sure I know the ranger has my name on his list?"

"Well, yeah." Rojo shrugged. "Us being pards and all."

"We're not *pards*, Rojo," Smith cut in. "We let you ride with us on Dade's say-so. Now that he's dead I don't know where that puts you." He looked at Leonard. "What do you say?"

"I say it looked like whoever took that bullet in the head got it put to him at close range," said Leonard, eyeing Rojo with suspicion. "How'd the ranger get that close? Did you not have Dade's back covered, the way a saddle pard should?"

"I ain't gonna lie, Trigger," said Rojo, making it up

as he went. "The ranger got past me. Had I been more alert, poor Dade would be alive right now. It was my fault. There. I've said it. I let the man down." He gave a remorseful look. "I hope wherever he's at he'll forgive me."

"I expect he's in hell." Trigger Leonard grinned. "If he's not, it ain't because he didn't try." He looked away, along the trail below, then back to Rojo. "What are you up to here, laying in wait like you're ready to ambush some sorry sucker?"

Rojo felt the mood lighten and he went with it. Grinning himself, he said, "Just *that*, Trig—laying in wait for some sorry sucker. You called it about right." He reached out for his rifle and Smith handed it over. "Now that you two have showed up I'm ready to ride on with yas, wherever you want to go." He had no idea what he would say if they agreed to him riding on with them. Luckily Mitchell Smith settled the matter quickly.

"We don't want you riding with us, Rojo. Now that Dade's dead, it's time you go off somewhere on your own, maybe steal chickens for a living." He gave an overbearing smile. "I always said you looked like a honest-to-goodness chicken thief to me."

"That's real funny, Mitch." Rojo kept his temper in check, but he reminded himself what he would do if he ever caught Smith with his back turned. He looked at Trigger Leonard. "What do you say about it, Trig? Can I ride with yas?"

"You heard Mitchell, Rojo. Dade is dead and you are on your own." He gestured a gloved hand toward the trail below. "Go on back to ambushing some unlucky bastard." He backed away and turned toward the path they'd walked up.

"But what about that ranger?" Rojo called out, acting as if it mattered whether or not they wanted him riding with them. "Three guns are better than two."

"That ranger has never seen me," said Trigger Leonard. "All he's looking for is my *name*. There's been no photo or sketch ever made of me that I know of. I could pass him on a street and say howdy and he wouldn't know."

"I sure hope you're right," Rojo called out, seeing them disappear into the brush where their horses stood waiting. Under his breath, he whispered, "You sonsabitches."

At their horses, Mitchell Smith looked back along the path and said, "Do you think anything that idiot said is true?"

"I doubt if much of it was worth listening to," said Leonard, swinging up into his saddle.

"Do you figure he killed Dade?" Smith asked, also swinging up.

"Ain't a doubt in my mind on that matter," said Leonard.

"What about that ranger?" Smith asked, nudging his horse along behind Trigger Leonard's.

"There's probably some truth in that," Leonard said over his shoulder. "I already heard he has my name on his list. But I'm not worried about it. He wouldn't be the first lawman I sent to hell." He grinned, staring straight ahead. "They don't call me Trigger for nothing."

"Where we headed?" Smith asked. "Now that

we've lost Dade and got shed of Rojo, we're a man short as far as pulling any serious robberies."

"We'll replace Dade easy enough," said Trigger Leonard. "As far as Rojo, we're lucky to get rid of him. I never trusted him."

"Neither did I," said Smith, looking back warily over his shoulder. "It might have been a mistake, not killing him while we had a chance. My skin always crawled when he stood behind me."

"Somebody will kill Rojo soon enough," said Trigger Leonard. "I'm more interested in riding into Sibley, see if I can get a look at that ranger. I might just want to shoot some holes in him and lay the matter to rest."

Smith grinned. "Sounds fair to me. I'm your backup man."

"What makes you think I *need* a backup man?" Leonard asked.

"It's not so much that I think you need one," said Smith. "I'm only saying just in case."

"That's better," said Trigger Leonard, staring ahead, his gloved hand resting on the handle of his holstered pistol.

No sooner were the two out of sight than Rojo went back to watching the trail from his rock perch. But the encounter with Heebs and Smith had unsettled him. He couldn't sit here forever, waiting for Texas Bob. For all he knew, Trigger Leonard and Mitchell Smith might change their minds any minute and come riding back to kill him. He couldn't take that kind of chance.

"Damn it," he said, standing, brushing his knees.

He had to slip in on Texas Bob under the shelter of night, maybe kill him in his sleep. That was riskier than catching him in an ambush, but sometimes circumstances forced you to throw caution aside and make a bold move, he thought.

Mary Alice had been alone long enough, she told herself, gazing out across the rocky hillsides looming above the cabin. The stillness had started to get to her, making her edgy, uneasy. *Once a city girl . . . ,* she reminded herself as she searched the dark afternoon shadows and called out the dog's name again. But it was more than the loneliness bothering her.

She had grown more and more concerned about Texas Bob. He'd been gone long enough to have found Sheriff Thorn and straightened everything out, hadn't he? "Stop it," she murmured aloud to herself, realizing that she'd been letting loneliness, and her nerves, get the better of her. She'd said she would wait here until Bob returned, so she would. *For how long, though?*

"Mercy," she sighed, tired of arguing with herself, tired of the silent days, tired mostly of the nights alone. Now that she and Texas Bob were together, she wanted them to *be together.* She smiled coyly to herself, knowing what she missed most of all. She called out the dog's name, holding a tin plate of food for him in her hand. What she missed was feeling Texas Bob's arms around her, she admitted, pushing a strand of hair back from her forehead.

"Plug, come and get it," she called out, trying not to think too much about her and Texas Bob right now.

This was the third time she'd walked out onto the porch and summoned the big dog to supper. Bob had told her Plug preferred to forage for himself. But once she'd started feeding the dog meat scraps, gravy and biscuits on the front porch of an evening, he had begun showing up like clockwork. By this time she would find him sitting at the open doorway, his tail brushing back and forth across the planks.

"Well, not tonight," she said, setting the tin plate down. When she straightened up and started through the doorway, she stopped for a moment and gave one last scanning glance around the rugged, darkening land. Had she heard a dog whine? No, she told herself, even as she listened closely for any other sound from within the dead silence, the encroaching darkness.

Raising her apron, she wiped her hands idly and stared down at the plate on the plank porch. There was something foreboding about the dog not being there as he had been the past nights. "Don't you worry," Bob had told her before he'd left. "Plug'll watch about you while I'm gone."

Yes, but where is Plug? she asked herself, looking back again across the hillsides, feeling the darkness creep closer in around her. She didn't like this at all. Something was wrong—something out there, she thought, smoothing her apron down and walking calmly but purposefully into the cabin. Suddenly she felt the sensation of eyes on her as she closed the door and shoved the heavy iron bolt into place.

From within the dark shadows of a large upthrusted boulder, Tommy Rojo had sat watching the door close, his rifle in one hand, a long boot knife in the other. He'd worked his way into the tight valley on foot over an hour earlier and sat patiently in the darkening shadows. He hadn't seen Texas Bob, but that didn't mean he wasn't around here somewhere, maybe hunting game, maybe on his way back to the cabin at this very minute, he told himself.

This had to be the hideout. This was where the two sets of hoofprints had led him. The woman had to be the whore from the saloon, he convinced himself. The thing he did not want to do was sit out in the dark and the cold, and then when Texas Bob came in for the night find it too dark to get a clear back shot at him.

No, that wasn't the way this was going to go, he decided, rising to a crouch and moving hurriedly from shadow to shadow down to the cabin porch. Ducking down below porch level, he waited for only a moment, then crawled like a serpent up onto the rough wooden planks and over beneath a window. He wasn't going to use the rifle on the woman. *No sir,* he thought, raising his face to a window and looking inside, seeing the woman stoke the hearth in the glow of an oil lantern.

He wanted this to happen quickly and silently, he told himself, laying his rifle on the porch beneath the window. He crawled slowly and carefully to the door, not risking his footsteps' creaking on the planks. He had to kill her quietly, not tip off Texas Bob with a rifle shot.

Gripping the knife handle tightly, he began to rise into a crouch, his free hand reaching for the door handle. With the woman dead, Texas Bob would walk through that front door not expecting a thing. *Almost too easy.* He grinned, ready to make his move. But just as his hand closed around the handle, he heard a low menacing growl behind him and turned his head slowly to see the big dog standing half on the step and half on the porch, its hackles raised, its fangs bared, glistening white. "Easy, boy," Rojo ventured in a whisper, seeing the dog poised, ready to spring forward into his face at any second.

But his words only seemed to enrage the dog. The growl grew deeper, louder. The dog stepped stiffly up onto the porch and closer to Rojo's face. The knife in Rojo's hand meant nothing to the animal. The rifle lay over ten feet away. Cold sweat beaded on Rojo's forehead.

"Who's there?" the woman's voice called out from inside. "Is someone there?"

"Yes, ma'am," Rojo said in a slim shaky tone, not wanting to trigger the big dog into action. "Pl—please, I'm— I'm . . ." He had no idea what to say next.

"You're *what*?" the voice said. Even in Rojo's state of terror he realized the voice seemed calm, almost as if the woman was toying with him. He managed to squeeze the door handle enough to feel the bolt in place.

He tried to think of something else to say, but before he could come up with anything the dog sprang into him. Rojo screamed long and loud, taking a stab at the dog but missing, and feeling the knife fly from his hand as he tried to clutch the big animal by its neck to keep its teeth out of his face.

Inside, Mary Alice heard the screams, the growl and

the ensuing scuffle against the closed door. She took her time slipping the bolt open, a double-barreled shotgun in her left hand, a thick iron fire poker in her raised right hand.

When the bolt allowed, the door swung open wide and Rojo spilled onto the floor at her feet, the dog atop him, the screaming man's face buried in the dog's snarling mouth. "Oh, a big knife!" Mary Alice called out above the melee, seeing the knife lying discarded on the porch.

"Get him off!" Rojo screamed, his words muffled by the dog's wet enveloping flews.

"I've seen bigger," Mary Alice said, still focused on the knife.

Suddenly Rojo realized the dog had turned his face loose and stepped off of him, Mary Alice having reached a hand down and grabbed it by the loose nape of its neck. "Get away from me, whore!" Rojo shouted, batting his blood-filled eyes, gasping for breath. But his reprieve was short-lived.

"Whore?" Mary Alice hissed, her face turning white with rage. "I'll show you what this *whore* can do!"

Rojo heard the *swish*ing sound of the iron poker swinging back and forth through the air and felt the bite of it at the end of each swing.

"You came here to stab somebody!" Mary Alice shouted as she beat him without mercy. "To kill some dumb helpless whore! Shame on you! This is not my first knife fight!" She screamed and beat him while the big dog bounced back and forth, excited, growling and barking wildly.

PART 3

PART 3

Chapter 14

———————

The first time Rojo regained consciousness, memory of the dog, the enraged woman and her iron poker came to mind, causing his swollen eyes to spring open as much as their sore and battered condition would allow. But to his waking horror both dog and woman still loomed over him, the dog growling, the woman having exchanged her iron poker for a double-barreled shotgun. "Oh *God*!" he managed to say just as the shotgun butt took a long swing sideways and crashed into the side of his already swollen, bloody head.

Upon his second awakening he used more caution. Opening one eye only a crack, he looked back and forth. The dog lay near a crackling hearth, sound asleep. Breathing a little easier, Rojo opened his other eye and looked back and forth at floor level, realizing he'd been tied tightly with a rope and enveloped inside a tight-fitting brownish bedsheet.

"So, you're awake," said Mary Alice, sitting at the

wooden table, holding a long needle and a ball of thick thread.

Rojo moaned and tugged at his tied wrists. She'd folded his arms across his chest, looped each wrist with a length of rope, drawn the ropes together tightly behind his back and tied them into a thick knot. His feet were tied securely together and the rope circled upward like the stripe on a barber's pole and ended in a floppy bow at his throat.

"What have you . . . done to me?" he gasped through swollen lips.

"Well, for one thing," Mary Alice replied, "I washed your face and sewed it up."

"Sewed it up?" As soon as she said it he recognized the tight painful sensation of stitches across his forehead, across his scalp, down the side of his black, swollen nose and beneath his chin. "The dog . . . ?" he asked in a trailing voice.

"Mm-hmm," Mary Alice replied in an offhanded manner, wrapping the remaining thread into a ball and sticking the needle in it. "Since I was sewing anyway, I went ahead and sewed you inside an old sheet I found under the wood box. So you can relax. You're not going anywhere. Even if you could, Plug would eat you alive."

Raising his head enough to look down himself, Rojo groaned and pleaded, "Shoot me, ma'am, please."

Mary Alice stood with one hand on her hip, the shotgun leaning against the table beside her. "Oh, now it's *ma'am,* is it?" she said. "Last night it was *whore.*"

"I want to . . . apologize for that, ma'am," Rojo

said haltingly. "A man says things . . . he doesn't mean, when his head's in a dog's mouth."

Mary Alice gave him a flat, unyielding stare. "You came to kill Texas Bob, didn't you?"

Realizing the pointlessness of denying it, Rojo sighed and said, "Yes, ma'am, that is . . . the gospel truth. I did. But I swear I never came to bring you any harm."

"You mindless fool," said Mary Alice. "I love Texas Bob. Coming to kill Tex *does* bring me harm. It's no different than if you came to kill me. Tex and I just happen to *love* one another. But what would a man like you know about something like that?"

Taking a breath, trying to clear his head and see what it would take to get out of his predicament, Rojo said quietly from within his tight-fitting cocoon, "Ma'am, there's nobody appreciates love more than I do. But your man Texas Bob is wanted for murder." He hoped he sounded official. "I wanted to take him to Sibley so he could face an honest trial by jury."

"I see," said Mary Alice skeptically. "Then you're a lawman?"

"In a manner of speaking, yes," said Rojo, his stitched-up face throbbing, aching painfully. "I'm under the authority of his honor, territorial judge Henry Edgar Bass."

"You're a bounty hunter," Mary Alice said flatly. "Judge Bass is the brother to the man Texas Bob killed in self-defense." She considered the situation, realizing the danger Bob was in if he hadn't yet found Sheriff Thorn and straightened things out.

"Yes, I am a professional manhunter, it's true," said Rojo. "But *self-defense*? That's for a jury to decide," he said, imitating the way he'd heard lawmen talk to people in the past, hoping it would work. He nodded toward a small wicker sewing basket on the table. "Now, if you'll take those scissors and cut me out of this concoction, I'll just be on my way, no harm done."

"No harm done?" Mary Alice looked at his purple ravaged face, then at white strips of scalp where she'd cropped his hair to skin level in order to sew his ripped flesh back down on his head. "You come sneaking around in the dark, peeping in windows, with a rifle." She shook her head. "There's been plenty of harm done. If Tex had been here, you would have killed him. Don't think you're getting out of here and taking off after him again."

As she spoke, she picked up the scissors and stood over him with them. Reaching down with the points she gathered a handful of the sheet at his crotch. "Ma'am, please, *no!*" Rojo begged, feeling the sharp scissors puncture the sheet.

"Calm down," said Mary Alice. "I'm cutting an opening front and rear so you can relieve yourself when the need arises." His voice had risen enough to awaken the sleeping dog. It stood and stretched and walked over to him curiously.

"You can't leave me trussed up like this! It's not human!" said Rojo, lowering his tone as he saw the dog step into sight. Grateful she wasn't going to use the scissors in some unspeakable manner, but now realizing she planned on him being tied and wrapped for a while, he said, "What are you going to do with me?"

"I'm taking you to town," said Mary Alice.

"Oh no you're not," said Rojo, struggling in vain for a moment before relenting with a moan. He pictured the town staring as she dragged him down the middle of the street sewn up in the bedsheet. "Ma'am, please don't take me into Sibley like this. I'm begging you."

"I have to," said Mary Alice. "It's either take you to Sibley or else kill you and hide your body out in the wilds," she said sincerely, snipping a second opening in the sheet. "I'm not turning you loose and I can't sit here any longer, doing nothing while the world falls down around me."

"I can't *ride* like this," Rojo offered, still hoping to get himself cut loose.

"There's a wagon wheel in the barn," Mary Alice said, more to herself than to Rojo. "I'll put you on it and pull it with a rope."

"Pull me on a wagon wheel? You can't do that," said Rojo. "All that dust will choke me to death! I'd never make it to Sibley."

"I'm not asking you to," Mary Alice said coldly. "Keep in mind that if you die that's one less problem for me to have to deal with." As she spoke Rojo watched her snip the scissors open and closed in her hand, as if in grim contemplation.

Judge Bass looked out of place seated at the battered wooden desk in the dusty sheriff's office, wearing his crisp white shirt and black linen suit. On the corner of the desk lay his black flat-crowned hat. With his head bowed over a stack of paperwork, he did not see the faces of Claude Price and Frisco Phil appear first at the window before they opened the creaking door and slipped inside.

Upon snapping his attention up from his paperwork, Bass said in surprise, "Well, it's about damn time! What took you two so long?"

Price and Frisco looked at one another. Then Price said, "Your Honor, you just can't believe the trouble we ran into out there."

"Trouble? What sort of trouble?" Bass jerked his wire-framed glasses from his eyes. Before they could answer, the judge said, "I suppose some trouble could be expected from a man like Texas Bob. The main thing is, you did drag him out of his lair. Am I correct?" He gave them a fierce stare.

"Judge Bass, this Texas Bob is a bigger deal than you or us either one realized," said Frisco Phil, stepping forward. "He's done a lot of other things you need to know about. He's killed Sheriff Thorn."

"Thorn is dead?" The judge stared, stunned. "You—you know this for a fact?"

"Yes, we do, Your Honor," said Price. "We heard shooting while we were on Texas Bob's trail. When we caught up to the gunfire we saw Thorn laying dead in the dirt beside the Cottonwood stage. Texas Bob robbed the stage and killed Thorn, and the two stage men too."

The judge realized the story he'd been told left a lot to be questioned, but he ignored that for now. Hearing the terrible things Texas Bob had done caused him to have to hold back a slight smile. "Do tell me you killed this monster, that his body is lying across a horse out there?" He sidestepped and craned his neck for a glance out the window.

"Uh, no, Your Honor," said Price sheepishly.

Seeing no body on any of the horses lined along the hitch rail in the waning evening light, Bass turned his chilly stare back to the two men. "Well, where *is* his body then?"

"I'm afraid he got away from us, Your Honor," said Price.

"So he's not dead," Bass replied coldly to Price. "I am very disappointed in you." His eyes swung to Frisco. "In *both* of you!"

"But we thought you'd be glad to hear about him robbing the stage and killing the stage crew, Judge," said Frisco. "That's just one more crime he's committed. We thought it would be useful information for you."

"The Cottonwood stage—Texas Bob robbing it," the judge said, letting things sink in a little more clearly now that he'd vented his anger. "I would never have pegged him as a stage robber."

"But then you never would have pegged him as a murderer if you didn't know he'd killed your poor dear brother," Frisco put in.

"Very true," said Bass, ignoring Frisco's mocking attitude. As the judge thought about what the two had told him, his eyes lit with possibilities. "This man killed my brother, went on the run to keep from answering for his crimes and now apparently has sunk to the level of a common criminal rather than face justice." He paused, then added as his mind worked over the situation. "Perhaps he had planned on the stage robbery to finance his flight from the country— to Mexico no doubt."

"No doubt," said Price.

"In fact I'd bet on it," Frisco cut in. The two looked blankly at one another. "There is one small problem, Your Honor," said Price. "Ranger Burrack is riding with him. They're headed here with the stage."

"But that's not a problem I can't handle!" said the judge, not about to let anything sway his sense of sweet revenge. "It's the ranger's job to bring in fugitives from the law." Smiling now, he said, "He brings him in, you two arrest him. He goes to trial and hangs. That's how justice is supposed to work—and work it will." His mood improved. "He robbed a stage, killed a law officer and two stage company employees. Yes, that will do nicely."

The two looked relieved. Then Price said, "So I figure we'll still get the reward, for doing the best we could?"

"Don't push your luck with me, Deputy," the judge warned. "You and I know you both have failed. There's no reward for *almost* bringing in Texas Bob Krey."

"But all this information, about the sheriff, the stage robbery and all," Price insisted.

"No reward, Deputy, so put it out of your mind. You're lucky to still be wearing a badge. Besides, after you two left, I sent out a professional manhunter to bring in Texas Bob in case you two failed, as now we see you have."

Frisco said guardedly, "Judge, there's a possibility this ranger and Texas Bob are both going to try blaming that stage robbery on us." He gestured between Price and himself.

"Oh?" The judge looked leery. "Now why, pray tell, would they attempt to do something like·that? Texas Bob is a murderer, but Ranger Burrack is known for his sense of fairness in matters of the law." He rubbed his jaw as he thought things over. "He'll take me to task. He's peculiar when it comes to seeing to it that the law is upheld in an impartial manner. I wouldn't be surprised if he tried to have me replaced as presiding judge over the case, if he had time to do it."

"A ranger can do that?" Price asked.

"He can *request* it, certainly. I don't want him to get the chance." Bass considered things, then said, "Too bad the Apache aren't on a raiding spree. They would cut the telegraph lines. We'd have plenty of time to make sure things go the way they should." He gave the pair a look.

"The Apache ain't the only ones who know how to cut wires, Your Honor," Price offered.

"I didn't hear you say that, Deputy." Bass smiled, knowing he'd made his meaning clear.

"It'll be our word against Texas Bob's anyway, is the way I see it," said Frisco, realizing the ranger hadn't seen them rob the stage, kill Thorn or do anything else illegal. "Whose word means more, a gambling, gun-fighting rounder's like Texas Bob, or a sworn deputy's like Price here, and me, a man sent to assist him?" Seeing the judge thinking his words over, he added quickly, "I could even be a sworn deputy myself if it helped matters."

"Indeed you could, and you will if you do as I tell you," said Bass, coming to some sort of conclusion. He looked at them both closely. "I don't know what went on out there, and I get the feeling it's better that I *don't* know. If both of you saw Texas Bob rob the stage, then yes, your word is certainly worth more than his, provided the ranger can't attest to anything different."

"He can't, unless he lies," said Frisco after the two looked at one another again.

"The ranger will not lie, I assure you. So, we've got Texas Bob for the stage robbery." Bass balled a vengeful fist and said, "But I want him to die for killing my brother. I don't care if it's a legal hanging or an out-and-out mob lynching."

The two looked at him, seeing how far he was willing to go to avenge his brother's death. "We'll back your play however you call it," said Frisco.

"Good," said the judge. He lowered his voice and said, "For a legal conviction to take place there is still something standing in the way." He stared hesitantly, thinking about Lady Lucky and her account of the shooting at the Sky High Saloon.

"Whatever it is, you just tell us, Judge," said Frisco. "Don't pussyfoot around about it."

"No, please, by all means, Your Honor," said Price. "We want to see to it Texas Bob swings for the stage robbery just as bad as you want to see him swing for killing your brother, Davin."

Bass saw something dark at work in Price's eyes.

He had no idea what these men were hiding from him, or what they'd been involved in since he'd sent them searching for Texas Bob. He dared not ask. He would soon have Bob where he wanted him. That was his only interest.

Chapter 15

During the night Trigger Leonard and Mitchell Smith had arrived at the Bottoms Up Saloon and Brothel. After a late evening of drinking they had taken adjoining rooms upstairs facing the street and spent the night with two of the brothel's doves, Mad Mattie Short and Sweet-face Hannah Lund. Both doves were up from the beds and gathering their clothes in the light of midmorning when they heard the stage horses come rolling along the dirt street.

"Take a look at this, Mattie," said Hannah, staring out the window and seeing Texas Bob jump down from the shotgun rider's seat and swing open the door.

Joining Hannah at the window as she finished pulling her dress down and straightening it, Mattie saw the boot soles of two of the dead men just inside the open stage door. "Uh-oh," she murmured. "Looks like it's been somebody's last ride."

"We better wake them up," said Hannah, taking a deep draw on her first thin cigar of the day. The two

watched the ranger step down from the driver's seat
and join Texas Bob at the open stage door.

Mattie looked hesitant. "Are you sure? I came near
getting slapped around last night. I don't want—"

"I'm sure," said Hannah, cutting her off. "He said
wake him if anything unusual went on in the street."
As she spoke she walked to the bed where Trigger
Leonard lay sprawled facedown, naked, snoring. His
right arm hung off the edge of the feather mattress,
his hand wrapped loosely around the neck of a whiskey bottle. "Here goes," Hannah shrugged. Nudging
his forearm with her toe, she said loudly, "Hey, Big-
horse Hairy, wake up!"

His snoring interrupted, Leonard only moaned at
first and cursed mindlessly. But upon feeling the whiskey bottle loosen from his fingertips and fall over on
its side, he snapped conscious and felt around frantically for it. When he raised it in his grasp and looked
at it bleary-eyed, making sure he'd corked it during
the night, he let out a breath and said gruffly, "The
hell do you want? You've been paid."

"But not enough," Mattie whispered with a look
of contempt.

"Come on, Big-horse, wake up," Hannah persisted,
reaching down and shaking him by his shoulder. "You
said wake you if we saw anything going on."

Leonard opened an eye to her. "Don't call me Big-
horse," he said in a thick-sounding voice.

Hannah shrugged again. "That's what you told me
to call you."

"Last night I told you to call me that," said Leonard, rising to the edge of the bed and twisting the cork from the whiskey bottle. "Not today." He swirled the whiskey around in the bottle, threw back a long drink and blew out a breath. "Now, what is it?"

Hannah stared at him for a moment, then jerked her head toward the window. "A stagecoach, one horse short and carrying bodies in it . . . a lawman driving it."

"A lawman?" The rest didn't seem to interest him, but now he sprang to his feet. With his free hand he snatched up the rifle leaning against the wall and hurried to the window. "Wake him up!" he ordered Mad Mattie as he peeped down at the street without being seen.

"Don't be shooting anybody from up here," Hannah said matter-of-factly. Then, on second thought, she said, "That wasn't included in the price." As she spoke Mattie raced barefoot into the other room and shook Mitchell Smith by his shoulder.

"Shut up, woman! You'll be taken care of!" Leonard growled over his shoulder at Hannah, without taking his eyes off the ranger's dusty sombrero, watching him reach inside the stage and fan flies away from the dead. "I'm not letting this chance get past me." He levered a round into the rifle chamber. "Bring me my britches!"

Staggering in from the other room, holding his trousers up at the waist, his wide gallowses hanging at his sides, Mitchell asked sleepily, "The hell's going on, Trig?"

"Ha! I'll tell you what's going on!" Cutting a sharp excited grin, rifle and whiskey bottle in hand, Leonard said, "The ranger is right down there on the street. He's fell into our laps!" As he spoke he held the bottle sidelong to Smith.

"You don't mean it!" Taking the bottle, Smith batted his bleary eyes and pushed his long hair back from his forehead. He took a drink, standing back from the window but looking down guardedly.

"Oh, I mean it, all right!" said Leonard, taking Hannah by her thin wrist as she handed him a chair from beside the bed. "You did good waking me, Sweetface," he said, his eyes going a bit soft for a second. "I want you to know that."

"I've never been so happy," Hannah said with a trace of sarcasm as she tugged her arm free. "Don't forget to pay us something extra."

"Yeah, sure," Leonard murmured idly as he stared down onto the street, his trousers hanging from his hand, his rifle going to his shoulder to take aim.

Mitchell Smith, having taken a drink of whiskey, stared wild-eyed at his naked partner. "Trigger! We ain't even dressed yet!"

"Dressed or not, I don't give a damn. I'm taking him down," said Leonard, looking down the rifle sights at the back of the ranger's riding duster. "Get yourself armed and back me up."

On the street, Sam waved the gathering townsfolk away from the stagecoach. "Give us some room, folks," he said, his eyes going up along the roofline across the street. As he spoke he felt the same way he'd felt many times when he'd found himself in someone's gun sights.

As the gathering crowd fanned flies from themselves

and stepped back grudgingly, the ranger looked closer at the open window above the Bottoms Up Saloon. But the window revealed nothing more than a thin curtain stirring on a breeze.

"Is that Sheriff Thorn?" a woman asked with a gasp, seeing the sheriff's bloody body through the open stage door.

"Yes, ma'am, I'm afraid it is," Sam answered, catching another glance along the roofline and going back to the open window.

"Is this the judge coming here, Ranger?" Texas Bob asked just between the two of them. He nodded at the large well-dressed figure walking along the boardwalk toward them.

"Yes, that's him," Sam said quietly. "I'm counting on you to keep your head if he gets testy with us."

"You've got it, Ranger," said Texas Bob. He held the shotgun out toward him butt first. "Do you want this?"

"That's not necessary," said Sam, without reaching for the shotgun. "You're not under arrest. You're not wanted for any crime that I know of. If you're through with the stage company's gun, stick it back under the seat."

"Obliged, Ranger," said Bob. He started to step over and lay the shotgun up under the seat. But before he could do so, the judge called out with a thick finger pointed at him, "Stop right there! Ranger Burrack, disarm that man immediately! Place him under arrest!"

Texas Bob stopped and stood facing the judge, the shotgun still hanging loosely in his hands.

Sam, unable to shake the feeling of being targeted from the saloon window, took another quick glance along the roofline, then stepped forward and said to the quickly approaching judge, "Stop where you are, Judge. I have no cause to arrest this man."

The judge stopped short ten feet away. "You do now. I'm charging him with the murder of Sheriff Thorn and the rest of those poor fellows lying there." His finger swung to the bodies inside the big stagecoach. "I further charge him with stagecoach robbery." He glared at Texas Bob. "Where is the stage money?"

Neither Texas Bob nor the ranger replied. They only stared. Sam felt relieved that Bob had hidden the money. Possession of the money would only have given the judge proof of his guilt.

"Very well," said the judge. "Refusing to answer me doesn't help your case in the least. Now do as I say, Ranger. Arrest him!" As he spoke he looked back and forth over the faces of the crowd, as if seeking their approval.

"Based on what evidence, Judge?" Sam asked skeptically.

The judge said smugly, "Based on the eyewitness accounts of sworn officers of the law, Ranger Burrack. Now arrest him! That's an order!"

In the window, Mitchell Smith said to Trigger Leonard in a lowered tone, "Well, are you going to shoot him?"

"Not just yet," said Leonard, a grin on his face as he glared at the street and listened to the exchange between the ranger and Judge Bass. "I don't want to miss this. Besides, like you said, we're not even dressed yet. Here, hold this." He handed his rifle side-long to Smith and stepped quickly into his trousers, keeping his eyes on the street below. "I can kill this ranger anytime. Maybe we'll watch for a while, get a chance to see the law in action."

Deputy Claude Price finished loading the shotgun he'd taken down from the rack inside the sheriff's office.

"Will you hurry the hell up?" Frisco Phil said, standing restlessly at the dusty window. He stood staring down the street toward the gathered crowd, keeping the judge's fine shiny derby in sight amid the sweat-stained flop hats, Stetsons and sombreros. "We've got this thing going our way. Let's not let it get away from us."

"Nothing is getting away from me ever again," Price said, clicking the shotgun shut and heading past Frisco and out the front door.

At the stagecoach in the street, Judge Bass waited impatiently for the ranger to carry out his order. But Sam made no attempt to arrest Texas Bob. Instead he stared warily at the judge and asked, "Who are these *officers of the law*, and what exactly did they witness?"

"I'll show you who they are," said Bass. Waving a hand above the crowd toward the sheriff's office as Frisco Phil and Price ran along the dirt street, he said as they stopped inside the circled bystanders and spread out, covering both the ranger and Texas Bob, "Deputies, is this the man you saw rob the Cotton-wood stage, kill its crew and murder Sheriff Thorn?"

Seeing Texas Bob's and the ranger's searing gazes upon him, Price averted his eyes, unable to face them. But Frisco spoke right up, shotgun in hand, saying, "Sure as the world, Your Honor. That's the man who did it." He grinned defiantly at Texas Bob.

"Why you rotten, murdering—" Texas Bob took a step past the ranger toward Frisco and Price. "These are two of the men who robbed the stage and did all the killing."

"Oh?" said the judge haughtily. "Then I suppose it will be your word against the word of two lawmen."

"This is nothing but a jackpot you're putting me in because of your brother, Judge," Bob said, his stare turning to the judge, his hands poised on the shotgun, raising it into a firing position.

Three feet behind him, Sam said, "Hold it, Bob. Let's not start a bloodletting here in the street." He watched the crowd step back, their eyes widening at the sight of so many shotguns in so small an area.

"Speaking of my poor brother," said Bass, "that is one more murder I intend to see you hang for."

The ranger noted that the judge seemed unconcerned about the many innocent bystanders. It was as if he wanted to goad Texas Bob into a gunfight. "He's trying to goad you, Bob. Don't let him," said Sam. "We've got our own eyewitness when it comes to you shooting Davin Bass. Lady Lucky will testify it was self-defense."

"Lady Lucky's luck ran out." The judge cut in with a dark stare at the ranger. He gestured with his hand toward Frisco Phil. "Tell them, Deputy," he ordered Frisco.

"She died in her sleep last night, from a mortal gunshot wound she received from *you*," Frisco said bluntly, his nasty smile still on his face. "She won't be testifying to anything." As Frisco adjusted the shotgun slightly in his hands, Sam caught a glimpse of the shiny new deputy's badge on his chest.

The sight of that badge somehow connected to Lady Lucky's death in Texas Bob's mind. Seeing the knowing look on the faces of the judge and the two deputies, he said, "You killed her, didn't you?" His eyes swung to the judge. "They killed her, and you had them do it! Just to make sure there was no witness to the shooting at the Sky High—"

"Arrest him, Deputies!" Bass demanded.

The ranger saw the judge back away; at the same time he saw the shotguns in Price's and Frisco's hands begin to rise. *Too many people are going to die here,* he thought, catching a glimpse of the stunned crowd. *Too many innocent people.*

Sam sprang forward, ahead of both the deputies and Texas Bob. His big Colt came up fast, but uncocked. Before the two deputies could put their killing plan into action, the Colt took a hard swipe sideways and knocked Texas Bob to his knees. The short-barreled shotgun flew from Bob's hands.

"There. He's under arrest. Everybody freeze," Sam shouted. He cocked his Colt now and swung it back and forth from the deputies to the judge. "This man is in my custody." Stepping forward quickly, he shoved Texas Bob facedown in the dirt and stood crouched over him, his left hand holding him in place.

"You had your chance, Ranger," Frisco said, still

tensed, ready to make his move. Beside him Price stood ready to do the same.

"Call your dogs off, Judge," Sam said tightly. His Colt stopped in full aim at the judge's large belly. "Nobody lives through a fight this close."

The judge needed no time to think it over. He knew the ranger's reputation and he saw the determination in his eyes. "All right, Deputies! That's enough! Lower the shotguns! Don't shoot, please! We've got our man!"

From the boardwalk out front of the Bottoms Up Saloon, Trigger Leonard and Mitchell Smith stood watching intently as the ranger dragged Texas Bob to his feet and guided him forward. "Now that beats all I ever seen," said Trigger Leonard. "A *ranger* squaring off with two *lawmen* and a *judge.*" He shook his head and shrugged, chuckling at the irony of it. "What the hell has this wicked ole world come to?"

"Beats me," said Smith, sounding disappointed. "I pulled my boots on the wrong feet to hurry down and see a rootin'-tootin' shoot-out. All I saw was a man get his head busted by a gun barrel and be dragged off to jail."

"Wasn't bloody enough for you, eh?" Leonard asked in a lowered tone.

"Not enough to pull me away from a warm bed and a bottle of whiskey," said Smith, leaning against a post, pulling his boots off to correct them. "I've seen more bloodshed at my family reunions, especially when my ma and pa was alive."

"Well, fix your boots and stick around," said Leonard, watching the ranger look back and keep an eye on the judge and the deputies as he escorted Texas Bob onto the boardwalk and through the open door of the sheriff's office. "I believe it's going to get bloodier by the minute around here."

Chapter 16

———◆———

At the door to the sheriff's office, Sam turned, gun in hand, and said to the two deputies who trailed him like wolves, "If anything happens to my prisoner, it better happen to me first."

The cocked Colt stopped them abruptly at the edge of the boardwalk. Sam's tone of voice caused the two deputies to spread their hands wide in spite of their shotguns. They looked to Bass for direction. "Stand down, Deputies," the judge said quietly, not quite sure himself what the ranger might do at any moment. "He has the right to use any jail in the territory. Give him room. He'll cool down."

Hearing the judge, Sam halted for a second in the open door and said, "I am as cool as I'm likely to get until I see justice done."

"Justice, indeed. Ranger, we are both after the same thing," the judge said smugly, concerned more with what the following onlookers heard them say.

"You're out for *revenge,* Judge," said Sam, with no

regard for what anybody heard him say. "Before this is over I've a feeling you will regret it."

"Ha." The judge scoffed. "When this is over I will have no regrets whatsoever. The guilty will have paid for their transgressions." For the crowd's sake he raised a finger for emphasis. "Remember my words when that time comes."

Seeing the judge pander to the crowd, Sam nudged Texas Bob forward, the tall broad-shouldered plainsman still staggering a bit from the blow of the gun barrel. When the door closed behind the ranger, Bass said to Price and Frisco, "All right, stay outside the door for a while. We've got the man we wanted in custody. He's not going anywhere."

"You got it, Your Honor," Frisco replied. He bounded up onto the boardwalk and took a position on one side of the door, his shiny new badge reflecting the midmorning sun.

Price stepped up and took the other side. "We should have shot him down while we had the chance," he whispered to Frisco. "Neither of these men are the kind you want to leave *alive*."

"There you go with the worrying again." Frisco chuckled, nodding toward the judge. "Look, man, we've got the law on our side." He rubbed his shirt cuff back and forth across his badge. "Hell, what am I saying? We *are* the law!"

At the edge of the boardwalk, Judge Bass turned to face the crowd and said, "All right, folks. I have taken care of everything. Sibley has lost its good and decent sheriff. But I swear to you, his killer will not go unpunished!"

The crowd only stared until finally an old miner stepped forward and said, "Texas Bob is a good and decent man too, Judge Bass."

"I will be the judge of that," the judge said with a condescending air. "This is a legal matter. Unless you are an attorney, I suggest you leave this matter to those of us who know the law."

"He'll get a jury trial, won't he?" a woman asked.

"Yes, of course he will," said the judge.

"What about an attorney?" a man's voice called out. "There's no lawyers within miles—none worth a hoot anyways."

"Territorial law says that if no attorney is available, a man can appoint whomsoever he pleases to represent him," said the judge. "For all I care he can represent himself." He paused for a second and, although no one made mention of it, said loud enough for all to hear, "I'll have none of you going off and deciding to take the law into your own hands. I won't stand for a lynching here in Sibley!"

The townsmen looked at one another, confused. "Who said anything about a lynching?" the old miner asked a man standing next to him.

The judge pointed quickly at the miner. "You there, stop it right now! I told you I won't have it. I admired the sheriff as much as any of you. But there will be no lynching in Sibley, even though we only have two deputies to keep things under control."

Beside the office door, Frisco leaned sideways and whispered to Price, "It's a pleasure to watch His Honor at work."

Inside the sheriff's office, once he had locked Texas

Bob safely inside a cell, Sam wet a cloth he'd found hanging above a pan of water in the rear corner, carried it to the cell and handed it to Bob through the bars. "I'm sorry I had to hit you out there, Bob," he said.

"Me too," said Bob, managing a thin tight grin. Pressing the wet rag to the back of his head, he winced, then said, "But I've been hit harder. I figure you was only trying to keep me alive, else I'd still be laying out there counting stars."

"I'm glad you realize it, Bob," said Sam. "Three shotguns blasting away in a crowded street like that—by the time it was over it wouldn't matter who was innocent or guilty. There wouldn't be enough of us left to bury the dead."

"I saw the judge and the deputies wanted it to happen," said Bob, "but the longer they talked the more I began to see what kind of jackpot the judge has me in. Finally all I saw was a hangman's noose waiting for me." He looked questioningly at the ranger. "I sure hope you've got something in mind."

"I'm not going to lie to you, Bob," Sam said. "Right now, with Lady Lucky dead and these two men wanting to frame you, I wish we'd never rode into Sibley."

"I'm not blaming you for anything, Ranger, no matter how this turns out," Bob said. "I know you meant to do the right thing." He paused for a second in contemplation, then hung his head slightly and said, "Lately I'm finding it harder to know what the right thing is. I killed a man fair and square. It wasn't something I wanted to do, but I had to kill him, to keep him from killing me. That should be the long and short of it."

Sam only stared at him. Beyond the front door, they heard the judge's voice call out to the gathered towns-folk, who had not only failed to move along but had actually grown in number.

Texas Bob nodded toward the street and continued. "But the man I killed was the brother of a territorial judge, so that changes everything. I didn't kill one of my *own kind* in self-defense. It turns out like I'm guilty of killing one of my *betters*." He turned his knowing eyes back up to the ranger. "That's how eas-ily the law can change these days, Ranger. That's how easy it is to go from being right to wrong."

"This man is not the law," Sam said. "He used to be, but he's gotten too big for it. I don't know where this thing is headed, but wherever it is, I'm with you. Don't give up on the law and don't give up on me." Sam let out a breath and added, "Most of all, don't give up on yourself. I hear what he's saying out there. He's planting the seeds for a lynching, even though he's talking against it. But I promise you this—there will be no lynching."

"What are you saying, Ranger, that you'll step out-side the law to keep me from hanging?" Texas Bob gripped the cell door with both hands. The water from the wet rag dripped from his closed hand and ran down the iron bar. "I don't expect that from you. I wouldn't ask it."

The ranger didn't answer right away. Instead he backed away from the bars, walked to the front window and looked out on the growing crowd. "Bass is trying to work the crowd into a lather."

"He wants me dead so bad, he doesn't care how it comes about," said Texas Bob.

"I'm afraid you're right," said the ranger. "But you'll be all right here while I go send off a telegram to the capitol, see if I can bring some attention to what Bass is trying to do." His voice dropped to a whisper. "Those deputies won't let anything happen to you so long as you don't tell them where the money is hidden."

"I'm not telling them anything," said Bob. "I'll be all right for now. Good luck, Ranger." He clutched the bars on the cell door.

Outside the front door, both deputies took a step sideways and looked at the ranger. On the edge of the boardwalk, the judge said to the townsfolk, "I want you all to go on about your business now. I have this matter in hand."

To the deputies, Sam said, "My prisoner is locked in his cell. I better find him there, safe and sound, when I return from the telegraph office."

Frisco and Price gave one another a look. "Telegraph office, huh?" said Frisco smugly. "I hope you do better than I did. I tried wiring home, but found the 'Paches had chopped down the lines. Dang them savages." He grinned. "Nothing is safe anymore."

Price cut in. "Nobody is going to bother your prisoner, Ranger, so long as he behaves himself." He nodded toward the remaining townsfolk. "We'll do our best to keep them from busting in and snatching him off to the nearest hanging pole, if we can." He gave Sam a knowing look.

Sam returned the look and said, "I believe it's in your best interest to keep him alive. Besides, most of these people know Texas Bob Krey. You'll have a hard time making him look like a thief and a killer to them." He looked Price up and down. "Meanwhile, I'm going to be doing my best to find out who really robbed the stage and killed the crew." He saw the tense nervousness in Price's face, and moved in closer to him, adding, "Once I start on a case I never let up until I know I have the right man on a rope."

Frisco chuckled as the ranger turned and walked away toward the telegraph office. "Don't let that fool rattle you, Dep," he said. "We're on top of this game."

"Don't start calling me Dep again," Price warned him flatly. "I'm in this to save my life."

"Ain't we all," Frisco said, cradling his shotgun and looking back out at the dissipating crowd.

When the last of the townsfolk had moved away, Bass shooing them with his hands as if they were sheep, the judge turned to Price and Frisco and asked, "Where was Burrack headed?"

"The telegraph office." Frisco grinned.

"Good. I'll be at the restaurant if you need to reach me." Bass nodded confidently. "The ranger will soon have to admit that this is one battle he's not going to win." As he spoke he stepped away along the board-walk. "I am the law here, whether he likes it or not." He adjusted his derby as he walked.

"Hear, hear. Well said, Your Honor," a voice called out from the dirt street beside him.

Looking down as he walked, Bass saw the smiling faces of Trigger Leonard and Mitchell Smith beaming at him with bloodshot eyes. "I hope you don't mind if we mosey along with you a ways, Judge," Leonard continued, inviting himself to step up onto the boardwalk beside the judge, Smith right behind him.

"Who might you be?" the judge asked gruffly, seeing the same sort of faces he had looked down upon from his bench for the past seven years.

"You can call me Mr. Leonard," said Leonard Heebs, giving Smith a passing grin. "This is my pard, Mr. Smith." He gestured toward Mitchell Smith.

"*Smith* indeed," said Bass, smelling whiskey on the two and speeding his pace along the boardwalk. "I venture to say of all the *Smiths* I've ever met in my profession, I've never yet met a real one." Looking sideways, he curled his nose at the reek of whiskey.

"Oh, he's a true Smith all right, Judge," said Leonard. "You can take my word for that."

"You two are drunk," said Bass. "Get your stinking selves away from me before I have the deputies haul you off to jail."

"Drunk we might be, Your Honor," said Leonard, keeping up alongside Bass. "But we are just two concerned citizens when it comes to how that murdering Bob Krey should be dealt with."

"Oh?" Bass slowed down a step. "And just how is that?"

Leonard's grin widened, knowing he'd struck a note with the judge. "He needs to hang. No two ways about it," he said. "In fact, I don't see why he even deserves a trial. The poor sheriff he killed wasn't given any consideration, was he?"

Bass looked at him squarely. "You don't even know the sheriff's name, do you?"

"No, not offhand," Leonard replied. "But he was a servant of the law. That's good enough for me and Mr. Smith here."

Looking impatient, Bass asked, "What is it I can do for you two?" As he spoke he reached into his trouser pocket and found some loose change.

Raising his hand as if to stop the judge from offering them a handout, Leonard said, "It ain't what you can do for us, Judge. It's what *we* can do for *you*."

Bass slowed only a little, giving him a questioning look.

Leonard's voice lowered. "You see, me and Mr. Smith are in and out of all the saloons and public gathering places. We're what you might call closer to the *common people* than an important man like yourself. We can say things and express ourselves in ways that you can't, you being the law and all."

"Meaning you can incite the crowd?" Bass asked, starting to get an idea of where Leonard was headed with his line of talk.

"Right you are," said Leonard. He gestured toward the foot traffic along the boardwalk. "You have to admit, your talk didn't exactly get them reaching for a rope, did it?"

"Reaching for a rope? How dare you imply such a thing!" Bass said, incensed.

"Come on, Judge," said Leonard. "We're all three

men of the world here—just from different levels of it." He gestured a dirty hand down his whiskey-soiled clothes. "If I'm wrong we'll take our leave now. But if I'm right, and you want this town to come busting forward with fire and brimstone in its eyes, then me and Mr. Smith are your huckleberries."

Bass paused for a second, giving himself time to consider Leonard's words.

Leonard turned a nod toward the street and began to veer away. "Come on, Mr. Smith. Looks like we misjudged the judge."

"Wait," Bass said quickly, stopping the two and stopping himself on the boardwalk. "I have to admit I wouldn't be disappointed if something like you're suggesting happened to Bob Krey. The man killed my brother."

"So we've heard, Your Honor," said Leonard. "That's why we offer ourselves to your cause."

Bass looked him up and down, seeing that this was probably the sort of lowlife who could stir a drinking crowd into a frenzy, given a little time and enough whiskey. "What is it you want from me in return if something like that should happen?"

"Now here's where I have to go out on a limb and trust you, Judge," said Leonard, guiding the judge from the middle of the boardwalk as he looked back and forth. "We all three know that if we instigate a lynching, that ranger is going to come at me and Smith with both horns down. All I ask is that when that happens, I can face him knowing that the law is going to be sympathetic to me having to blow his damned head off."

Bass just looked at him for a moment, trying to picture him shooting the ranger, knowing how many fast guns had stood and fallen before Sam Burrack's big Colt. "Sure," he said, "if that's all you want. I promise you the same as I promise any man who stands before my bench. Whosoever has acted only in a manner of self-def—"

"Save it, Your Honor," said Leonard. "All I need to know is where we stand. Now me and Mr. Smith are going to get to work." He wiped his hands on his trousers. "I can tell you from experience, though, the more money I can wave in a bartender's face, the quicker I can get a crowd liquored up. It's been proven time and again." He grinned expectantly.

"I thought as much," Bass grumbled, reaching down into his trousers again, this time avoiding the loose change and finding a thick roll of bills. "I better see some results," he warned, keeping the money out of sight as he passed it into Trigger Leonard's dirty hand.

"You rest assured," said Leonard. "You'll hear a rope creaking from a pole before you know it. Just think kindly of me when I kill that ranger."

"I never heard you say that," the judge replied solemnly, looking away from the two and tugging down on his vest. He glanced both ways quickly. "In fact, I think it best if this entire conversation never happened."

Leonard gave Smith a quick glimpse of the money before tucking it away inside his clothes. He gave an even wider grin this time and said, "Hell, *what* conversation, Your Honor?"

Chapter 17

Inside the telegraph office, Sam asked a young clerk about wiring a message to the commission of the territorial court in Bisbee. At the counter, a rough-looking lineman with a thick beard and a strand of telegraph wire plaited and strung around his neck said with a scoff, "You'd do as well tying a message to a rock and throwing it toward Bisbee."

Sam gave him a scorching look. The young clerk cut in. "What Lon here means, Ranger, is that the lines are down. We haven't been able to send anything out of here for the past day and a half. Lon is going out tomorrow morning to search for it."

"Yep, that's so," said the burly lineman, Lon Beck. "But if it's the 'Pache cutting them, I'd just as soon leave them down a while, let everybody get back into practice writing letters again." He gave a gruff smile, recognizing the ranger. "No offense intended, Ranger Burrack. Sometimes I talk when I ought to listen. The fact is, I don't like hanging atop a pole when there's 'Pache slipping around."

Seeing that the lineman hadn't meant anything by his remark, the ranger nodded and said, "No offense taken. I understand your concern. What if you had a rifleman covering you while you tracked down the break and repaired it?"

"If you be that rifleman, Ranger, I expect I could be swayed into doing it." He narrowed his gaze and asked cagily, "This message ain't something that's going to help the law convict Texas Bob for anything, is it? Because if it is, I ain't going, 'Pache or no 'Pache."

"No," said Sam. "I believe Texas Bob is innocent. I'm trying to send a message that will keep him from hanging for a crime he didn't commit."

"Then I expect I'll go along with you," said Lon. "As much as I enjoy seeing a good hanging, I have nothing but respect and admiration for Texas Bob Krey. I've never known him to come up bad on anything."

"Neither have I," said the ranger. Then he stood quietly while the lineman considered it.

"Well," Beck said after a pause, speaking as he rolled down his shirtsleeves and stooped to pick up a wooden toolbox full of repair wire and hand tools. "To be honest, as long as I've been in this trade I've never personally known of the 'Pache cutting any wires." Hefting the toolbox he said, "But that's just what you call a personal observation."

"This is one time I'm certain the Apache had nothing to do with it," said Sam. "Whatever the case, I've got to get it repaired quick and get a message to Bisbee."

As the big lineman straightened up, he said, "I hope you realize that the break can be anywhere between here and the next office—that's in Kiley, nearly a hundred miles across the hills."

"I understand it could be, but I'm betting it's not far from Sibley," said the ranger, opening the door for the big dusty lineman.

Watching the ranger and the lineman walk out of the telegraph office and head for the restaurant where the judge had entered the door and taken a seat, Frisco Phil said with a dark laugh, "There goes one awfully upset lawman."

"You need to take him more seriously, Frisco," Price warned, watching the two walk along the street, Beck carrying his toolbox and looking over toward the jail.

"I'll take him more serious when the time comes," Frisco said coolly. "There's not many times in life you find a judge and a lawman going at one another over a couple ole boys like us. We better enjoy it while it lasts, is what I say."

Price just looked at him. He'd made up his mind. At the first sign of something going wrong he was in his saddle and headed out of here, he thought. To hell with Frisco Phil, he told himself, eyeing Frisco up and down. He'd had nothing but trouble since he'd thrown in with this ne'er-do-well. Nodding toward the lineman walking with the ranger, he said, "They'll find that broken line in no time. I told you we should have gone farther out."

"Don't start telling me how to cut lines," said Frisco testily. "I know how to cut a damn line."

Price just glared at him.

At the boardwalk out front of the restaurant, Sam told Beck, "Meet me at the sheriff's office as soon as you get your horse and mule."

"Right you are," Beck replied. He cut away to gather his animals from the livery barn while Sam walked inside the restaurant. He walked straight to Bass' table as an old man wearing a white apron poured the judge a steaming cup of coffee. Seeing the ranger's demeanor and the look on his face, the old waiter shrank away, coffeepot in hand.

"I just came from the telegraph office, Bass," Sam said, noticeably dropping the judge's title. "I don't think it will surprise you to hear that the lines have been cut."

"Oh? Cut down by some raiding Apache, no doubt," Bass said, giving him a blank stare.

Sam didn't reply. Instead he spoke in a calmer tone, looking down at the judge, keeping the conversation between the two of them. "I'm headed out with the lineman to find the break. I hope for everybody's sake you keep your two deputies away from Texas Bob."

"It's the law Bob Krey must answer to, Ranger, not me," Bass said in a rehearsed and insincere tone.

Sam took one more try at reaching the judge, showing him the error of his ways. "There are times when a man finds he's overstepped himself, and needs to back up and get his actions in check before he ruins his whole life, Bass."

"Do tell, Ranger," the judge said smugly. "It's ironic you should say that to me." He pointed a finger at the ranger. "You have overstepped yourself in such a manner that it will be hard, if not impossible, for you to ever make recompense. You have sided against my court in favor of a murderer."

"He's not a murderer, Bass, and we both know it. I'm not here to argue this case with you. I'm coming to you one last time and telling you to step back and look at what you're doing. I have never agreed with your decisions, but I've always respected your office, until now."

"He killed my brother!" Bass said, pounding the tabletop. "For that he hangs."

"Any man who kills has killed somebody's brother, or father, or son. From your bench you've had to tell the family to accept the verdict the law hands them and go on with their life. But now it appears that the law you ask them to live by doesn't apply to you. You hold yourself above the very law you administer."

"Yes, indeed I do consider myself an exception, Ranger. If not for me this place would continue to be a barbaric wasteland for the next thousand years." He thumbed himself on the chest. "I am the exception because I have done what I have done to tame this land!"

Sam shook his head slowly. "Don't you see, Bass? Every man I ever face down has his reason why the law doesn't apply to him—some because fate dealt them a bad start, some because whatever they put their hands to didn't turn out the way they wanted it. Everybody has their excuse. But these excuses are the very reason we have the law. The law is there to rein us all in, make us abide things in spite of how wrong we feel we've been done. Don't let go of those reins because this time it's you who's been wronged. Don't ally yourself with lowlifes. Be what you're supposed to be. Do what's right no matter how bad it hurts you to do it."

Bass stared squarely at him. "Are you quite through with your lecture on ethics, Ranger?"

Sam stopped and took a breath. "Yes, I'm through talking, Bass. I figured I owed you that talk for the years you've put into serving this territory. But now you're just one more gone-wrong, in a place overfilled with gone-wrongs. Stay away from my prisoner, and stay out of my gun sights. We're on opposite sides of the law, you and me." He turned to walk to the door.

Before he left, Bass said to him, "You pious fool! Tell me, Ranger, how far will you go to stop me from doing what I know needs to be done? Will stopping me be your excuse for not reining in when the time comes to cross the line of legal restraint? Will it justify you spilling blood to save Texas Bob Krey?"

Without answering the judge's question, Sam said, "Nothing justifies spilling blood, Bass. But some things make it easier to live with."

Bass sat there tapping his fingers on the tabletop, watching the ranger walk to the door and out onto the boardwalk. For a moment he considered the ranger's words, but then he shrugged, not taking them to heart. The old waiter appeared with a steaming plate of eggs, gravy and fresh hot biscuits and asked the judge meekly, "Is everything all right, Your Honor?"

Bass breathed deep, shook out a white cloth napkin,

stuffed it down behind his collar and spread it on his chest. "Yes, just fine, thank you," he said curtly. "I hope these eggs are fresh."

"Oh yes, Your Honor," said the old waiter. "For you, nothing but the best."

Before riding out of Sibley, Sam walked back to the sheriff's office and through the door without a word to the deputies standing out front. At the cell he said to Texas Bob, "I tried wiring Bisbee to tell the commission what's going on here. But the lines have been cut."

"I'm not surprised," said Bob, holding the bars with both hands. "Now what?"

"I'm riding out with a lineman to find the break and repair it while there's still time," said Sam. "I'm counting on you being all right here until I return."

"These two are going to want to find out about the money. I can play them off for as long as I need to," said Bob, glancing past the ranger toward the door. "But I don't know about a lynch mob."

Sam gave a grim smile. "You've got two armed deputies who have every reason not to want you lynched."

"I know," said Bob.

"Look at it this way," Sam added. "Bass wouldn't have been baiting the crowd for a lynching if he was sure of himself. He at least has enough respect left for the law to keep up a pretense."

"I suppose that helps—some," Bob said, calm but with a look of uncertainty.

"I'll get back to town as quick as I can, Tex," said Sam. "You have my word on that."

"Obliged, Ranger," Texas Bob said as he watched the ranger turn and walk out the door.

At the hitch rail out front, Lon Beck sat atop his horse, a lead rope to his mule in his free hand. The mule carried his toolbox, along with a canvas-covered load of other tools and supplies necessary to the lineman's trade. When Sam stepped out the door he saw the two deputies standing close to the edge of the boardwalk, talking to Beck.

"I'd be careful who I sided with, *Lineman*, if I was you," Sam heard Frisco Phil say to him.

"I've never been careful who I side with," the burly lineman said. "But I've never had to. I always side right to begin with."

"Not this time, you didn't," Frisco said, his hand tightening on the shotgun stock. "This time you've started rubbing the wrong cat the wrong way."

The lineman slipped a hand down to the large bowie knife sheathed at his hip. "I didn't think much of you as a bartender, Page. I think less of you as a deputy. You once asked how fast I could put a knife through the air. Still wondering?" He glared at Frisco.

Coming up behind Frisco, and seeing that Price wasn't wanting any part of this, the ranger said, "Pull that trigger, Frisco, and cut my trouble in half."

Phil stiffened, but he lowered his shotgun. "We'll meet up some other time, *Lineman*," he said to Beck, still trying to intimidate him.

"Yeah, I hope so," said Beck in a low, menacing tone. "You can sling me a beer and light my cigar." He kept his hand on the big bowie's handle until Frisco lowered the shotgun the rest of the way and he and Price stepped back to the front door of the sheriff's office. Sam called out to Price, "Keep in mind Texas Bob is *my* prisoner. He better be treated fairly, fed and looked after."

Price started to reply, but Frisco cut in, saying sharply, "He's *your* prisoner, *you* feed and water him when you get back."

Sam didn't respond, knowing it would only make matters worse.

"I never could tolerate a mouthy bartender," Beck said as Sam swung up onto his horse. The two watched Frisco closely until they backed their horses into the dirt street and turned and rode away.

On the boardwalk, Frisco Phil said to Price, "I don't feel like you had my back covered, Deputy. I had the strangest thought that you was going to leave me hanging all alone out there."

"Think what you will," said Price. "I'm only looking out for myself and my interest from here on." He leaned back against the front of the building with his shotgun under his arm and watched the ranger and the lineman ride away.

For the next hour, Sam and Lon Beck rode their horses along at a brisk walk, searching the telegraph line running alongside the trail. Before they'd gone twelve miles, Beck stopped suddenly and pointed at a down line alongside the trail ahead of them.

"Looks like you was right, Ranger," he said. "Whoever did this was too lazy to stray very far from town." He looked warily out and back and forth across the rough terrain. "No 'Pache did this. It's too close to town. They would have cut the lines fifty miles out just to aggravate a fellow."

Riding closer to where the line lay on the ground, Sam said as he drew his rifle from its saddle boot, "I've got you covered. Let's get it up and get on back to town before Texas Bob's luck runs out. I don't trust the judge or the deputies as far as I can spit."

"You can ride on back now, Ranger, if it makes you feel any better," said Beck. "Had I known it was this close to town I would've rode out alone, hours ago."

"I'm here now," said Sam. "I'll wait for you." As he spoke he scanned out across the land and spotted a single rider coming toward them slowly across the rise of a hillside.

"What have we got coming here, Ranger?" Beck asked as he stepped down and walked to the mule for his tools.

"I don't know," said Sam. Looking closer through the wind and sand, he recognized the lone rider to be a woman, pulling a travois behind her horse, a big dog trailing alongside her. "While you work I'll ride out a ways and find out, unless you need my help."

"Naw, go ahead," said Beck. "I'll likely have this wire spliced and strung before you get back."

Sam turned his horse, rifle in hand, and set the big animal into a trot across the rolling hillside. As he drew closer to the woman, she stopped the horse and sat with her hand on the stock of the shotgun lying in her lap.

"Easy, Plug," Mary Alice said sidelong to the dog,

who stood with his head lowered, a deep growl rumbling inside his chest.

"Wha-what's going on up there?" Rojo asked, half delirious from fever and pain. "Is it Indians? Is it? You best cut me loose now, you hear? Please don't leave me trussed up this way."

Mary Alice did not answer until the ranger drew close enough for her to recognize him. Then she said over her shoulder to the babbling Rojo, "Shut up back there. It's not Indians. It's Ranger Sam Burrack."

"Oh no." Rojo groaned in humiliation. "Please, go ahead and shoot me!"

Chapter 18

When the ranger slowed to a halt fifteen feet away and looked down at the big dog, Mary Alice called out, "Ranger Burrack, he won't bother you." Then to the low-growling dog she said, "Hush up, Plug, settle down." Upon Mary Alice's urging, the dog circled slowly and quieted, sensing no danger from the oncoming horseman.

"Ranger," Mary Alice called out anxiously, "have you seen Tex? He was headed to find Sheriff Thorn and straighten everything out with him!"

"Slow down, Mary Alice," Sam called out, nudging his horse forward now that the dog had stopped growling and stood watching him closely. "Texas Bob is in Sibley, in jail."

"In jail?" Mary Alice looked worried. "He can't stay in jail in Sibley! Price will kill him! He's already tried it once."

"I know all about it, Mary Alice," Sam said. "I'm only leaving him alone long enough to get the telegraph lines repaired. He's in my custody. I arrested him to keep him from getting shot down in the street."

"He's innocent, Ranger," she said, breathing a little easier. "Lady Lucky will tell you that."

"If I didn't think he was innocent, I wouldn't be out here with the lineman, fixing this line so we can wire Bisbee and tell them what's happening." He let her relax for a second, then said, "But here's some bad news. Lady Lucky is dead. She can't do a thing to help clear him."

"Oh, no, not Lady," Mary Alice said, her eyes welling for a moment until she told herself there was nothing she could do for Lady Lucky. Texas Bob's situation demanded her full attention. "What will happen now?"

"First thing, I'm trying to get us another judge, one who has no dog in this fight."

"Huh?" Mary Alice looked confused.

Sam said patiently, "A judge who has no personal interest in the case."

"Oh," said Mary Alice, looking a little embarrassed at her lack of understanding him. "I'm afraid I'm not thinking as straight as I should, Ranger. A lot has happened."

"I understand," said Sam. Leaning to one side, he looked around her and back at the travois behind her. "Who do you have back there?" As soon as he'd asked, he heard a low groan from the travois, followed by mindless babbling.

"A bounty hunter, or so he says," Mary Alice said. "He came snooping around trying to catch Tex unawares. But the dog near ate him alive. I tenderized him with a hearth poker. But I sewed him up best I could afterward," she added quickly.

"That was considerate of you." Sam winced at the thought, but nudged his horse forward, having a good idea who he'd find lying on the travois.

"His name is Tom Rojo," Mary Alice said, seeing the ranger step his horse back for a closer look.

"I would have guessed that, Mary Alice," the ranger said. "I warn everybody not to turn their back on him. I expect I needn't warn you."

"No, I wouldn't let him out of my sight," Mary Alice remarked. "He's half out of his head right now."

"I would have guessed that too," Sam said. He stopped alongside the travois and looked down at Rojo's swollen, battered, stitched-up face, barely recognizing him. "How's bounty hunting treating you, Tommy?" he asked dryly, seeing the battered man wrapped up like a mummy, save for his gruesome face.

"Ranger, you've got to get her to turn me loose!" Rojo gasped. "She's the devil! Look at me! Look what she's done! I can't go into town like this!"

"Careful what you ask for, Tommy," said Sam, looking at the red puffiness along his stitches, the black bruises striping his face and head. "If she turned you loose out here, where would you go? What would you do?" He nodded at Plug, who sat watching intently. "Like as not this dog would make another run at you before you got five yards."

Rojo's eyes went wildly to Plug. "Somebody needs to shoot that dog! He's the devil! I swear he is!"

The dog's ears perked up, as if he knew Rojo was talking about him.

"You're talking crazy, Tommy." Sam gave a faint smile. "These are not devils. She was just protecting herself, and this dog was just doing his job." Circling his horse back to Mary Alice, he said, "I'm in a hurry to get back to Sibley as soon as the lineman finishes his repairs. Can you keep up?"

"If I can't, you ride on without me," Mary Alice replied. "I'd rather you get back and keep an eye on Tex. I'll be right along."

"Ranger, don't leave me here!" Rojo begged.

Sam ignored him and asked Mary Alice, "Did you make this yourself?" He gestured toward the travois behind her horse.

"No," said Mary Alice. "I was hauling him on a wagon wheel. But yesterday an old Mexican happened along on foot and made this out of some oak saplings. Good thing too. Dragging that wheel was wearing this horse to death." She patted her horse's withers as she spoke.

"That was no Mexican!" Rojo shouted, sounding half delirious again. "It was the devil!" he raved. "I saw his horns! He's still following us! I saw him twice over there, watching us!" His hand raised shakily and pointed along the horizon to their left. "He's not gone! I swear he's not!"

Mary Alice saw the questioning concern on Sam's face and reassured him. "I'll be all right, Ranger. Plug won't let Rojo get out of hand."

"I'm asking Lon Beck to stay behind and ride in with you," Sam said.

"All right," said Mary Alice. "I know Lon. He'll knock Rojo cold if he acts up."

"Lon *is* the devil!" Rojo cried out behind them with an insane laugh. "All of yas—devils!"

Sam shook his head. With no more to say on the matter, he turned his horse and rode back to the broken telegraph wire.

"Who is that back there?" Beck asked, wiping his dirty hands on a cloth that hung from a leather tool belt around his waist.

"That's Mary Alice, one of the doves from the Bottoms Up in Sibley. I'm hoping you don't mind riding back to town with her. She's got a wounded bounty hunter named Tommy Rojo on a travois. Tex's dog has worked him over pretty good."

"Good for him," said Beck. "I know Mary Alice. She lit out with Texas Bob. I'd be pleased to escort her on into town." He loosened his tool belt and hung it over his shoulder. "I told you I'd have this fixed by the time you got back here," he said.

"Good work," said Sam, looking up at the line, spliced and restrung from the pole.

"I left a tag in case you want to send your message from here," said Beck. "It'd save you some time."

"You bet I would," said Sam. He looked at a long wire hanging from the top of the pole, connected to the main line.

"Then let's get it done," said Beck, taking a striker plate and telegraph key from his supplies. "I'll have you ready in less than a minute. Just tell me what to say and I'll tap it on out for you. It'll be in Bisbee before you drop a rock." He grinned. "Ain't science remarkable?"

"It is," Sam said seriously. Considering things, he

said, "Once I get this sent, I'd appreciate it if you wouldn't tell anyone in Sibley I sent it."

"If the clerk is at the set, he'll hear it," said Beck. "But like as not he won't write it down, since it's not coming directed to anybody in Sibley."

"Good," said Sam. "I'm ready when you are."

The ranger had sent the message to Bisbee and headed back to Sibley by the time Mary Alice arrived at where Lon Beck sat waiting, leaned back against the pole where he'd made the repairs. The additional wire he'd attached at the pole for the ranger to tap into lay coiled at his feet. On the distant horizon all that remained of the ranger was a drift of trail dust.

"Hello, Lon," Mary Alice called out as she rode closer and stopped her horse a few feet away.

"Good day to you, Mary Alice," Beck said, tipping his sweat-stained hat. "The ranger said for me to escort you safely to Sibley, if that's all right with you."

"That's all right with me, Lon," said Mary Alice, "but I need to tell you right off, that me and Tex are together now."

"Proper like?" Lon asked, standing, dusting the seat of his trousers. He looked her up and down while the dog circled wide, came in close and sniffed at him. Beck let the dog sniff the back of his hand, then patted the big animal on its rough head.

"As proper as it gets without any words said or a preacher swearing us up," said Mary Alice. She paused, then added, "I'm not in the business anymore, so if you sat there and thought yourself into a frenzy on anything happening between us on the way to town, I hate to tell you, but it ain't going—"

"Ah, Mary Alice, you hush," said Beck, cutting her off. "If you're with Tex, that's good enough for me." He looked down at the dog, stopped scratching its head and watched it butt his hand, wanting more. "I admit I had considered it while you rode up." He looked from the dog up to her. "But enough said. If you're out of business, that's the end of it." He turned to his horse and took the mule's lead rope in one hand. Plug stayed beside him, still butting at him.

"Back, Plug," Mary Alice said. But the dog continued to press for a pat on the head.

"Pushy, ain't he?" Beck said, rubbing the dog's head one more time before climbing into the saddle. Plug stepped back, circled and stood beside Mary Alice.

"He's the devil!" Rojo cried out from his travois.

Beck looked back at Rojo. Once atop his horse, he led the mule around Mary Alice and looked down at the babbling, feverish bounty hunter, then winced and said, "You and this dog did all that to him?"

"Yes, we did," said Mary Alice, almost apologetically. "But I sewed him up as quick as I could. I think he'll be all right, once his fever breaks. Don't you?"

"I expect that depends on what you call all right." Beck chuckled darkly.

"You are one pig-ugly sight, Mr. Rojo," he said, backing his horse and mule a step, preparing to ride on to Sibley.

"Ranger Burrack warns everybody not to turn their

backs on him, Lon," Mary Alice said as the lineman rode up bedside her.

Beck looked back over his shoulder at the securely wrapped Rojo and said, "Well, I'm always one to follow sound advice, but I think we're safe for now."

Rojo raved and babbled out of his head.

Before the party of humans, horses, and the dog had traveled a mile, Beck slowed his horse and mule and said quietly to Mary Alice, "Don't look, but somebody is tagging along with us just over the rise."

Staring straight ahead, Mary Alice said, "Not a band of wild Apache, I hope."

"Naw, it's no band of 'Pache. If it was I would never have seen them," said Beck. "This is only one person, I'm thinking."

"What are we going to do?" Mary Alice asked, appropriately concerned.

Beck leaned forward. "See where we go through those chimney rocks ahead?"

"Yes," said Mary Alice, staying calm.

"When we get in there, you take this mule and horse and I'm going to slip up on foot and find out who it is, and why they're following us. Most likely some greedy bounty hunter like Rojo back there."

"It's *the devil*," Rojo bellowed, catching only a portion of the conversation.

Beck and Mary Alice rode on for the next twenty minutes, not looking over at the rise of land parallel to them. Once the trail meandered upward through the tall chimney rocks, the lineman handed Mary Alice his reins and lead and slipped down from his saddle. "Move ahead a half mile, then circle back for me," he whispered, walking alongside the mule and taking down a short-handled shovel from his tools.

"What about a shotgun?" Mary Alice asked.

"No," said Beck. "I've got this bowie knife if I need it." He patted the big knife in its fringed leather sheath on his hip. "I don't want to make any noise, in case anybody else is out there."

Shovel in hand, Beck hurried up out of sight onto the thinner trail running along above them. He chose a thick chimney rock twenty feet high and took cover behind it, just off the trail. Within moments he heard footsteps crunching along the narrow rocky trail. Giving himself a tight smile for being right, he waited until the steps drew closer, then drew the shovel back for a good solid swing. "I don't know who you are," he muttered to himself, "but if you'd announced yourself when you had the chance . . ."

The man on foot heard the whooshing sound of the shovel swinging through the air, followed by a loud vibrating metallic *twang* as it slapped him flat in the face.

"There now. Let's take a look at you," said Beck, stepping out over the man and seeing a wide straw sombrero land a few feet away. Stooping, he pulled aside a brightly striped serape that had flung up over the man's face as he flew backward and fell—knocked cold—to the ground.

Knowing it would be a while before the man came to and explained why he was following them, Beck looked back along the trail, then sat down against the rock and rolled himself a smoke. By the time he'd finished the cigarette, Mary Alice rode into sight, saw him and called out to him, keeping her voice low and even, "Is everything all right, Lon?"

"For me it is," Beck said, satisfied that the man had been traveling alone. "His nose looks broke. He's gonna have a dandy headache."

Riding closer, Mary Alice looked down at the man on the ground while the dog hurried forward and sniffed at the bloody gash across the bridge of his nose. "Oh, no!" she cried, recognizing the serape and straw sombrero instantly. "It's the old Mexican who built the travois for me!"

"Really?" Beck didn't look too concerned. "Why do you suppose he was following us?"

"I don't know," said Mary Alice, stepping down from her saddle and taking a closer look at the old man's bloody face. "Wait a minute! I know this man! Rojo was right. This is no Mexican! This is the miner, Andrej Goran. The Croatian."

"The who?" Beck asked, taking a closer look for himself, the shovel lying on the ground near his feet.

"He was at the Sky High Saloon the night it burned down. Tex dragged him out, saved his life."

On the ground, Andrej groaned and moved his head back and forth groggily. "I— I have been, hit upon . . . most badly," he managed to say.

"He's speaking English!" Mary Alice said.

"Yeah," said Beck, sounding unimpressed, "if you want to call it that."

"No, you don't understand!" said Mary Alice. "He couldn't be a witness to the shooting because he didn't speak English. But he does speak it!"

"Oh?" Beck looked skeptical. "Then why didn't he say so when this all happened?"

Andrej shook his head slowly, trying to regain his senses. "It is not always wise for one to speak English when one is a foreigner," he said haltingly. "But I speak it now because the man who saved my life is in trouble."

"You're headed to Sibley, to help Texas Bob?" Mary Alice asked, her voice cracking a bit with emotion and gratitude.

"Yes. I saw everything that happened," said Andrej. "I disguised myself as a Mexican so I could travel safely."

"A Croatian disguised as a Mexican, so he can be *safe*?" said Beck. "That's not something you hear of every day."

"I wanted to tell you who I was when I helped you build the frame to carry this man on," said Andrej, pointing at Rojo on the travois. "But I was afraid." He touched his fingers to his flattened nose. "As it turned out, I could have done no worse."

"Wait," said Mary Alice. "Let me get you some water! Stay awake. Please!" She hurried over and grabbed a canteen of tepid water from her saddle horn.

Chapter 19

After giving the Croatian a long drink of water, Mary Alice sat beside him and pressed a wet bandanna to his bruised forehead. She let him rest until the impact of the shovel blow stopped ringing and echoing inside his aching head. On the travois, Rojo settled down after a while, stopped babbling and closed his eyes. "Why does he call me the devil?" Andrej asked, sounding more conscious now, not trying to speak above the ring of the shovel.

"Pay no attention to him," Mary Alice said. "He calls everybody the devil."

Andrej's eyes went to Lon Beck and the shovel lying near his feet. "Why did this one hit me?"

Before Mary Alice could answer, Beck said bluntly, "I hit you because I thought you were following us."

"I *was* following you," said Andrej.

"See? There you are." Beck shrugged to Mary Alice. To Andrej he said, "Out here, it's not a good idea to follow folks—as you can see." He gestured toward Andrej's flattened nose and swollen forehead.

Andrej shook his head slowly in bewilderment. "I do not understand Americans. I follow you because I want to go where you go."

Beck shrugged again. "You should have asked."

"But that doesn't matter now," said Mary Alice in a soothing voice. She held Andrej's miner's hand between hers. "You just relax, clear your mind and tell me what you saw that night in the Sky High Saloon."

Andrej took only a second to summon up the memory, then began. "Well, I was passed out drunk. . . ."

The old miner told his version of what had happened, his account identical to what Lady Lucky had said after the fire. When he finished, Mary Alice and Beck looked at one another. Beck looked doubtful. "If he says he was passed out drunk, nobody is going to listen to him."

"Maybe . . ." Mary Alice hesitated for a moment, then said to Andrej, "Maybe you shouldn't mention that you were drunk."

"But, why should I not?" the old Croatian asked in his stiff English. "I *was* drunk. I go to Sibley to tell the truth about what happened. How can I not tell them that I was drunk if it is the truth?"

Lon Beck let out a breath and looked away impatiently, out across the rugged terrain.

"Sometimes the truth has to be cleaned up a little before it's told," Mary Alice said. "But don't you worry, we'll have you telling the truth the way it sounds best by the time we get you to Sibley."

"The way it *sounds best*?" Beck said, giving her a dubious look.

"Yes, that's how it has to be," said Mary Alice,

undaunted. Then to Andrej she said, "Come on, let's
get you onto your feet and walk you around some."
Struggling with him, she helped him stand and walked
him in a circle with his arm draped over her shoulders.
Beck sighed, picked up his shovel and walked to the
mule. "Once you get the truth sounding the way it
should, you can try it out on me. If it's not good, you
can work on it some more," he called out over his
shoulder, sticking the shovel into the tied-down
supplies.

In the Bottoms Up Saloon, Trigger Leonard and
Mitchell Smith had been busy all afternoon, buying
rounds, offering comments, praising Sheriff Mike
Thorn and cursing Texas Bob as a cold-blooded murderer. "It's not our town," said Trigger Leonard. "Me
and Mr. Smith are only passing through. Maybe it's
none of our business, but I can't understand why men
will stand around and do nothing when a fine lawman
like Thorn has been shot down like a dog." As he
spoke his voice grew louder and his eyes scanned
around the crowded saloon. He made sure everybody
heard him.

A big miner wearing a ragged shirt and a battered
bowler hat called out to him down the bar, "For it
being none of your business, you sure are running
your mouth about it, mister."

"Who said that?" Leonard looked back and forth,
then homed in on the big miner. Drinkers standing at
the bar between the two stepped back, anticipating
trouble. "I happen to care about the law," Leonard
said, thumbing himself on the chest. His right hand

fell instinctively to his holstered Colt. "When I see a man like Thorn killed, I've got a right to speak my mind on it." He reminded himself that he was here to stir up the crowd, not get into a fight. He took his hand off his pistol.

"I've got a right to speak my mind too," said the big miner. "I've never known a better man than Texas Bob. You've been sore-talking him ever since I walked in here. I think you're just an agitator." He narrowed his gaze on Leonard. "What is your angle in this, mister? Who's buying your dinner?"

The words stunned Leonard for a moment. But he recovered quickly and said with a red face, "You talk a bold game for a man unhealed." He looked the man up and down, noting his lack of a firearm. "Somebody give this man a gun! I won't be accused."

"I don't want a gun," said the miner, rolling up his ragged shirtsleeves. "Instead of giving me a gun, put yours on the bar, stranger," he said to Leonard. "I'll break you up for kindling."

"Hold it, gentlemen!" said Smith, acting as though he and Leonard weren't together. "This is not the time to fight among yourselves! There's a man in that jail who needs hanging!"

"That's right," a drunken teamster called out. "I don't know Bob Krey. But I *did* know Sheriff Thorn. I'm sick of seeing time and money wasted on trials. Krey's a murderer. Hang him! It's that simple!"

"Here's a man who makes sense!" said Smith. "Somebody get a rope. Let's go do what needs doing!"

From the open front door of the sheriff's office,

Frisco Phil smiled as a roaring cheer came from within the saloon. "It won't be long now," he said to Price, who stood at the battered desk, a cup of coffee in hand. "They're building up a strong head of steam."

Price turned and faced Texas Bob, who stood holding the bars with both hands. "Look at all the trouble you've caused, Krey," he said seriously. He started to say more, but before he could, Frisco cut in.

"It won't matter much longer," Frisco said to Texas Bob. "They'll soon come charging in and take you away from us." He grinned and gave a shrug of helplessness. "What can we do to stop them? Just us two hardworking deputies up against an angry mob, them all liquored up and bent on hemp justice. Hell, we won't stand a chance. Will we, Deputy Price?"

"No," Price said flatly, staring at Bob. "I suppose we'll have to step aside and let them have him, unless there's something in it for us."

Bob only returned the stare, offering no response. He knew Price was hinting at the stage money.

"All right," Frisco said impatiently. "Let's not dally around like three schoolgirls!" He walked over to the cell and said, "We want that money, Bob Krey, and we want it now."

"What money?" Bob asked calmly.

Frisco's gun came up quickly from his holster and cocked only inches from Bob's chin. "You know what money! Now where is it? I won't ask you again."

Texas Bob stared him coldly in the eyes. "If I die the money dies with me. If I live, the money is all mine. That's a fifty-fifty chance of me staying alive and getting rich. I can't turn those odds down."

Frisco batted his eyes, looking confused. "What does he mean by that?" he asked Price.

"Well, I'll be danged." Price looked surprised, but only for a moment. Walking to the cell, he said, "Don't tell me that our *honest, decent, do-gooder* Texas Bob has a greedy streak in him!"

"Then I *won't* tell you, Price," Bob said. "I don't think you're smart enough to understand." He turned to Frisco. "Tell me something, bartender. If you found a bag of money laying in the dirt out there, nobody around, what would you plan to do with it? Would you come toting it back to town, like a good little boy, so it can end up back to a bank somewhere?"

Frisco grinned. "Not even if I'd been kicked in the head by a mule." He uncocked his pistol and lowered it a little. "But that's just me. Call it the way I was raised." His grin widened. "The question is, What about you? What's the first thing *you'd* think?"

"The first thing I thought was 'What a piece of luck,' " said Bob. "There I was, running from a crime I didn't commit." He looked back and forth between them as he spoke. "I come upon a bag of money stolen by the very man who jackpotted me in the first place." He centered his gaze sharply on Price for a second. "I figured you owed me that money, Price. All I had to do was make it to Mexico and I'd be set for life. Let the law chase its tail, far as I was concerned."

"Ha! I knew it!" said Price, slamming his fist into his palm. "I knew that no man could be as good as you had everybody thinking you are, Mr. *Texas Bob!*" He sneered Bob's name, unable to contain his glee.

"I wish Mary Alice and all those moony-eyed doves could see you now! You're as phony and no good as the rest of us!" He spread his arms toward the ceiling, as if exposing Texas Bob to heaven. "But I saw through it! I was right! I was *right*!"

Frisco and Bob stood watching, bemused. "Jeez, Price!" Frisco said after a moment of stunned silence. "I'm trying to find out where our money is. Can you give me a hand here?"

Bob cut in, saying, "First of all, it's not your money, bartender. It's *mine*." He thumbed his chest. "As far as where it's at, you'll never hear it from me." He gave them a determined stare.

"Then kill him," Price said. "I don't want it getting out, what happened out there."

"Kill him?" Frisco looked astonished. "How are you going to explain killing him?"

"He tried to break jail," Price said stubbornly. "What's the difference? You said yourself, Judge Bass will go along with whatever we tell, so long as it ends up Texas Bob is dead."

"Don't talk crazy," said Frisco. To Texas Bob he said, "I have never yet seen money that can't be shared among reasonable gentlemen willing to cooperate."

"You have now," said Texas Bob. Nodding at the gun in Frisco's hand, he said, "Go on and shoot. I'm not giving it up, not after what Price here put me through. Call this my act of parting vengeance." He gave Price a triumphant look.

Frisco turned angrily to Price, his gun tightly in

hand. "See? You and your danged vengeance! I ought to shoot *you*! You pigheaded son of a—"

Price cut him off, his hand poised on his holstered gun butt. "Can't you see he's trying to play us against one another?"

"Yeah, I see that," said Frisco, "and he's doing a dandy job of it! I want that money. Shenlin, Roby and Kane all three died getting it. I *want* it!"

"In that case you better make sure nothing bad happens to me," said Texas Bob. He turned, walked to his bunk and stretched out on it.

"If you won't shoot him, I will," Price said angrily, stepping forward, his gun coming up cocked and pointed.

"Wait!" said Frisco, stepping in front of Price. He said to Bob, "Are you saying something *can* be worked out between us?"

"Not if I'm killed by a lynch mob," Bob said matter-of-factly, propping his arms behind his head, relaxing.

"Bolt that door!" Frisco demanded of Price. "Nobody's taking him out of this cell until we know where that money is hidden!"

"The judge is not going to like that one bit," Price warned. "He'd as soon they drag him out of here, save the trouble of having a trial."

"To hell with what the judge wants," said Frisco. "I want that money."

From his bunk Bob said coolly, "You want the money, I want out of here without getting lynched. What did you say about *reasonable gentlemen* finding a way to share it?"

Frisco gritted his teeth, turned and walked to the front window, hearing cursing and gunshots coming from the direction of the Bottoms Up Saloon. "They're liquoring right up, Price," he said. Walking quickly back to the cell, he asked Texas Bob, "What do you have in mind? Three-way split?"

Bob considered it with a grimace, then said, "All right, three ways is better than nothing, provided I don't hang in the process."

"Then it's a deal," said Frisco, a new grin coming to his face. "Now tell us where it is."

Bob, saw he could play his hand no further without offering something to the pot. "I hid it beneath a cactus!" he lied.

"Oh, a *cactus*! There, you see?" said Frisco, still grinning. "He hid it under a *cactus*." His pleasant mood suddenly turned black. "In a territory full of cactus from here to hell and back!" He turned on Bob and said, "I'm getting my fill of you too, Texas Bob." He gripped his pistol tightly.

"The best thing for you to do right now is settle down and keep me from hanging," said Bob, seeming to make himself more comfortable. "Tonight, when everybody is asleep, we'll take three fresh horses and slip out of town. It'll be morning before anybody knows we're gone. By the time they get onto our trail, it'll be too late. We'll ride straight to the money, split it up and go our own ways."

"I'll get us some horses lined up," Frisco said, "as soon as we see how this lynch mob is going to act."

"Wait a minute, Frisco!" said Price, looking at him

in disbelief. "We're busting him out? We're riding him to get the money? We're going to *trust* him?"

"Have you got any better ideas how we'll get the money?" Frisco snapped at him.

"What about the ranger?" Price asked. "No matter how much of a head start we get, Burrack will be right up our shirts."

Frisco looked at Texas Bob. "Does the ranger know where the money is?"

"Do I look that stupid?" Bob lied. "I hid the money before I rode down to the stagecoach and joined Thorn. I didn't even tell *him* where I hid it."

"Then he won't know where we're going," said Frisco. "We'll cover our tracks, hit some high trails, cut through some streams. The ranger might be good at tracking, but I'm better at hiding."

As Frisco spoke, a roar of cursing and cheering resounded from the direction of the Bottoms Up Saloon.

Price gave him a serious look, clutching his shotgun close to his chest. "I can't believe I'm about to stand off a lynch mob for a man I'd have given anything to see hang."

"Get your mind right, Deputy," Frisco demanded, "or you'll be giving up your share of the stage money."

Chapter 20

The ranger rode hard and fast all the way back to Sibley. When he arrived on the dirt street, the crowd from the saloon had just spilled out onto the street, milling and shouting and firing pistols wildly into the air. Taking a deep breath, Sam slowed his horse almost to a halt, then nudged it forward at a cautious walk. As he neared the main body of the drunken crowd, he slipped his rifle from his saddle boot and held it propped up on his lap.

"Uh-oh, a lawman coming," a drunken voice called out from the boardwalk.

In the street guns lowered and fell silent. Eyes turned toward the ranger. The crowd settled slowly as he rode to the heart of it. At the center of the crowd stood a burly retired army sergeant named Sheppard Kerns, who worked part-time as a bouncer at the Bottoms Up. Sam looked at the rope hanging in his thick hands, seeing the noose he'd tied in one end of it.

"Drop the rope, Kerns," Sam said calmly, still stepping his horse toward him. "I won't allow a lynching here, and you know it."

"It's not what you'll allow, Ranger," said Kerns in an angry, drunken voice. "*We the people* will decide what goes on here today. We're sick of the robbing and killing, and the law doing nothing about it!" A drunken roar from half the gathered townsmen cheered him on. "We're sick of town funds going to providing trials when we already know the man is guilty as sin to begin with!" Kerns shouted, shaking the noose in his hand.

"Shep doesn't speak for us, Ranger," a man called out from the right. "We're here trying to stop them from hanging Texas Bob. He's an innocent man!" But the ranger didn't take his gaze off of Kerns.

"It sounds like Bob Krey has as many folks on his side as he has against him, Kerns. If you're speaking for half these men, what about the other half? Aren't they the people too?"

"Not if they don't side with us, they're not," said Kerns. "Sheriff Mike Thorn was a damn good man— a good friend of mine. I'm seeing to it his killer swings!" Again he shook the noose.

"Sheriff Thorn was a good friend of mine, too," Sam said to Kerns, nudging his horse up even closer. The big man spread his feet shoulder width apart, making a rigid stand for himself in front of a throng of supporters. "You know me—I don't play favorites and I don't bend the law. I know Texas Bob is innocent. But even if he was guilty, I would still be sitting here, stopping you from lynching him."

"You sound awfully sure of yourself, Ranger," said

Kerns. "I don't see nothing being stopped. I fought for this country. I *earned* the right to stand here today and speak my mind."

"Nobody earns more rights than the next man in this country, Kerns," Sam said. "We're all born with the same amount." He leaned down a little, trying to keep the conversation between them. "You've spoke your mind. Now drop the rope and back off."

"I'll do more than *speak* my mind, Ranger!" he bellowed, taking a step forward, grabbing Sam's horse by its bridle. "Rush him, men!" he shouted.

Kerns' supporters surged forward—but then stopped abruptly. The ranger's rifle rose high in his gloved hand. The butt stock slammed down with a sickening thud on the big sergeant's forehead.

The crowd gasped in unison. "My God, he's killed Shep!" a voice cried out. The big man dropped spread-eagle on the dirt, his glazed eyes wide open, staring blankly at the sky. A thin trickle of blood ran down his upper lip. The rope lay loosely on his broad chest.

"He's not dead, but he'll wish he was when he wakes up," Sam replied, looking at the big oval knot already rising in the center of Kerns' forehead. His rifle swung toward Kerns' supporters. "So will the lot of you if you don't break it up out here and go about your business."

"You tell them, Ranger!" a voice called out from the other group of drunken townsmen. "What about Texas Bob's rights? He was a veteran same as Kerns here." The man pointed down at the knocked-out bouncer.

"Texas Bob's a killer!" shouted one of Kerns' supporters.

"And a thief," another voice shouted.

"You're both damn fools, and black-hearted liars to boot!" another townsman replied heatedly.

"All of you break it up," Sam said in a stronger tone of voice. "The middle of the street is no place to settle anything."

"That's a damn funny thing for you to be saying, Ranger," a man shouted with a dark laugh. "You settle everything in the street!" He gestured a hand down at the ground. "Look at poor ole Shep laying here."

Inside the saloon, watching from the corner of a dirty window, Trigger Leonard gritted his teeth and cursed under his breath. "That blasted ranger."

Beside him Mitchell Smith said, "Yeah, we should have shot him dead as soon as we saw him riding in. Nobody would have known we did it."

"That's not the way I want it to play down," said Leonard. "Once I kill him, I want the world to know I did it. But I want it to be legal-like—one-on-one."

Across the street, at a second-floor window of the Markwell Hotel, Judge Bass pounded a fist on the window ledge, watching as the ranger began dispersing the crowd in all directions. "Damn you, Sam Burrack!" he said aloud to the dusty windowpane. "Why is it so hard, killing Texas Bob?"

In the street, Sam stepped down from his saddle, rifle in hand, while Kerns' supporters lifted him from the dirt and carried him inside the saloon. Looking back and forth warily, Sam caught a glimpse of the two gunmen lurking about inside the bat-wing doors.

"If I catch anybody inciting a lynching, they'll get the same as Kerns, or worse," he said. "Sheriff Thorn is dead. Out of respect for him, let the law take its course."

One of Texas Bob's defenders called out, "The law has broke down here, Ranger! Anybody can see that with one eye shut." The man pointed a finger toward the Markwell Hotel. "The only thing Texas Bob did was make the mistake of *defending* himself against Judge Bass' brother!"

"Amen!" another voice called out. "Now that the law's gone to hell, it's up to us to protect our own. The next time they come to lynch Bob, we'll be armed and ready for them!"

"That's enough of that kind of talk," Sam called out, unable to take sides but a little glad to hear that not everybody wanted to see Bob Krey hang. "The law is not broken down in Sibley. As long as I'm here it's not going to be." He gave another glance toward the saloon doors, knowing that somebody in there was behind the drunken uprising.

Inside the saloon, seeing the ranger staring toward them, Smith whispered sidelong to Leonard, "All right, he's accusing us. Here's your chance! Go get him." He almost nudged Leonard out the doors in his excitement.

"Get away from me!" Leonard hissed at him. He stepped back. "I'll get him when I'm damn good and ready! Don't ever act like you're going to push me into something!" He turned toward Smith, his hand poised above his gun butt.

"I didn't mean nothing!" Smith said, raising his hands in a show of peace. "I just thought that—"

"Never mind what you thought," said Leonard, his temper still flaring. "Don't ever crowd me! I won't take it!"

Outside, Sam heard heated words being exchanged, but not well enough to hear them clearly. He waited for a moment, watching the remaining townsmen go their ways, some of them back inside the saloon. Then he looked above the doors flapping back and forth, not knowing who stood in there, yet almost certain their conversation had been about him. Whoever it was, they would reveal themselves soon enough, he told himself, stepping back to his horse and picking up the reins. Meanwhile, he knew he had plenty to keep him busy.

Out front of the sheriff's office, Price and Frisco had been standing, watching the angry crowd come out of the saloon and begin mustering up its courage in the street. Now that the ranger had arrived and taken the situation in hand, Price let out a tense breath and said to Frisco, "I never thought I'd be glad to see the ranger ride in."

"Right in time, too," said Frisco, keeping his voice lowered. "As soon as we get that money, we're killing Texas Bob. No two ways about it."

"You'll get no argument from me," said Price, still gripping the shotgun as the ranger led his horse toward them from out front of the saloon. "I'd rather kill him than protect him. That's for damn sure."

When the ranger arrived and had hitched his horse

at the rail out front of the sheriff's office, he stepped up onto the porch and walked to the door without a word to the deputies.

"Just so's you know, Ranger," Frisco said before Sam entered, "we weren't going to let that crowd take this prisoner out of here without a fight."

Sam only looked at him curiously, stepped inside the office and closed the door behind himself. Seeing the look on Price's face, Frisco shrugged. "I felt like I ought to say something."

At Texas Bob's cell door, Sam smiled, seeing Bob seated on the side of his bunk, a cup of coffee in his hand. On the bunk beside him sat a food tray with an empty plate and scraps of food on it. "Well," said Sam, "it looks like things have taken an upward turn for you since I left town."

Standing, walking over to the cell door, Bob said in a whisper, "We talked about the money. They can't do enough for me now."

"I bet," said Sam.

Nodding in the direction of the saloon, Texas Bob said, "I heard some shooting and yelling going on. Did you put it down?"

"Yes," said Sam. "It might make you feel good to know you've got as many folks for you as you have against you."

"Yes, it does help to hear that. Obliged, Ranger," Bob said, tipping his coffee cup toward Sam.

"I get an idea there wouldn't be any talk of a lynching if somebody wasn't in the background pushing for it," Sam said. "This town is drinking too much for this time of day."

"Were you able to find the line break?" Bob asked quietly, keeping an eye toward the closed door.

"The line is fixed, and. the message is sent to Bisbee," said Sam, also in a quiet tone. "But that's not all I found. Mary Alice is riding into town with the lineman. She's got Tommy Rojo with her. Your dog just about ate him alive."

Tex looked concerned, gripping the bars. "Is she all right?"

"She's just fine," said Sam. "So is your dog. I don't know if Rojo will ever look the same again."

"Plug got him bad, did he?" Texas Bob asked.

"No worse than he deserved," said Sam. "Rojo is a back-shooter I warn everybody about. He went snooping around there for you. If your dog hadn't tipped off Mary Alice . . . I hate to think what Rojo is capable of."

"As long as she's all right," Bob said, sounding relieved.

"She is." Looking around, Sam said quietly, "What about you?"

"If it helps any," said Bob with a faint smile, "I've got these two doing exactly what I want."

Sam didn't reply. He understood.

On their way to Sibley, Andrej Goran, Mary Alice and Lon Beck decided it would be best if the Croatian slipped away from the group and camped out near town until they talked to the ranger about him. By the time Mary Alice, the lineman, the dog and Rojo arrived in Sibley, the afternoon sun had sunk low in the western sky. Sam had grained and watered his

horse and eaten his evening meal. Tension had eased
between him and the two deputies, so much so that
when drinkers from the saloon began to gather once
again in the dirt street, Price stuck his head through
the office door and told Sam.

"It looks like they're back at it, Ranger," he said,
unable to identify Mary Alice or Beck in the quickly
waning light.

"I better see what this is about, Tex," Sam said.
Standing up from the desk chair, he picked up his rifle
and jacked a round into the chamber. On his way to
the front door he said over his shoulder, "Let's hope
it's Mary Alice and Beck arriving. They should have
been here half an hour ago." He stepped onto the
boardwalk between the two deputies and out onto
the street.

Out front of the Bottoms Up, Trigger Leonard and
Mitchell Smith stood before a newly gathering group
of onlookers. Smith stooped slightly and squinted for
a closer look at Tommy Rojo lying wrapped in the
dusty bedsheet. "Is that *Rojo*?" he asked himself
aloud, sounding more than just a little drunk. Then
he chuckled and said, "Good Lord, it *is* that idiot!
Look at this, Trigger! Rojo has fell face-first into a
barrel of straight razors!"

"Tommy?" Trigger Leonard grinned. "Man! What
in the world happened to you?"

Laughing, Smith said, "I told you, he fell face-first
into a barrel—"

"Shut up Mitch, damn it," said Leonard, cutting him
off, still angry over what had happened earlier. "He
can talk for himself."

Smith quieted down and stood staring at Rojo with a sullen look on his face.

"Yeah," Rojo said, giving Smith a look of hatred. "I'm hurt here. You think this is funny? I was attacked by that dog." He nodded toward Plug, who had sat down in the dirt and busied himself licking a front paw. "I'm lucky to be alive," he added. "I'm ruined for life."

"You was ruined already, Rojo," Smith said solemnly, still stinging from Leonard's harsh words.

Atop their horses, Mary Alice and Beck waited until they saw the ranger approaching from the sheriff's office before stepping down to the street. Seeing the two men standing over Rojo on his travois with the townsmen gathered behind them, Sam stopped beside Beck and looked them over.

Upon seeing the ranger look him up and down, Smith said, "What's the matter now, Ranger? Any law against standing on the street in Sibley?"

"None at all," Sam said evenly, "so long as you behave yourselves." He let them see plainly that he was sizing them up, running their faces through his mind for the slightest recognition. He decided these two were the ones who'd been watching earlier from inside the saloon. He looked from Smith to Leonard; neither of them looked familiar.

"*Behave* ourselves?" Leonard sneered, his thumbs unhooking from his holster belt and his hands dropping to his sides. He said to Smith, "Hear that, Mr. Smith? The ranger here must be used to correcting schoolboys."

"Yeah, I heard it." Smith stepped to the side, put-

ting a little room between himself and his partner.
Sam knew that move. It was the move a man made
when he and his pal had worked it all out between
themselves. This one had been told to stay out of it,
he decided, looking at Mr. Smith. The other one had
said he wanted this lawman all to himself. But looking
closely at Leonard, Sam could tell he wasn't quite
ready yet. The rifle in Sam's hand had him unsettled.

Sam used that to his advantage. Sliding his thumb
over the rifle hammer, he calmly cocked it, lifted the
rifle one-handed and let the barrel point toward Leonard's belly. "Do I know you boys from somewhere?"

Something about the ranger's move with the rifle
suddenly rattled Leonard. One minute he'd been
standing there ready to call the ranger down—a one-on-
one gunfight. The next minute his plan had crumbled.
He gave a nervous sidelong glance at Smith, feeling
sweat form at his hat brim. He couldn't answer. How
the hell had he let himself get covered by a rifle?

"No, you don't know us, Ranger," Smith said stiffly,
seeing Leonard wasn't going to answer. "We're—
we're not from around here." He'd raised his hands
chest high in a show of peace as soon as he'd heard
the rifle cock. He couldn't believe Leonard had let
the ranger get the drop on them. He gave Leonard a
confused look.

Leonard's mouth had suddenly gone dry, his hand
feeling less steady than it had only a moment ago. He
backed up a step, his legs feeling weak. The townsmen
behind him parted and gave him room to retreat.

As the two backed away, then turned and walked

woodenly back into the saloon, Beck asked the ranger, "What was that all about?"

"I'm betting those two are behind the lynch mob that was just about to make a move on Texas Bob when I got back to town," Sam said, watching the men until they were out of sight. The townsmen had also started drifting back to the saloon.

"Is Bob all right, Ranger?" Mary Alice asked anxiously.

"He's holding up real well," Sam said. "I expect he'll be glad to see you."

She started to walk away toward the sheriff's office, but before leaving, she said in a hushed tone to Sam, "I heard one call the other *Trigger*." She gave Sam a knowing look.

"Obliged, Mary Alice," Sam said. He looked down at Rojo. "I suppose you were going to tell me that, right, Tommy?"

Rojo just looked away and mumbled hoarsely under his breath.

"We've got a witness to the shooting at the Sky High, Ranger Burrack," Mary Alice said barely above a whisper, calling his attention away from Rojo and back to her.

"Oh?" Sam looked first at her, then at Beck.

"Andrej, the Croatian," Mary Alice said. "It turns out he does speak English. He was just afraid to. We've got him hiding out at the old Minion Mine shack until we come for him."

"Good," said the ranger. "Now get on to the sheriff's office and see Texas Bob. It'll do him some good."

As soon as Mary Alice had walked out of sight, Sam asked Beck, "Is she fooling herself, or does the Croatian speak English well enough to help us out?"

Beck thought about it for a second, then grinned and said, "Both. He spoke English well enough when he showed up and told us his story. Since then both his English and his story have improved, if you know what I mean."

Sam shook his head. The way things were shaping up, he doubted the case would ever make it to trial anyway.

On the ground, Rojo looked up and said, "Will somebody cut me loose and hold that dog back while I get out of here?"

Sam reached down, pulled a long knife from his boot well and sliced the bedsheet from Rojo's chin to his crotch while Rojo held his breath. "You take it from there," Sam said. He slipped a hand down onto Plug's head as if to steady him into sitting still.

"You bet I will," said Rojo, ripping and pulling at the sheet until he staggered to his feet and threw the remnants of it to the ground. The dog only growled and watched as he stamped off toward the Markwell Hotel, where Judge Bass' silhouette filled a window on the second floor.

Chapter 21

When Bass realized that Tommy Rojo was walking straight to the hotel, he cursed under his breath, "Damn you, Rojo. This is all I need." Watching him walk closer, in the dim light of the oil lamps lining the street, the judge felt a sudden uneasiness come upon him. Hurriedly he stepped over to his leather travel bag, rummaged inside it and came out with a small-framed ivory-handled Remington pistol. "There now, that's better," he murmured, checking the pistol, making sure it was loaded. He turned the shiny gun back and forth in his hand as he hurried over and made sure the door was locked. Then he sat down in a chair facing the door, crossed his thick legs and waited, the Remington cocked in his hand.

Moments later he heard a commotion down at the front desk as the night clerk tried to stop Rojo from climbing the stairs. Then, predictably, he sighed, listening to Rojo's footsteps move upward and stop at his door. Taking a breath, Bass said, "Yes, who is it?" when he heard the knock.

"It's me, Tommy Rojo—the bounty hunter," Rojo called out though the thick oak door.

"Go away. I'm not seeing anyone this evening," Bass replied. "I'm much too busy."

"I'm hurt, Judge. We need to talk," Rojo said pitifully.

"I don't know why," Bass said callously.

"We had a deal going, Judge," Rojo said evenly. "I nearly got myself killed trying to help you. Now let me in." He jiggled the brass doorknob and knocked again, harder this time.

"Our only deal was for you to deliver Texas Bob," Mr. Rojo," said Bass officiously. "But did you do that? No. Bob came in with the ranger. Perhaps I should offer the ranger your reward."

"I brought the woman to you," Rojo said through the thick door, staring into a swirl of hand-polished oak grain.

"Indeed," Bass said sarcastically, his hand growing restless on the Remington. "I saw just how you *brought her in*! You forced her and the lineman to wrap you up like a raving asylum lunatic and drag you behind her horse, eh? What a clever idea, Rojo!"

Rojo gritted his teeth, feeling the pain intensify in his jaw, his forehead. "What's the difference? I brought her, Judge," he said, trying to keep from flying into a rage.

"Well, yes, that's true," said Bass. "I have to admit, you did *arrive* here with her."

"There. You see?" Rojo nodded, settling some.

The judge continued. "The problem is, I didn't want

her! I only wanted Texas Bob Krey! There was no reward for Mary Alice!"

"You said bring *them* back, Judge! I heard you say it. *Them* means *them*—either one or both!" Rojo said, starting to rant out of control.

"Are you sure you're a bounty hunter, Rojo?" Bass said indifferently. "I get the feeling you're nothing but a complete fool."

"Open this door, Judge, or I'm breaking it down," Rojo threatened, his face throbbing in pain. He'd had all he could stand of people for a while. It was time he made things go his way.

Bass smiled thinly to himself. *It's about time . . .* He raised the gun and held it firmly pointed at the door, at about chest level to Rojo, he estimated, prepared to fire.

But Rojo took a deep breath, knowing how sore and stiff he felt now, and how much more sore and painful he would be after flattening a big oak door. "All right, Judge. Listen to me," he said, keeping control of himself. He could feel the blood rush to his stitches and throb with each thump of his pulse.

Bass let out an impatient breath, wondering if the Remington's bullet would go through the door and still be capable of killing Rojo. But as he wondered, Rojo continued, saying, "Mary Alice and the lineman brought the Croatian back with them. He's going to be a witness for Texas Bob."

"No, he isn't," said the judge. "He doesn't speak English. That's the law of the territory."

"He speaks it, Your Honor," said Rojo. "I heard

him speak it. And I heard his account of what happened. He says your brother started the whole damn thing. He says it plain as day, and in English as good as any I've heard lately."

"Where is he?" Bass asked, his voice sounding more interested.

"They've got him hidden," said Rojo. "They thought I was asleep, but I was faking. I heard where they sent him to. He's waiting for the ranger to come get him."

"Blast you, Rojo, tell me where he is!" the judge demanded.

Now it was Rojo's turn to grin to himself, as much as his stitches would allow. "Not through this big ole door, Your Honor," he said. "We need to talk face-to-face. The way I see it, we need one another."

Rojo stood in silence, listening beyond the door to what he thought could be a gun hammer being lowered. Then he heard footsteps come to the door; the latch clicked open, the footsteps walked away. Finally, the judge said in disgust, "All right, Rojo, come in. But don't you dare touch anything."

Don't touch anything? Rojo had to wait a few seconds longer to let the judge's insult roll off his back. Then he swallowed his anger and pain, opened the big door and stepped inside.

"Rojo, I have to tell you that I am greatly disappointed in you," the judge said right away, almost before Rojo had closed the door behind himself. "I sent you to perform a job for me, and look at you—" He gestured a hand up and down Rojo. "You pathetic wretch! You look like something that has been mistaken for carrion and ravaged by vultures! What can we possibly have to do with one another? Tell me where this Croatian is, so I can have him protected until it's time to bring him into court."

Rojo clenched his fists at his sides and kept himself from flying into a rage. He hurt all over. "Judge, let's stop playing kid games and pretending you're upholding the law. You want this Croatian brought in, and I'm the man who can do it for you." He thumbed himself on the chest.

"Oh, can you now?" Bass said sharply. "So far I have seen no sign that you are capable of anything. You certainly didn't turn out to be much of a bounty hunter! Have you now changed professions and become a hired assassin?"

Hired assassin? *Damn right!* It hadn't occurred to Rojo until that very moment, but . . . "That's what I'm doing, Judge," he said. "To hell with all this bounty hunting. Let's cut to the bare bone. I kill men for money. If you want this man dead, he's dead. The only question now is, How much?" He rubbed his thumb and fingers together in the universal sign of greed.

"I would never pay one man to kill another, Mr. Rojo," Bass said with a sincere expression. He considered Rojo a fool. He wasn't about to tell him outright to kill the Croatian. He leaned back in his chair, the Remington lying across his lap. "But let's just suppose for a moment what it would mean if this case makes it to trial and this man doesn't make it to court . . ."

When Mary Alice arrived at the sheriff's office, she and Texas Bob hugged and kissed through the bars.

Enough to make a man sick, Price had thought to himself, turning and walking out the front door. She whispered into Tex's ear about Andrej Goran being a witness. Tex listened and pretended for her sake to be excited about the news. His plans were made. There was no way he could get an honest trial from Judge Edgar Bass. He wasn't going to come out of this alive if he relied on the law. He accepted that; he knew what he had to do.

"That's wonderful, Mary Alice," he whispered when she'd finished telling him. For a long moment the two lovers stood pressed together, the bars between them not important.

"I miss you something terrible, Tex," Mary Alice whispered through the bars.

"I miss you too," Texas Bob whispered. He closed his eyes, imagining they were somewhere else for a second. His arm through the bars, he stroked her hair, feeling the warmth of her overtaking the cold and the hardness of the iron bars.

"You don't think it will help, having the Croatian as a witness, do you, Tex?" she asked quietly.

"To be honest, no," Bob replied. "Or maybe it will help me as far as the shooting at the saloon goes. But there's the charge of stage robbery and murder." He shook his head. "The fact is, I've got a judge who wants me dead." He gave her a thin hopeless smile. "What worse hand can a man draw?"

"Oh Bob, what are we going to do?" she whispered, putting her face back against the iron bars, near his chest.

"I want you to stay strong, and have faith, Mary

Alice," he said. "No matter what happens." He wanted to tell her not to worry, that he was leaving tonight, but he didn't dare.

"I'm getting you out of here," she decided all of a sudden, unable to bear the thought of him hanging for crimes she knew he didn't commit. She gave a guarded glance around the office, her eyes glistening with tears, and whispered, "Tonight, when the deputies are sleeping. I'll bring a gun to the back window." She nodded up at the small barred window in the rear wall of his cell.

He wasn't about to tell her he'd made plans with the two deputies. If she knew, she would want to ride along. He didn't want her involved. He couldn't risk giving Price and Frisco an upper hand. "No, Mary Alice. Listen to me," he said sternly, turning her face up to his. "I don't want you breaking me out of here. It's too dangerous."

"No, it's not," she insisted. "I'll be careful. Nobody will see me. Nobody will ever know."

He knew he couldn't change her mind. "All right, but not yet. Not tonight."

"Then when?" she asked, wiping her eyes on the back of her hand. "The ranger says Bass is going to push this case as fast as he can before anybody from Bisbee can do something to stop it. Meanwhile," she said, "what about the lynching? Ranger Burrack said he had to hurry back here to keep something like that from—"

Texas Bob cut her off gently. "Don't worry about a lynching. Bass tried it; it failed." He pushed a strand of hair from her face. "Seems I have a good reputation in Sibley." He smiled. "I hope that doesn't surprise you too badly."

"No, Tex, that doesn't surprise me at all," Mary Alice said, again pressing herself to the iron bars to be near him. "You're a good man. Everybody knows it. I always knew it, and so did all the girls where I work. . . ." She let her words trail hesitantly.

"It's okay for you to say it, Mary Alice," Bob whispered into her cheek. "I know where you worked. It doesn't mean a thing to me. You know that, don't you?"

"Yes, I know that," she whispered back.

"We're going to be all right, Mary Alice," Bob said. "I want you to believe that. Will you?"

"Yes, I will," she said.

"Promise?" Bob asked.

"I promise," she whispered in reply, clinging to him.

"And promise you won't show up here tonight trying to stick a gun through the window?"

"All right. Not yet I won't," she said. "But if things get any worse, I'm taking you out of here. I promise you that too."

Out front of the sheriff's office, Price and Frisco watched Tommy Rojo trudge along the dirt street, his shirt bloodstained and tattered, his head ragged, half shaved, and stitched in every direction. "One dog did all that to him?" Frisco asked, wincing at the sight of Rojo.

"One dog and one whore," Price said, nodding toward the inside of the sheriff's office.

Frisco chuckled. "That's one tough little gal is all I can say."

"Yeah," said Price. "That's something you might want to keep in mind."

"Noted," said Frisco. "But I've never met a whore who can do something like that to me, dog or no dog."

Price just looked at him and shook his head.

Rojo made his way on up the dirt street, the glow of the oil streetlamps casting dark shadows on his gruesome face. "Sonsabitches," he growled under his breath when a man and woman veered quickly out of his path toward the Bottoms Up Saloon. "There's nothing wrong with me," he shouted over his shoulder at them. "You ought to see yourselves!"

Under his breath he muttered as he looked back and forth all along the dimly lit street, "I see that dog, I'm killing him." He felt his empty holster and added, "Soon as I find myself a gun."

Chapter 22

Inside the Bottoms Up Saloon and Brothel, Trigger Leonard and Mitchell Smith sat at a table in a darkened corner. The two had given up on raising a lynching party, at least for the time being. "I never seen a man that well liked in my life as this Texas Bob," Leonard said, brooding over a glass of whiskey before raising it to his lips and draining it in one long drink.

"Hell, it wasn't our fault," said Smith, hoping to cheer his partner up. "We liquored everybody up, but they just didn't get into a serious killing mood." He nodded around the saloon. "Look at them. All we managed to do was liven them up."

"And that blasted ranger," Leonard growled, not seeming to hear Smith trying to console him over the failed attempt to get support for a lynching. "I had the chance to kill him and *didn't*! What the hell happened to me out there?" He pounded a fist down onto the tabletop, the sound of it going unheard beneath the din of the drinking crowd and the rattle of a tinny piano. "I wasn't scared. I swear I wasn't. It was just strange, the way he lifted that rifle into play, getting the drop on us before I could even start any trouble with him! It was like he already saw what was coming and stopped it."

"Don't feel bad," Smith offered. "I've heard he has a way of drawing his Colt and getting the drop on a man before he expects it." He shrugged. "I reckon that's just his way. One minute you're ready to make a play on him, the next minute the play has been made. *Bang,* you're dead."

While Smith spoke, Leonard had stared at him with a sour expression. "Are you through?" he said bluntly.

Smith shrugged. "I'm only saying—"

"I *know* what you're saying!" Leonard growled. "And I know what you think! You're thinking I'm afraid of that ranger!" He scooted his chair back and made the motion of rising to his feet, his hand on his gun butt. "What's the matter, don't you have the guts to come right out and say it?"

"Trig, you're wrong!" Smith pleaded, seeing the look in his partner's red-rimmed eyes. "I know you're not scared of him, or anybody else! I'm your pal, remember? I'm on your side, right or wrong!"

Leonard's shame had gotten the better of him. Instead of standing, he took a long breath and let it out slowly, trying to free himself of his whiskey-fueled rage and humiliation. "Damn it! Why didn't I kill him?" He backhanded a shot glass off of the table. It flew across the room in a low straight line, missed a pair of drunken dancers, hit the brass mud-splattered foot rail and shattered in a spray of broken glass. In the din and clamor only one drinker standing nearby even noticed. He looked down for a second toward the disturbance, then looked back to the woman who stood leaning on the bar beside him as if nothing had happened.

"Next time you will," Smith said, glad to see the worst of Leonard's storm had passed.

"Yes, that's right. And there *will* be a next time," said Leonard, giving him a harsh, expectant look. "You can count on it."

Knowing how easily one wrong word could rekindle their drunken argument, Smith looked all around nervously while searching for the right thing to say. When his eyes came upon the bedraggled Rojo walking into the bustling saloon, he gave a smile of relief and said, "Well well, if it ain't ole *Dog-meat* Tommy Rojo!" Smith waved Rojo to the table, seizing an opportunity to change the subject, or at least put someone between himself and Leonard's drunken fury.

Upon seeing a fresh customer enter her world of gray smoke and whiskey vapor, a young dove started toward him from the bar. But then, at the sight of Rojo's face and ragged bloodstained clothes, she stopped short and backed away. Rojo cursed her under his breath and walked to the table where he'd heard Smith call out to him.

Sliding a chair out to seat himself, Rojo said to Smith, "I'd consider it an act of kindness if you'd not use the name Dog-meat. We all know how names have a way of sticking to a fellow." He sighed and slumped into the chair. "I swear, I feel like I've been through hell in a pushcart. You ain't going to believe what I've—"

"Who said you can sit down here, *Dog-meat* Tommy?" Smith grinned cruelly, cutting him off.

Looking at the brooding Trigger Leonard for some sort of permission, Rojo saw only a caged stare that revealed nothing. Rojo tapped his fingers on the table-top for a second, keeping calm. "All right," he said, rising from the chair, "if I'm not welcome—"

"Aw, sit down, Dog-meat Tommy," Smith said, chuckling darkly. "I'm funnin' with you."

"All right," Rojo repeated. He let out another breath, nodded and sat down. "I'm serious about the Dog-meat name, Mitchell. I'm obliged if you won't get that started."

"Why, what's wrong with Dog-meat Tommy?" Smith said, getting rid of some of the anger Leonard had forced onto him by passing it along to Rojo. "I saw that dog a while ago. He's gone all over town, bragging about how he ate you from the head down."

Rojo tried to be a sport. "That's funny." He gave a weak halfhearted grin, then turned to Leonard, seeing that Mitchell wasn't going to let up. "Trig, I've got some business we ought to talk about, if it's all right with you."

Leonard only stared.

"What kind of business, Dog-meat?" Smith cackled, cutting in.

Rojo just looked at him, keeping calm, then said to Leonard, "It's *gun* business. I've been offered a piece of work. I might need some help—"

"Gun business? You don't even have a gun, *Dog-meat*," Smith said, his digs getting worse by the minute. "You couldn't shoot anybody if you wanted to!"

"Wanna bet?" Rojo said tightly. His stitches throbbed, as did his forehead.

"Bet what, Dog-meat?" Mitchell laughed.

"That's enough, Mitch," said Leonard, interested in what Rojo had to say. He poured the last drops from a whiskey bottle into his mouth. "Get us a bottle, and a couple of shot glasses."

"And hurry back," Rojo said, getting in a dig of his own, seeing the look on Smith's face.

Smith glared at Rojo, but then said, "All right, I'll get a bottle and glasses. I'm needing to relieve myself anyways." As he stood up he said to Rojo, "The dog said he thought you'd be a bull elk, but you tasted more like pure pussycat." His grin went away. "If you ever *find* yourself a gun, come see me, *Dog-meat*."

Rojo watched him walk halfway to the bar, call out to the bartender for a bottle and two glasses, then walk out the back door.

"Now then, Rojo," said Leonard, "tell me about this business proposition you've got for us."

Still staring at the back door, Rojo said, "I've got a man who wants me to kill a fellow for him. He's paying five hundred dollars." He turned his eyes from the door to Leonard.

"Five hundred? For killing just one man?" Leonard looked impressed.

"This is an important man who wants it done," said Rojo.

"Aw, I see." Leonard grinned. "You mean like a judge or something?"

"Something like that," said Rojo, his eyes wandering to the back door.

Leonard nodded. "Yeah, five hundred sounds good, till you figure cutting it three ways."

"Right." Rojo nodded. Then he stood up without another word on the matter and walked toward the back door. On his way, he veered close to the crowded bar and slipped a big Dance Brothers pistol from a drinker's holster without being noticed. Stepping out back, he closed the door behind himself and walked up behind Mitchell Smith, who stood relieving himself into a urinal ditch alongside the public jakes.

Smith, staring off into the black-purple sky, suddenly felt his skin crawl; hair rose on his forearms. *Oh no!*

Rojo raised the big pistol and shot him squarely in the back of the head. "Found one," he said, a blue-orange bolt of fire streaking from Smith's forehead out across the darkness. Smith splattered facedown into the urine-soaked mud, smoke curling from the back of his head.

Turning, Rojo walked back into the loud sound of drunken revelry and deafening swell of piano music. Veering back along the crowded bar on his way, he slipped the smoking gun back into its unsuspecting owner's holster, picked up the two shot glasses and a bottle the bartender had set there, and walked back to his chair and sat down.

"Two ways," he said to Leonard, standing the bottle in front of him. "Mitchell ain't coming."

Leonard stared at Rojo in silence for a moment, letting it all sink in, having seen him walk out the back door and return so smooth and effortlessly. "Oh . . ." he said after a while, watching Rojo fill two glasses and slide one over in front of him. "Well . . . I suppose that's that," he offered. "Let's go do this piece of work. I need to get away from here for a while anyway, get my mind clear and think some things through."

"I'll be borrowing Mitch's horse, rifle and whatnot, if it's all the same with you," Rojo said, lifting his shot glass as if in a toast.

Trigger Leonard gave a knowing look, raising his shot glass in return and smiling. "If he's not objecting, neither am I."

In the middle of the night, Texas Bob lay on his bunk, fully dressed, boots on, waiting for the deputies to arrive. Once freed from this cell he had no doubts he could handle Price and Frisco Phil when the time came. The main thing was to get out of here, away from the threat of a noose hanging over his head.

Ranger Burrack had done all he could to try and keep him from hanging, but it wasn't enough. There were times when being in the right made no difference, not when you had a man like territorial judge Henry Edgar Bass out for your blood, he told himself.

He wished he could have told Mary Alice what his plans were, but he was certain she would understand once she realized why he had to do it this way. *I'll be back for you,* he said to her in his mind as he sat up on the bunk, hearing quiet footsteps cross the board-walk and open the door.

The door closed softly. Without lighting a lamp, Price walked across the darkened office and stopped at the cell door. Bob heard the metallic sound of the key slipping into the lock. "It's me, Texas Bob," Price said, turning the key and swinging the door open enough for Bob to step out of the cell.

"Where's Frisco?" Bob whispered, walking across the floor toward a peg on the wall where the ranger had hung his hat. He took his hat down and put it on.

"He's out back with the horses," said Price. As Bob turned toward the front door, Price stepped in front of him, blocking his way. In the light of a streetlamp glow coming through the front window, Bob looked him up and down and saw the handcuffs in his hand. "I've got to put these on you, Bob, just until we get to where the money is hidden. Frisco and I agreed."

"Yeah, but I didn't," said Bob. "I'd be a fool to go out there handcuffed with you two. You can put those away or lock me back in the cell." He decided that his next move would be to take Price to the floor, knock him cold and make his getaway alone if he had to. He took half a step forward.

"No matter. Let's go," said Price, stepping aside, offering no argument on the matter. The two slipped out the door onto the dark empty boardwalk and around the corner of the building. "I also need a gun," Bob said.

"You'll have to ask Frisco," Price said, to Bob's surprise.

A few yards down a dark alley running between the

sheriff's office and a land title building, Frisco called out in a low whisper, "Ask me what?"

"He wants to know if he can have a gun," Price said, slowing to a halt, letting Bob get a couple of steps ahead of him.

"A gun?" Frisco chuckled. "Not on your life, Texas Bob." He stepped out from a group of four horses. Even in the darkness, Texas Bob could see his forearm crooked around Mary Alice's neck. "But just so's everybody gets the right idea about who's in charge here, tell your boyfriend what I've got sticking against the side of your head."

Bob froze in midstep. Mary Alice gasped and struggled against Frisco's arm. But he held her tight. "You better tell, Dovey," he warned her. "Before he tries something stupid and gets you both killed."

"He's—he's got a gun to my head, Tex," Mary Alice said breathlessly. "Turn and run! Get away! Please don't try to—"

"Whoa now!" said Frisco, cutting her off with a hard press of his forearm against her throat. "Enough of that kind of talk!"

"Turn her loose, Frisco!" Texas Bob demanded. "I'm keeping my part of the deal! You don't need her!"

"Oh, you're going to keep your part of the deal all right," Frisco said, cocking the pistol against Mary Alice's head. "But with my gun against the dove's head, let's just say your heart will be more into it."

Texas Bob stared, trying to figure his next move. Behind him, Price stepped in, stuck a gun into the small of his back and jiggled the handcuffs on his finger. "Put your wrists together in front of you, Texas Bob," he said with sarcasm. "Let's see how these babies fit."

Across the street in a darkened room of the Markwell Hotel, the ranger sat at the window in a straight-backed chair, watching the dark mouth of the alley entrance. A moment earlier, he'd seen Texas Bob and Claude Price slip out of the sheriff's office and around the corner of the building. His face showed no expression of surprise, only a keen interest.

Wearing the same look of rapt interest, the big dog sat at the window ledge staring down as if he knew full well some sort of plan was afoot. "Easy, boy. He's all right," Sam had whispered, hearing a low whine when the animal caught sight of Texas Bob moving along the boardwalk, then disappearing from sight. The ranger's gloved hand reached out, patted the dog's big shaggy head reassuringly, then rested there.

A moment later the dog turned his head from the window and faced Sam in the darkness, whining long and low, as if asking the ranger's permission. With his free hand, Sam picked up a piece of jerked beef from a plate and held it down to the dog's wet cold muzzle. "This isn't your fight," he said quietly. "Here, have some supper, rest yourself. I'll bring him back to you."

Chapter 23

When Andrej Goran heard the first soft clink of a horse's iron shoes against the stone-covered hillside leading up to the abandoned mine shack, he did not wait to hear the sound again. He crept around quickly in the grainy predawn darkness, pulled his heavy miner's boots on, gathered his coat and hat, and picked up the tin miner's pail he'd found lying on the floor filled with the modest food supplies Mary Alice had given him.

Instead of using the door and leaving footprints in the thick dust coating the floor and the front porch, Andrej crawled out through a hole in the wall. But in his haste, he knocked over a hide-tanning frame that stood leaning against the side of the building. Hearing the sound, Tommy Rojo stopped his horse at the crest of the hill and reached an arm out, stopping Trigger Leonard, who had insisted on riding a couple of steps behind him.

"Shhh! Hold it! Did you hear that?" Rojo asked in a whisper.

"No, I didn't," Leonard said flatly, his head pounding like a bass drum from the whiskey he'd poured down himself after his public humiliation by the ranger. He stared at Rojo, not liking to be told by anyone to *shush*, especially a lowlife loser like Dogmeat Tommy. *Most* especially when he hadn't been saying anything in the first damn place, he thought, seething to himself.

"Well, I did," Rojo whispered, drawing Smith's rifle from the saddle boot and cocking it across his lap. "Keep your eyes open."

Keep your eyes open? "I'll try," Leonard said dryly, his jaw clenched. He nudged his horse up beside Rojo's, slipping his Colt from his holster, looking all around the littered, weed-stricken yard of the Minion Mining Company.

"Look! Over there!" Rojo said, pointing with the rifle to a pile of scrapped wagon wheels, pick heads and shovels at the far side of the yard. "I saw somebody move!" The rifle exploded in his hand, less than three feet from Leonard's aching, unsuspecting head.

"My God, man!" Leonard raised a gloved hand to his ringing ear.

"Come on! There he goes!" Rojo shouted, gigging his horse into a run across the dark yard. Leonard cursed but followed, his Colt out, ready to fire.

On the other side of the yard the hillside broke off sharply, so sharply that the Minion Mining Company had built a fence there years ago to keep its employees from walking off into the darkness and plunging headlong onto stones and cactus some forty feet below. But Andrej had not seen the broken board fence or the steep drop as a hazard. He saw it as his advantage. As soon as he'd arrived and looked the place over, he'd decided to keep the horse Mary Alice had given him—the one that had once belonged to Rojo— somewhere at the bottom of that deep chasm, for just such an emergency.

At the fence, Andrej squeezed between two loose boards and hurried along an eroded, one-foot-wide stretch of loose-rock ground. Near the end of the broken fence, he scrambled down off the edge onto a long thick hemp rope he'd found coiled up in the corner of the shack. He'd tied the rope to the base of a cotton- wood stump clinging by its roots to broken ground.

Gigging his horse back and forth in the littered mine yard, Rojo called out stiffly, his face stinging with pain from his effort, "Come out, come out, wherever you are!"

Huh? Leonard stopped his horse and stared at Rojo again. What was wrong with this fool? He was ready to call this deal off and go back to Sibley. Maybe if he felt better . . .

"I see him! Come on!" Rojo shouted suddenly, spurring the horse toward the broken fence, where he'd just caught a glimpse of Andrej going over the edge in the grainy early light. Rojo pointed the rifle and fired again one-handed as he rode.

The wiry Croatian lowered himself quickly, hand by hand down the steep bank of dirt and loose rock. His boots stirred up a dusty avalanche around him as he dug and kicked and scurried downward.

"Down there!" Rojo shouted, jumping from his sad- dle, running to the fence, shoving his way through it and aiming the rifle down at the cloud of gravel and dust. "I've got him!"

Right behind Rojo, Leonard winced as another rifle shot exploded. Yet, looking down and seeing the Croatian drop the last few feet to the ground and take off running to the cover of boulders along the hillside, Leonard joined in, firing his Colt until it clicked on a spent round.

"Damn it!" said Rojo. Wide-eyed with the excitement of the chase, he looked around at Leonard. "What do you think? Did we hit him?"

Not wanting to be this close to Rojo with an unloaded gun, Leonard spoke as he punched the spent rounds from his Colt and hurriedly replaced them. "I don't think so," he said. "At least not enough to slow him down any. There he goes!" He nodded down at the wiry Croatian as he ran in and out of sight from rock to rock, like a ground squirrel, the tin pail looped over his shoulder by a long strip of rawhide.

Rojo raised his rifle to his shoulder in reflex, but then held his shot, seeing no way to get a bead on the running miner. "Damn it!" he cursed again, lowering the rifle as Andrej disappeared behind another landstuck boulder. A second later, the Croatian reappeared, this time in the saddle, batting his boots to the horse's sides. "Hey! That's my horse!" Rojo said, recognizing the animal even in the grainy morning light. He grinned. "He won't get far. That horse'll stop dead still when he hears it's me."

Leonard drew his head away as Rojo raised two fingers to his lips and let out a loud shrill whistle. But instead of stopping dead as he'd predicted, the horse appeared to panic and speed up, almost bolting out from under the Croatian, who had to hang on to the saddle horn and clamp a hand down on his straw sombrero.

Leonard made no comment, but only looked away for a moment.

"I guess you can't depend on any animal anymore," Rojo said, watching the horse cut in and out of the rocks as if fleeing for its life. "Dogs, horses, they're not really our friends, the truth be known." He watched with a disappointed look as the horse sped out of sight.

"He laid that rope as his getaway," Leonard said, avoiding the animal subject altogether. "Good thinking on his part."

"Yeah," said Rojo, "but it won't get him very far." He stood and backed away from the edge. "We'll ride him down easy enough. I know that horse. It's not a long-winded runner."

Leonard just looked at him and kept his mouth shut. He was pretty sure he'd have to kill Rojo before this job was over.

The ranger had tried to leave the dog behind, securely locked in his room until the cleaning lady came in the morning and opened the door. But when he'd left the hotel room he'd heard the animal whine and run back and forth frantically. On his way down the stairs he'd heard a loud crash of window glass and realized what had just happened.

Hurrying out front, Sam had arrived on the street just in time to see the fragments of broken glass and the dog racing out of sight into the blackness of the alley. "Crazy dog." All he could do was shake his head. "Don't get yourself killed out there," he murmured, turning to his horse at the hotel's hitch rail.

Once atop his horse and on the trail, he'd seen the dog's tracks in hot pursuit of the horses, following his owner's scent. Thinking about it, he decided maybe it was a good idea, having the dog ahead of him once he headed into the rocks on the trail of Bob and the deputies. He had a good idea where they were headed, but he wanted to lag back and give Texas Bob plenty of breathing room. No sooner had he had picked up their trail than he'd counted four separate sets of hoofprints instead of three, another good reason to keep his distance until the right time, he thought.

By first clear morning light, he'd ridden up into rock country on the same trail he and Bob had brought the stage in on. Judging by the closeness of two sets of hoofprints, he speculated that the fourth horse was carrying Mary Alice. It made sense, he told himself, Price and Frisco Phil taking her along as a hostage— a sure way to keep Texas Bob from making any move that might get her hurt.

The ranger pictured two of the horses riding close together, one of the deputies holding a gun on the woman. With that picture in mind, he rode on steadily, judging the distance between himself, the dog and the four riders on the high rocky trail ahead. He'd allowed them a half hour head start, to keep himself from being spotted crossing the flatlands. Now that he'd made the cover of the hills, he needed to close that gap, get ahead of them, atop of them if he could, he thought, looking up along jagged broken cliff lines. He knew about where they were going. With any luck he'd be there waiting.

Three miles ahead of the ranger, the big dog loped on, tired but still running, the scent of his owner and the woman having grown stronger. Now that the riders had traveled up into the rock country, the winding trails had forced them to slow their pace. At a turn, the dog slowed to a walk. Then he came to a halt, seeing Price standing half hidden behind a large rock. Price and Frisco had heard something on their trail and Price had elected to stay behind to investigate.

"Bob's blasted hound," Price cursed out loud to himself, taking a step closer. "I'll clip both your ears off!" Raising his rifle to his shoulder, he took quick aim and fired. His shot fell short, missing the dog but kicking up dirt that stung the dog's forelegs and sent it scurrying out of sight. "That'll do," he said, stepping back into his saddle. Turning his horse to the trail, he hurried to catch up with the others.

Forty yards up the trail, Frisco turned in his saddle and asked, "What was the gunshot?"

"Bob's dog was following us," Price said, slowing beside Frisco, seeing Bob looking back from a few feet ahead.

"Did you kill it?" Frisco asked, holding the reins to Mary Alice's horse, keeping the horse and its rider close at all times.

"Naw, I wasn't trying too hard," said Price. "I sent him running, though. That's the last we'll be seeing of him."

Texas Bob and Mary Alice both looked relieved

that the dog hadn't been shot. Frisco shook his head and spit. "You don't know nothing at all about dogs, if you think that," he said, looking back along the trail.

"I expect I know as much about dogs as the next fellow," Price said. "If he does come back I'll send him flying again." He gave Bob a cross look. "Next time maybe I will take closer aim."

Frisco chuckled and pointed back along the rocky trail. "Then maybe you ought to do it now. Here he comes."

"Damn dog. He's as hardheaded as his master," Price said, levering a fresh round into his rifle chamber.

"He's harmless. Leave him alone," Texas Bob said, his cuffed hands gripping the saddle horn tightly. He shouted at the advancing dog, "Get out of here, Plug! Go, boy! Go on, get!"

"This time I'll make a good dog out of him," Price boasted, raising his rifle.

But the dog, either from his master's command or from seeing the rifle pointed at him, ducked quickly out of sight behind a large rock. Once out of danger, he barked loudly.

"Good boy." Bob and Mary Alice both breathed in relief.

"Let's go," Frisco said to Price, "if you're all through playing with the doggie." He gestured Bob on ahead, keeping Mary Alice's horse reined in close beside him, his Colt still in hand.

Price gave a sour look, shoved his rifle down into his saddle boot and nudged his horse forward, grumbling, "Danged dog will be pestering us this whole trip."

Even as he rode forward, the big dog slipped from behind the rock and loped along the side of the trail, warily keeping the cove of rock and cactus between himself and Price's rifle.

Less than a mile to the left of the four riders, the ranger had heard the shot. He'd stopped for a moment and stared in that direction as the echo resounded along distant canyon walls. Then he'd pushed on, gaining ground on the riders, using a stretch of higher flatlands to his advantage. For the next hour and a half he'd stopped his horse only long enough to allow it to draw tepid canteen water from the crown of his sombrero.

When Texas Bob led the other three down from the rock trail and onto the spot in the sand where he'd found Sheriff Thorn and the stagecoach, he pointed across at the rise where he'd found their bag of money lying on the ground. "Turn her loose, Frisco," he said. "You'll find the money under a flat rock right up there, to the right of where you laid it."

Frisco said, "Nice try, Texas Bob," making no effort toward turning Mary Alice's horse loose. Instead he pulled its reins tighter against him and tightened his grip on the Colt. "Take us up there," he demanded. "I'll turn her loose when that money is in my hands."

They pushed on toward the top of the rise, wind whipping up dust and licking at the tails of Price's riding duster. As their horses climbed the loose sandy incline, Price looked back in time to see the dog circle wide of them and duck out of sight into a stretch of brush and cactus. Topping the rise, Bob led them to the flat rock and stepped down from his saddle. He stooped and turned the rock over with his cuffed hands. Lifting the bag, he turned it upside down and poured the money into the sand.

"Well, I'll be damned," said Frisco, looking down at the money. "There's only one rock on this whole hillside. You'd think one of us would have looked under it."

"Turn her loose now," said Bob, having no idea what his next move would be. His only interest was in seeing Mary Alice free and riding away. After that, he would deal with his own fate, whatever it might be.

Frisco started to speak, but something drew his attention toward the other side of the rise. "What was that?" he asked Price, tightening his grip on the Colt.

"The wind," said Price, not wanting to step away from the money even for a second.

"Ride over and see," said Frisco.

Price just stared at him. "It's the wind, or the dog. Either way, let's get on with the money."

Frisco looked back down and wagged his Colt at Texas Bob. "Bag it up," he said.

"Turn her loose," Bob insisted. "Let her ride away. You've got your money. I kept my end of the deal. Keep yours."

Frisco gave Price a guarded look. "Think I should turn her loose, Deputy?"

Price made the slightest move of a finger, his hand resting on the rifle across his lap. "Sure, why not," he said, both of them knowing these two would never leave here alive.

"All right, dove," said Frisco, throwing the end of her reins to her. "Take off."

But Mary Alice only straightened the reins and backed her horse a step. "I'm not leaving without Tex," she said with finality.

"Get out of here, Mary Alice!" Bob said, the empty bag hanging in his cuffed hands. "Ride hard and don't look back. I'm begging you."

"Uh-uh," said Mary Alice. "We both go or we both stay. I'm not leaving."

"Suit yourself, dove." Frisco chuckled darkly, giving Price another look. "You can both sleep in the sand till Judgment Day." He cocked the Colt, ready to fire it.

Past Frisco, Texas Bob saw the ranger stand up on the other side of the rise, thirty feet away.

"Drop the guns, both of you," the ranger called out.

But Bob knew that Frisco was already making his move, turning the Colt toward Mary Alice. In a wild desperate attempt to stop him, Bob leapt forward and swung the empty bag, slapping Frisco's gun hand away and spraying his face with a flurry of sand.

Price swung his rifle toward the ranger. But Sam's first rifle shot punched him in the chest and sent him flying from his saddle into the sand. Sam stepped forward with deliberation, levering another round into his rifle. Atop his horse, Frisco recovered quickly from the face full of sand and turned his Colt toward Texas Bob. "I said drop it," Sam shouted, stepping closer.

"Go to hell, Ranger!" Frisco bellowed, swinging his Colt from Bob toward the ranger.

The ranger's second shot lifted him from his saddle as well and flung him over the edge of the rise. Frisco slid a few feet in the loose sand, then came to a stop on the long hillside, spread-eagle, his chest bloody, his dead eyes staring blankly at the sky.

Walking closer, Sam watched Price reach a bloody hand inside his vest pocket. "Don't try it, Price," he warned, levering another round into his rifle.

Price coughed and chuckled grimly, blood trickling from his lips. "Or what? You going to . . . shoot me?" he said haltingly. His hand fell from his vest pocket and dropped the watch fob he'd taken from Thorn's body. Sam stopped and looked down at the blackened finger of Jeuto Vargas. "You know where I . . . got that, Ranger?"

"It belonged to Sheriff Mike Thorn," Sam said, recognizing the grizzly trophy, "and I know the only *way* you could have taken it from him."

"Yeah," said Price. "We killed him." A look of regret came to his face. "We killed him . . . killed poor old Teddy Ware, and Norbert Block too." He shook his head. "What a no-good sumbitch . . . I turned out to be. All I wanted . . . was to be admired." He managed to raise his eyes and point up at Texas Bob as Bob and Mary Alice stepped forward, Bob's shadow falling across Price's face. "Like . . . this damned . . . do-gooder . . ." he murmured, his words trailing off with his final breath.

Slipping over the rise and in between them, the big dog stuck his muzzle down to Price's face as if to make sure he was dead. "Get back, Plug," Bob said gently, reaching down and patting his big shaggy head.

Chapter 24

With Texas Bob's wrists freed from the handcuffs and the bodies of Price and Frisco Phil lying over their saddles, the three stood for a moment, the ranger turning the watch fob back and forth in his hand. "Some evidence," he said. "But the court will have no choice but to accept my testimony. Price gave a dying confession. A dying confession to a lawman is not hearsay. Bass will have to give up on the charges." He looked at Texas Bob and said, "But as bad as this has all gone for you, I couldn't have blamed you if you'd managed to get away, take the money yourself and cut for Mexico."

"Maybe I would have, Ranger," Bob admitted, his arm looped around Mary Alice's waist. "But I could never have lived with myself, doing something like that. It's not my way." He smiled down at Mary Alice, then said to Sam, "Does that sound foolish, Ranger?"

"To some it does," Sam replied. "But not to me. I expect if a man *is* right, he *stays* right." He let out a breath and pocketed the watch fob. "I understand if you want to turn your horses toward Mexico right now and not look back. I can explain all this. You won't have to be there."

"Obliged, Ranger," said Bob, "but it doesn't feel right to me. I think a man ought to speak for himself. Don't you?"

"You know I do." Sam gave a thin smile. "I just thought I'd make the offer." He slipped his rifle down into his saddle boot. "Bass has tried everything to kill you, Tex. The townspeople of Sibley thought too highly of you to go along with a lynching. A man whose life you saved came all the way back to testify for you. You must be doing something right." He swung up into his saddle. Mary Alice and Texas Bob did the same. The dog stopped licking his paws and fell in behind them as the horses turned toward the trail back to Sibley.

In the afternoon they turned onto a less-used trail that ran through a stretch of rocky hills and past a string of abandoned mines, including the Minion Mining Company. They stopped abruptly when they heard a volley of pistol and rifle shots exploding a short distance ahead of them. "Andrej!" Mary Alice gasped.

Seeing the ranger already boot his horse up into a run, Bob handed Mary Alice the reins to the two dead men's horses and said, "Wait here!"

But no sooner had he said it and ridden away than Mary Alice slapped her reins to her horse and followed, leading the two horses, the dog racing right along behind her.

A half mile ahead, in a maze of rock, sand and cactus, Andrej Goran's terrified horse had stumbled and fallen on a steep path leading down into a draw. The wiry Croatian slid, rolled and tumbled, and came to his feet, running without looking back. When he got to a place where he saw nothing but high rocks all around him, he looked back, saw the two gunmen riding down on him and ran up into the steep jagged rocks and began climbing.

"We've got him now," said Rojo. He slid his horse to a halt and looked at Trigger Leonard, who stopped right beside him. "You need to go back, climb around and get up there, in case he makes it to the top." He pointed up along the edge above the climbing Croatian.

"Like hell," said Leonard, still suffering his hangover and long since worn-out from the long hard day in the saddle. "He's not getting away." He nudged his horse forward, gun in hand. "I'll plug him dead center first."

Rojo stared at the back of Leonard's head for a moment, his hand tightening on his rifle stock as Leonard rode forward. "All right then, *Trig,*" he called out angrily, "why don't I just go myself?"

"Good idea," Trigger Leonard said without looking back.

Rojo stared a second longer, almost raising his rifle as he cursed under his breath. But then he took his thumb from over the rifle barrel, turned his horse and rode hard back along the trail.

Stopping his horse in the center of the sandy draw, Leonard stepped down from his saddle, spread his feet shoulder width apart and raised his big Colt with both hands. He took close aim on the climbing Croatian and started to fire. But at the last moment he realized that if he shot the man right there, he'd have to climb up a good ways himself to drag the body down.

"Damn it," he said, letting his gun hand fall loosely to his side. He rubbed his temples. His head pounded. His ears had been ringing all day from Rojo's rifle shot so close to his head. "Hey up there," he called out, cupping his pounding forehead. "Come on down here! I won't hurt you."

"To hell you go, is what I say to you!" Andrej called out without looking back or slowing down.

"To hell I go?" Leonard sighed and shook his aching head. "Damn foreigners." At his feet lay the tin pail that had fallen off the Croatian's shoulder. He kicked it away. "All right, then, let's get it done!" He cocked the big Colt and started to raise it again.

"Drop the gun," the ranger shouted, stepping down off the narrow path. Behind him, his horse stood beside the Croatian's horse, looking it over as the dusty animal stood shaking itself off.

Leonard lowered his gun, but didn't drop it. Instead he turned, letting his gun hand once again fall to his side. "Well well now, look who's here," he said, certain the ranger had not noticed that his Colt was already cocked. "Ranger, I have been miserable all day and all night, ever since I let you buffalo me in the street."

"I said drop it, Heebs." Sam stood with his gun down at his side. Without taking his eyes off of Leonard, he noted the Croatian had stopped climbing and had looked around and down to see what was going on. "I won't tell you again."

"You know it's me, huh?" said Leonard, without dropping the gun. "Then you ought to know I'm not going to drop this gun. Now that it's just you and me, I think we ought to finish this little contest fair and square. We'll both just holster these shooting irons—" As he spoke, he prepared himself to make a move. As soon as the ranger holstered his gun, Leonard would fire. That would do it. He had the ranger cold—

But before he'd finished his thought, his whole body stiffened and flew backward. The sky streaked madly past his wide eyes as the ranger's bullet punched through his heart and sent him sprawling onto the sandy ground. "What contest?" Sam murmured under his breath.

From atop the high rock wall above the draw, Rojo belly-crawled to the edge and looked down at the ranger standing over Trigger Leonard's body. A few yards back, he saw Texas Bob and Mary Alice walking their horses down into the draw. He looked at the bodies slung over their saddles, a grim reminder of where he and men like him stood with the ranger.

"Uh-oh," Rojo said, seeing the ranger look up toward him. From his position he couldn't that see Andrej Goran had turned and started climbing back down. He did see Mary Alice bend down and pick up the tin pail by its rawhide strip. Beside her he saw the dog poke its nose into the pail, sniffing the contents. He had a clear shot from here, Rojo told himself, at the dog, at Texas Bob, at the ranger himself if he wanted to take it.

He raised the rifle to his shoulder and looked down

the barrel, looking from face to face of each of the people he could kill, and at the dog. It was time to make a decision. He closed his finger over the trigger. Then he stopped. *No, wait . . .* This wasn't the time to start a gunfight. No matter who he shot down there, the others would start shooting back. This was the time to make a getaway.

Judge Bass had no idea what had happened the night before in Sibley. The jail stood empty when he'd arrived there this morning, yet it didn't appear there had been a jailbreak. The key hung in the lock of Texas Bob's cell. There was no sign of a struggle. Both deputies were gone. A window had been broken out of the ranger's room at the Markwell Hotel. What had gone on here? He'd spent the day wondering about it, certain that everything was connected somehow— the window, the jail, the missing deputies.

Earlier he'd seen the telegraph clerk and learned that the ranger had a telegraph from Bisbee waiting to be picked up. The telegraph had him more than a little concerned. He'd tried to get the clerk to reveal what it said, but the fellow wouldn't budge. He'd even offered a bribe. Nothing doing. Whatever was going on here, it was time for him to clear things up and get on across the territory.

Since nobody had enough guts to lynch Texas Bob, he supposed he'd have to do it. *Legally,* he chuckled to himself. Once Rojo killed the Croatian there would be no witnesses other than the deputies, if they ever returned. They would say anything he told them to say. That was one good thing about having surrounded himself with lowlifes. They would do anything for a dollar. He knew he could never trust them, but then, he'd never intended to.

In the late afternoon he took a toothpick from his lapel pocket and stuck it between his teeth on his way from the restaurant back to the sheriff's office. He needed to check every once in a while until they returned. He wasn't about to mention Texas Bob's being gone until he knew more about it. For all he knew, the deputies could have ridden him out somewhere and put a bullet in his head. He smiled to himself. That wouldn't be too bad, he thought.

When he'd stepped up onto the boardwalk and to the door of the sheriff's office, an old townsman had started at the far end of the street, lighting streetlamps against the encroaching darkness. "Another day in Hell's Paradise," he grumbled to himself, opening the door and stepping inside. He closed the door and stepped over to the battered oak desk. Taking a long match from a tin match holder, he raised the globe on an oil lamp and started to light it.

"Don't strike that match, please, Judge," Tommy Rojo whispered, hunkered down against the front of the cell, his rifle standing between his knees.

"Rojo!" The judge turned, startled, the unstruck match still in hand. "What on earth are you doing here, hiding in the dark like some crazy man?"

"The ranger is after me," said Rojo. "He killed poor Trigger Leonard, and he'll be coming right here after me any minute."

"What are you talking about, you fool?" Bass said.

"What do you mean he killed Trigger Leonard? Who in blazes is Trigger Leonard?"

"You know, Leonard and Smith, the men you hired to stir up a lynching?"

"Oh, those two," said the judge with a sour expression. "Don't mention those miserable wretches. They found Smith dead in the public urinal ditch this morning. Poor bugger had been lying there all night with his brains blown out, drunks relieving themselves on him."

"Yeah, that's terrible." Rojo kept himself from smiling. "So, now Leonard is dead too. He rode with me to kill the Croatian. The ranger attacked us, killed him deader than hell."

"Wait a minute," said the judge. "Do you mean to tell me *you* didn't kill the Croatian?"

Rojo lied. "No, I killed him! He's dead, just like you wanted him. That's why I came here to find you, to get paid, so I can get out from under this ranger dogging me. I'm telling you he's right behind me. Him and Texas Bob and the whore from the Bottoms Up."

"What?" The judge stiffened. "The ranger has Texas Bob with him?" He looked all around the office as if the deputies might appear out of thin air. "What the devil is going on? Where's Price and Frisco Phil?"

Recalling two bodies lying facedown over their saddles, Rojo said, "I don't like bringing bad news to you, Your Honor. But I've got a pretty good idea they're both dead."

Bass only stared at him, stunned speechless for a moment. Finally he managed to say, "*Dead?* Both of the deputies?"

"The ranger has two bodies over their saddles," said Rojo. "If it's not the deputies, I'll be awfully surprised." He hesitated, then said, "I'll be needing my money now, Your Honor. I don't want to be here when he arrives. I hate to say it, but I don't believe he likes me much."

"My goodness," said Bass, not even hearing Rojo. He stood staring off into space, letting things sink in. "He has freed Texas Bob and killed two officers of the law." He seemed to be wondering what sort of charges he might bring against the ranger. "He is simply running loose, doing as he pleases, isn't he?"

"Well, yes, I suppose you might say that," Rojo said as if giving it consideration. "But that is none of my business. I want my money, so I can put some miles between him and me."

"Your money. Yes, of course," said Bass, as if snapping out of a mild stupor. He reached inside his coat, took out a roll of bills and began counting off the blood money he'd promised Rojo. "You did your job. I suppose you have this coming."

"Obliged, Your Honor, and it's been a pleasure doing business with you," Rojo grinned, his dirty hand stuck out for his pay.

From outside, the ranger's voice called out, "Judge Bass . . . Tommy Rojo. This is Arizona Territory ranger Sam Burrack. Both of you come out of there with your hands held high."

"Oh no!" Bass said. He stopped counting and glanced at the window, money in both hands.

"Tell him I'm not here," Rojo whispered nervously.

Bass glanced out at the tired horse standing at the

hitch rail. "They *know* you're here," he said sarcastically.

"How?" Rojo whispered, looking bewildered.

"Is that not your horse out there, ridden half to death?" Bass asked, already knowing what the answer would be.

"Dang it!" Rojo cursed through clenched teeth.

"Allow me to handle this," Bass said. Without stepping away from the desk, he called out through the open window, "Ranger, what on earth are you trying to pull here? Where are the deputies, Price and Frisco Phil Page?"

"They're right here, Bass," Sam replied. "Both of them dead across their horses. So is Trigger Leonard Heebs, one of the men you sent after Andrej Goran. Luckily we got to Andrej first."

"What?" Bass said, giving Rojo a cold stare. "You said you killed the Croatian! You lying idiot. I should never have trusted a fool like you!"

"Andrej will be a witness for Texas Bob," the ranger continued. "He saw your brother start the gunfight that night at the Sky High Saloon. Your game's over, Bass. Come on out. For your own good send Rojo ahead of you."

"Give me that money, Judge!" said Rojo. "I'm cutting out the back door and getting out of here!"

Bass stood staring at him across the battered desk, money in hand. "We'll beat this if you do exactly as I tell you."

"I'm beating it, all right," Rojo said, his hand out, snapping his fingers toward the money. "I'm beating it out of here as fast as I can! Give it to me!"

"I'm a judge, you idiot!" said Bass. "Listen to what I'm telling you! This ranger can't match me when it comes to legal skills!"

"It ain't legal skills that put them three facedown over their saddles, Judge!" Rojo argued. "You stay and hash it all out in court if you want. But give me my money so I can skin out of here!"

"*Your* money? Your money for *what*?" Folding the money and stuffing it back inside his coat, Bass said, "Keep your stupid mouth shut and pay attention, you fool, and maybe you'll learn something here."

Rojo seethed, watching the judge turn and walk to the open front window. "Ranger Burrack," Bass called out, "there have been several mistakes made here in Sibley. But I trust that you, myself and even Texas Bob Krey can work them out, if we apply ourselves like reasonable people."

Sam called out, "Bass, get away from there, don't turn your back on—"

But the ranger's words came too late. Texas Bob, Mary Alice, Andrej and Sam all four ducked aside as the judge's forehead exploded in a long streak of blood, bone fragments and brain matter. The impact from the rifle shot at close range picked him up and tossed him half out the open window. He hung there limply, head down, his arms swinging back and forth above the dusty boardwalk.

Sam winced at the sight, but then went back to the task at hand. Waving Texas Bob and the others aside, he called out, "Rojo, lay down your gun and step out here with your hands up." From all parts of town came the sound of slamming doors and running feet, a murmur of voices.

"I'm going to hang for this, ain't I, Ranger?" Rojo called in a sobbing voice.

"It's likely, Rojo," Sam said. "But you did it. Now you got to pay for it."

"I can't sit around wondering how it's going to feel, hanging!" he said. "You understand that, don't you, Ranger?"

"I do," Sam replied. He sidestepped, taking himself farther out of the circling glow of a streetlamp. Then he walked to the middle of the street and stood in silence.

"Boy oh boy," Rojo called out. "I sure wish I'd been a different kind of person my whole danged life!"

The ranger didn't answer, but to himself he thought, *I wish you had too, Tommy.* He watched the door burst open, and he heard Rojo yell as he lunged out, his rifle blazing, but the quickly levered shots going wild.

The ranger's rifle bucked once in his hands. The shot silenced Rojo's rifle and sent him back onto the boardwalk, dead, the rifle flying from his hands and landing in the dirt.

As the ranger stepped forward, he levered another round into his rifle chamber out of habit. But he saw right away that he wouldn't need it. The killing had ended. Standing on the boardwalk, he looked down at Rojo's wide, frightened eyes. He looked over at Judge Bass hanging down from the window, bleeding into the dust on the boardwalk planks.

"My goodness!" said the telegraph clerk, who had eased up beside him, "I almost walked smack into the middle of this!"

The ranger just looked at him.

"Yes, it's true!" the clerk said. "I saw you ride into town and I immediately came running. I have a telegraph from Bisbee for you. It appears important."

"From Bisbee," Sam said, giving Texas Bob a look as he and Mary Alice stepped up beside him.

Bob watched closely as Sam read it, shook his head and folded it back up. Seeing the questioning look on Texas Bob's face, he said, "Bisbee says they appreciate the importance of the situation here. They're going to try to have somebody here by the end of the month."

Texas Bob let out a breath. "You saved my life, Ranger. I'm obliged."

Sam didn't reply. He touched the brim of his sombrero, turned and walked toward his horse.

Mary Alice looked at the ranger, then at Bob, and asked in surprise, "You're obliged? Is that all you're going to say, Tex, after everything he's done? You're *obliged*?"

"Yep," Texas Bob replied quietly. He watched the ranger walk away, his rifle hanging loose in his hand, a tail of his duster lifting on a chilled evening breeze. "It's enough said between us. Between men like the ranger and men like myself."

Ralph Cotton brings the Old West to life—
don't miss a single page of action!
Read on for a special preview of the next
Ranger Burrack adventure. . . .

Nightfall at Little Aces

Coming from Signet in March 2008

Emma Vertrees stood in her backyard spreading a damp white bedsheet along the clothesline. She stopped what she was doing when she saw the four armed riders move their horses at an easy gait along the alley toward the livery barn. Three of the four men seemed to not even see her as they passed by single file, no more than thirty feet away. But the last man turned his eyes to her and touched the brim of his hat. Emma stood rigid, giving no response.

There was nothing unusual about armed men riding into town. In fact, an *unarmed* man in Little Aces, New Mexico, would have been more of a rarity. But being the wife of a town sheriff for over seven years had conditioned Emma to closely watch the comings and goings of armed men, especially those riding in off the southwestern badlands.

She had learned intuitively to read a man's purpose by the manner in which he rode into town along the dirt street. It was a skill her husband, Dillard, had learned as a lawman, and while it was not something one person could teach to another, having been made aware of it, Emma had learned. She had gotten good at it, she reminded herself, watching the four men stop their horses halfway up the dusty alley beside the livery barn.

These men rode into town with a purposeful bearing about them, yet she sensed no immediate danger. They were cowboys, she determined; and while cowboys could turn as wild and unpredictable as the wild broncs and range animals they lived among, they were for the most part not bad men.

But with cowboys you can expect most anything, she recalled Dillard telling her. She pictured him saying so as she touched a wet cloth to his most recently bruised, or sliced, or punctured flesh—battle scars acquired on the streets of Little Aces. *Enough of that,* she told herself, feeling a bitterness slip into her thoughts.

She let the picture of her husband pass from her mind and watched the four dust-streaked young men saunter toward the battered wooden table where Blind Curtis Clay sat, his sightless eyes fixed straight ahead.

"I keep hearing how fast you are with your big Remington, Blind Man," said one of the four, a cowboy named Hank Lindley. As he spoke he lifted his Colt quietly from his holster. "I figured it's time I rode in and found out for myself."

Clay heard the faint sound of gun metal sliding up across holster leather. His were the only ears to detect the sound. Others might have heard it had they been listening for it, but Blind Curtis never missed such sounds. Nor did he take such sounds for granted. His ears distinguished in sound what his eyes could not see in the engulfing darkness that lay before them. He sat perfectly still behind the wooden table out front of his shack in the alley alongside the livery stables.

"My, my," was Clay's only response. His large black hands lay atop the table, the big Remington between them on an oilcloth, like some demon at rest. A silence passed as he smelled whiskey, beer, cigar smoke, horse and sagebrush on the four young cowboys standing before him. Clay finally asked, "What kind of gun do you have pinted at me?"

Hank gave his friends a half smile, not even wondering how the blind man might know that the Colt was directed at his broad chest. "It's a Colt *pinted* at you," Hank said, a bit mockingly. But he tipped the barrel upward. "Does that make any difference?"

Clay seemed to consider the question for a second, then said, "Naw sir, I expect it don't."

"I ought to warn you, I'm fast," said Hank, the half smile still on his face. "I've been practicing ever since I heard about you."

"I thank you most kindly for telling me," said Curtis Clay, "but I take on all comers."

"What I'm saying is, I'm *danged fast.*" As Hank spoke, he looked at a tall hickory walking stick leaning against the table beside the blind man.

"Are you more than fifty cents fast?" Curtis asked respectfully.

"Oh yes," Hank said confidently. "I'm more than fifty cents fast. I might be five dollars fast. Are you sure you want to try me?"

With no expression on his broad face, Curtis said flatly, "You're the one come looking."

Three of the four cowboys exchanged grins and nodded. "He got you there, Hank," said Dennis Barnes. "I expect you'll have to put up or shut up."

"Yeah," said Rupert Knowles, "I don't mind telling you, I'm betting a dollar on the ni— I mean, *Mr.* Clay here," he corrected himself. "So get your money up and let's get on with it."

"Not so danged fast," said Hank, giving Rupert a stern look. "Before I put up any money, I ought to get some kind of idea what I'm up against."

The fourth cowboy, a serious-looking young man named Omar Wilkens, stood to the side, eyeing his companions and Blind Curtis Clay with equal contempt. "What a waste of time," he grumbled to himself, hearing Hank Lindley begin to have second thoughts. "I'll be at Little Aces." He turned back to where he'd tied his horse alongside the others. "You can let me know who wins."

"Stick around a minute, Omar," Dennis Barnes called out. "This will be a hoot."

"I've got better things to do," Wilkens growled under his breath, snatching his horse's reins and flipping himself up into the saddle.

"Oh yeah? Like what?" Barnes barked.

Wilkens didn't bother answering. Instead, he jammed his spurs to his horse's sides and sent the animal bolting away in a hard run.

Standing at her clothesline, Emma Vertrees fanned the dust that had billowed and drifted across her small backyard behind the running horse. As the young man sped past her yard, he once again touched his hat brim toward her—and once again she ignored his gesture. Now she watched him rein his horse down to a halt at the end of the alley, where he turned the animal and sat gazing back toward her.

He nudged the horse forward at a walk back toward her yard. She looked away from him quickly, still hoping that ignoring him would send him on his way. But she was wrong. As she stooped slightly and picked up a damp pillowcase from her metal laundry tub, she watched peripherally as the horse drew nearer, sidling up to the weathered picket fence at the edge of her yard.

She wondered if it would be a good idea to simply walk away from her task and watch from inside her kitchen window until the young man left. *Yes,* she told herself, *that's the proper thing to do.*

"Begging your pardon, ma'am," he said as she straightened and turned toward the back door. "That was most inconsiderate of me."

She stopped. An apology? She hadn't been expecting that. She wasn't sure what she had expected, but it certainly wasn't an apology. She tried to make herself walk on to the door, yet something in his voice compelled her to turn back toward him. As she did so, she idly held a hand to the collar of her gingham dress. Her only response was a curt but tolerant nod, one that forgave yet dismissed him. That would be enough, she told herself. This was no rowdy drunken range hand. This one showed at least *some* signs of proper upbringing.

But as she once again started to turn away from

him toward the door, he threw a leg over his saddle and slid down over her picket fence into her yard. Before she could object, he had twirled his horse's reins on the fence and come walking toward her. He took off his battered Stetson and held it respectfully at his chest.

"I hope my kicking up dust hasn't spoiled your whole wash," he said, coming closer and stopping seven feet from her. "I should have been paying more attention. I don't know where my mind was."

"That's—that's all right," Emma replied awkwardly, not knowing what else to say.

"No, ma'am, it's not all right," said Wilkens. As he spoke he looked down at the damp clothes wrung tightly and piled in the washtub. "A woman has enough to do without some dumb ole boy like me making more work for her." He gave her a wary smile—a nice smile, she thought. But his smile only brought her attention to his face, his eyes. Something in his eyes caught her and held her.

"It's no trouble, really," she said, realizing he was beginning to make too much of the matter. "We haven't had any rain . . . it's got the ground so parched . . ." Was she staring? Yes, of course she was. She knew it, yet she couldn't bring herself to look away. If she looked away now, it would be even more obvious.

"Where are my manners today?" the young man said, chastising himself. "I'm Omar Wilkens, one of Major Gentry's cattle hands." He took a step closer, as if somehow she'd given him permission. "And you, ma'am?" he asked politely. "That is, if I might be so forward?"

His question was forward indeed, she told herself. But for reasons she did not understand she answered him without hesitation. "I'm *Mrs.* Vertrees—wife of *Sheriff* Dillard Vertrees."

"Oh." Her words caught Wilkens by surprise. He hadn't been in the high grasslands surrounding Little Aces for long, but he'd been here long enough to know that the sheriff in Little Aces was Vince Gale, not Dillard Vertrees. Yet he recalled something about the name Vertrees. What was it? "Well then, Mrs. Vertrees," he said, realizing he would have to think about it later. Right now he needed to say something. "I'm honored to have made your acquaintance, even under these circumstances."

Her acquaintance? They had not been properly introduced. How dare he. Remaining composed, she said a bit sharply, "I must ask you to leave now, Mr. Wilkens." Before finishing her words she stooped to pick up the metal tub of damp clothes under the pretense of having to re-rinse everything. "As you can see, I have much work to do."

"Yes, ma'am. I understand," said Wilkens, but instead of turning away, he stepped between her and the metal tub and picked it up before she could reach the handles. "First, allow me to take this for you," he said. He stood up holding the tub, his Stetson still in hand.

"No," said Emma, sounding more firm on the matter. "I will not allow it."

"Please, Mrs. Vertrees, it's the least I can do," said Wilkens, his voice respectful, innocent, a young man speaking to an older woman.

Emma relented, looking toward the wooden washing machine standing on three legs beside the water trough nearer to the house. "That *is* courteous of you, Mr. Wilkens." She gestured toward the water trough as she stepped toward it. "If you will, please, set it down right there."

"Yes, ma'am," Wilkens replied. He set the tub beside the trough.

"Now, if you'll excuse me," Emma said curtly, walking away toward the rear door.

"Allow me, ma'am," Wilkens said. Anticipating her move, he hurried ahead of her to the door and opened it for her.

Emma walked warily inside. She did not like the way she'd permitted him to put himself so close to her, to her home, her place of safety. Yet she had done so almost before realizing it.

As soon as she stepped through the door, she turned around quickly, expecting to have to stop him from inviting himself inside. "Look, Mr. Wilkens—" Her words stopped short as she saw him closing the door behind her.

Hearing her speak his name, Wilkens re-opened the door slightly. "Yes, ma'am?"

"Nothing— Thank you, Mr. Wilkens," Emma said, relieved, and at the same time feeling foolish. She noted that he had already placed his Stetson atop his head in preparation to leave. With a twinge of guilt she said in reply to his earlier remark, "Likewise, it's good to make your acquaintance."

He smiled hopefully. "Yes, ma'am. I look forward to seeing you again soon."

Wait, no! Her words weren't meant to offer him encouragement. She wanted to explain that to him, but it was too late. The door closed quietly in her face. *What have you done?* she asked herself.

Stepping away from the door, she ventured a guarded look out the kitchen window. "Omar Wilkens," she said almost cautiously, under her breath, as if to record his name in her memory. At the rear of the yard, she saw him hop up onto the picket fence, over it and into his saddle.

Beside the livery barn, Dennis Barnes gigged Rupert Knowles and gestured toward Wilkens riding away from Emma Vertrees's yard. "Look who's leaving the woman's place, Rupert," he said with a chuckle. "Do you suppose Omar don't know about her?"

Rupert glanced at Wilkens for only a second, then shifted his attention back to the wooden table where Hank Lindley sat facing Curtis Clay. "I don't know Omar from a broken boot heel—what he knows or doesn't know," said Rupert, irritated by Barnes's interruption. "I've got money bet here."

On the table in front of Lindley, his Colt lay disassembled on a one-foot-square oilcloth, the same as the cloth lying in front of Curtis Clay. The blind man's Remington pistol had been laid in pieces between his resting hands. At each man's elbow sat his wagering money. On Clay's five-dollar bill stood a bullet, holding it down. Lindley's money consisted of three dollar bills held down by a handful of loose quarters.

Clay had heard mention of *the woman*, and he knew which woman Barnes referred to. He had heard Wilkens's horse leave moments ago, then heard it ride back a shorter distance—he knew where the young cowboy had been, and he'd also heard him leave. "Are we all set?" Clay asked, his face showing no expression, his cloudy blind eyes hidden behind a pair of dark shaded spectacles.

"Yeah, I'm ready when you are," said Lindley.

Clay put away his concern for Emma Vertrees and patted his hands gently down on the parts of the Remington, getting a feel for their location. "Somebody say 'go,' " he said bluntly, his hands going back to the tabletop, relaxed yet poised.

Barnes grinned. "Just like that? You don't want them to say 'get ready, get set' first?"

"If you need them to, they can," Clay said respectfully.

"No, I don't *need* for them to. I'm ready." The smile had left Lindley's face as he heard Rupert and Barnes stifle a laugh. With his eyes fixed on the blind man's face, Lindley said, "Barnes, say 'go' for us."

Barnes stalled. "It don't seem natural, just saying 'go,' without no warning or nothing else."

"Just say it, dang it to hell!" Lindley growled at him. "Let's get this over with."

"All right," said Barnes. A tense silence loomed for a second, until he said loudly, "Go!"

Clay's black hands worked deftly, almost in a blur,

snatching piece after piece of the Remington from the tabletop and fitting them into place. Across from him Hank Lindley did the same. He worked fast, but not fast enough. Before his Colt had been half assembled, he heard the spin of the big Remington's cylinder and heard Rupert say in awe, "Damn! He's done!"

Lindley let the cylinder to his Colt fall back onto the tabletop in defeat. He stared at the Remington looming before him in Clay's hand and said, "This is rigged. Nobody is that fast putting a gun together."

"Rigged? Rigged how?" Rupert asked. "You seen it with your own eyes. How could you rig something like this?"

"I don't know, but it's rigged, I'm telling you." As Lindley spoke, Clay heard the rustle of his shirtsleeve and the slightest jingle of coins as he reached over, picked up the five dollars in bills and coins and set the money over in front of him. "But I've never crawfished on a bet," Lindley added in disgust.

Relieved, Clay touched the money lightly with his fingertips, counting without giving the appearance of counting. "How close did you get?" he asked quietly. "I never heard your cylinder click."

"Not very danged close." Rupert laughed. He rubbed his finger and thumb together toward Lindley, reminding him of the dollar bet he'd made. His laughter cut short as Lindley snatched a dollar from his shirt pocket and tossed it at him.

"Never mind how close I got," Lindley said grudgingly. "I'll be coming back. I'm going to try you again."

"I'm always here and you're always welcome," Clay

said respectfully. This was what many of them said after he'd won their money. *I'm coming back . . .* But they never did.

He sat silently as Lindley finished assembling his Colt and the three cowboys mounted their horses and rode away toward the dirt street. When the dust had settled and he could no longer feel the gritty dryness of it in his nostrils, Clay stood up, shoved the Remington down into his waist behind his shirttail and picked up the tall hickory walking stick leaning against the table.

"Come on out here, Little Dog," he said to a growth of weeds and debris on the other side of the alley. "Take me on over to the woman's fence. We best ought to see about her."